Ruby Dreams
of Janis Joplin

FLYOVER FICTION   Series editor: Ron Hansen

Ruby Dreams of Janis Joplin

A Novel

Mary Clearman Blew

University of Nebraska Press | Lincoln and London

Publication of this volume was assisted by
a grant from the Friends of the University
of Nebraska Press.

Library of Congress Cataloging-in-Publication Data
Names: Blew, Mary Clearman, 1939– author.
Title: Ruby dreams of Janis Joplin: a novel /
Mary Clearman Blew.
Description: Lincoln: University of Nebraska
Press, [2018] | Series: Flyover fiction
Identifiers: LCCN 2017050530
ISBN 9781496207586 (softcover: acid-free paper)
ISBN 9781496208767 (epub)
ISBN 9781496208774 (mobi)
ISBN 9781496208781 (web)
Classification: LCC PS3552.L46 R78 2018
DDC 813/.54—dc23 LC record available at
https://lccn.loc.gov/2017050530

Set in Sabon Next by Mikala R Kolander.

For Ali
pianist extraordinaire

Acknowledgments

I want to thank the University of Idaho, which granted me sabbatical leave to mull over and write the early draft of *Ruby Dreams of Janis Joplin*. Thanks also to Joy Passanante and Jeff P. Jones, who read the whole of the novel in manuscript and made detailed and insightful notes; to Rochelle Smith, Debbie Lee, Peter Chilson, Alexandra Teague, and Michele Leavitt, who read and commented on chapters of the novel; to Dan Faller for allowing me to borrow the name of his band, Daniel Mark Faller and the Working Poor; and special thanks to Brian Davies (Cryin' Brian on the steel) for sharing his stories of life on the road with a country-western band and also for the years he has been a member of my family. My warm thanks to Sean Prentiss for his friendship and the many conversations we have shared about the music Ruby and her friends play, listen to, and love. Thanks to my wonderful daughters, Elizabeth, Misty, and Rachel, who put up with my absently calling their friends by one of my characters' names. And my thanks to two women no longer living who have contributed to *Ruby Dreams of Janis Joplin*: Miss Grace Pennock, graduate of the Boston Conservatory of Music, who taught me to play the piano; and Patricia Konopatzke, British war bride, who told me stories of her life after leaving London to live in a town very like my fictional Versailles, Montana.

1

The hiss of the Greyhound's air compression brakes wakes me from what might have been sleep. The pain in my abdomen is much worse. Lights flash past the bus windows, hitting my eyes like blows after miles of rolling through darkness. It must be past midnight; we must be arriving somewhere, I don't know where, but maybe it's Versailles, in northern Montana, because I remember buying a bus ticket to Versailles. I think I remember. My mind hasn't been right for days.

Versailles. Pronounced *Ver-sails*. Brazos used to say "Ver-sigh." Brazos, damn him. Thinking about Brazos is making something real for me that I don't want to be real.

The lights stop moving as the bus pulls up in front of the Greyhound station. People behind me and ahead of me get to their feet, stretching and looking around for belongings. I want to hunch over in my seat and close my eyes, but that's not possible. The bus driver has jacked open the hydraulic door at the front of the bus, and I must drag my backpack from under my seat and get off like everyone else.

After the air conditioning in the bus, the night air feels warm and smells of diesel fumes and lilacs. It's lilac season in Versailles for sure. Nowhere, at least where I've been, do lilacs bloom so late into the spring, and their perfume is like a promise that won't be kept. Same old sidewalks, same old worn-out brick storefronts, and same old bar signs still flashing their neon cocktails and cowboys, so it must not be past closing time.

How many years have I been gone? Ten? I'm not sure of anything, and apparently my body has led me back here after my mind went blank, but surely the girl I used to be stole the last of Gall's cash and bought an airline ticket out of Anchorage, Alaska, to Spokane, and then another ticket, on the Greyhound, for the slow ride and many stops with people getting off and other people getting on, people with somewhere to go, down through eastern Washington and across Idaho to the high prairie of Versailles, Montana.

Now what.

I can't just stand here pretending I don't feel the pain in my side while other people's luggage is dragged out of the belly of the Greyhound and stacked on the sidewalk. A man in a Seattle Seahawks sweatshirt finds his suitcase and gives me a look as he walks past, seeing a woman by herself at this hour and not a pretty woman but a scary-looking woman with long tangled hair and dirty clothes.

I shoulder my backpack and limp down the street. Hardly any traffic at this hour. Hardly any air current, not even a muddy whiff of the Milk River. Businesses closed and locked behind iron security bars I don't remember. Trees in their iron cages hanging their leaves over the sidewalks, drained of color and etched into a single dimension by the overhead lights. A recessed door opens in a concrete facade, and somebody stumbles out and leans on a parking meter, regaining his balance. A burst of guitars floods across the sidewalk before the door closes, canned country music, lyrics I know—*break all the windows, sweep the glass away*—and I realize I'm walking past the Alibi Bar and Grill, right here where it always was, and I'm seeing the last face I saw before I left Versailles ten years ago, Isaiah's face.

Isaiah stands in front of the door to the Alibi. He's still nineteen years old. He holds out his hand—Ruby, come with me.

Who the hell are you? She's coming with us, says Gall, and with his words, Isaiah disappears.

The drunk leaning on the parking meter is gone, too.

Weather in Versailles, on the Montana highline, is more extreme than anywhere else in America. One July the thermometers hit 117 degrees above zero and the following January dropped to minus 56. The hot summers and freezing winters buckle the highways and erode the prairies that stretch around the town in every direction and encourage people to stay put and let their faces erode along with the prairies. Why do I know this? Because the girl I used to be knew it. The girl I used to be left Versailles one night in the back of an old Volkswagen van with a couple of rich kids from Boise, Idaho—Gall Margarus and Brazos Keane—who had recruited themselves a drummer and started their own band, and that girl never came back.

Now I'm back, with my guilt and my riddled memories, and I think about opening that door into the Alibi and climbing on a bar stool, filthy as I am, and hoping somebody will buy me a drink. But my feet are making my decisions tonight, and my feet keep walking to the end of Main Street and then up the grade toward the plateau, past the closed and shuttered auto dealerships with their pennants hanging limp over the rows of used cars, past the darkened strip malls, past the corner where somebody tried to start a Thai restaurant that now has gone to weeds. All the traffic lights are on automatic blink.

At the top of the grade my feet give up, and my knees buckle under me. I try to tell myself I've stopped to look back, but really I'm doubling over to get my breath, alternately shivering and sweating with my backpack slipping off my shoulders, and now I'm curled up on the pavement with my arms around the backpack, which seems to help.

Here on the crest of the plateau I feel the air current, the warning of rising wind. Night clouds race through a glitter of stars. Below me a stream of lights maps the main grids and thoroughfares of Versailles, the bridge over the Milk River, and the highway that runs north to Medicine Hat, Canada. Behind me, farther along the plateau, the lights of the airport. To the east lies the faraway glow that is the tiny town of Broadview; to the west are the security lights around the shopping mall and the security lights around the baseball field at the college. At this hour the town's ugliness hides behind the glow of lights through the darkness.

No. The pain hasn't gone away. I'm crouching in the weeds with my arms around my backpack and my throbbing abdomen, and I'm retching, not that I've eaten for hours, but my mouth is full of black bile, and I'm floating on the screaming spasms.

But the sky to the east is lightening, its stars fading. I've lost track of time, but the early dawn of late spring must be near. And Isaiah is back. Isaiah is smiling, glad to see me, and he takes my pale hand in his dark hand and helps me to my feet. Isaiah is nineteen years old, and I am sixteen again, and Isaiah leads me into a residential area called the Orchards because somebody once tried to plant cherry orchards here. Streetlights in the Orchards are far apart, and cottonwood trees reach across the rambling graveled streets to touch each other's new leaves, and darkened houses sit behind their flower beds and lawns with hardly a porch light burning, nobody stirring to wonder who is passing.

By now the sky has lightened to gray, the stars are gone, and so is Isaiah, but I have stopped at a familiar gate in a white picket fence. Behind the gate a graveled walk leads to a shadowed porch. Somewhere from the back of the house a light shines, and the faint sound of a piano ripples into the dawn. Someone is playing a Debussy étude, a piece I once played on that very piano, and my fingers start to move, as though the pickets of the gate are piano keys.

The thread of the étude draws me through the gate and around the house. I'm shivering now, my teeth chattering, but while I can hear the piano, I can crawl as far as the giant blue spruce in the backyard.

The blue spruce is even taller than I remember. Its boughs sweep the lawn and rise toward the last stars. I drop to my knees and crawl through the protecting boughs into the warm hidden space of needles and the scent of resin, and I feel as safe as I did when I hid under here as a child.

I push my backpack against the trunk of the spruce for a pillow, and I draw up my knees and shrug my arms for comfort inside Gall's old T-shirt. My mind is ragged, but from the ticket counter at Anchorage International through the dingy old Spokane airport and the dingier Greyhound bus station, the endless ride in the dark, and then the long walk up the grade to the Orchards, a memory in the muscles and bones of my body has brought me to the blue spruce, where I listen to the pianist repeating the Debussy étude and wait for Isaiah to find me in the dark.

I waken to the pain, which has its own spinning motion and its own high and relentless sound. Also relentless is something warm and wet on my neck, and I squint against brutal shafts of sunlight through the spruce needles to see a bundle of white fur squirming with happiness at finding me. He pauses in his licking to fix me with black button eyes while his stump of a tail wags in rapid-fire staccato. He is Jonathan, so named because he is an American dog, still alive and still remembering me after all these years.

"Jonathan?" calls a woman's voice. Then the lower boughs move, and a deeply lined face materializes in a frame of spruce needles as though from another age. Hazel hawk's eyes, an arched hawk's nose, and a cloud of hair I remember as iron gray but now is pure white.

"*Ruth?*"

I can't answer. I would scream if I tried.

Strong cool fingers on my forehead. "Ruth? You're on *fire*."

5

2

The room in the Budget Motel in Anchorage is wallpapered with a repeating pattern of antlered elk emerging from low firs under a cloudless blue sky. It's important to know how many elk in the room, exactly, and I keep counting and losing track of my count. Somebody keeps interrupting me, calling my name, and I turn away to keep counting, but the voice is relentless, and sooner or later I must open my eyes on a window whose white blinds deflect none of the hard light striking the chipped metal table with its closed drawers or the blank screen of a television hanging from a ceiling mount. I don't want to see any of those things, so I close my eyes and will myself back into the room with the elk.

"Ruth?"

The voice will not go away. The pillow under my head is thin; the texture of the sheet is coarse. I force my eyes open to sick green walls, the foot of a bed, and a flimsy white blanket that covers me to the chin. A needle is taped to a vein in my arm, and a tube leads from the needle to a pouch of liquid hanging from a rack.

"Ruth?"

Why do you have two names? Bill the Drummer once asked me. Which would you rather be called?

Doesn't matter. Ruth or Ruby, whichever, I told him.

"Ruth?"

At last I turn toward the voice. The pianist sits in one of the cracked vinyl armchairs with her back, straight as ever, to the window. Her face is shadowed, but light falling from the window casts a white nimbus over her hair.

"Are you thirsty, Ruth?"

I nod, and she pours water from a carafe into a paper cup. When I try to sit up to drink, I feel a sting in my abdomen, and I realize the high-wire screaming pain is gone, leaving only the stinging sensation and some tenderness. I've lived with the pain for so long that its loss is an absence of the familiar—*Gall, whatever they've done with you, wherever you are, will you be the pain I feel now?* But I sit up on the pillows and sip water and set down the cup and run exploring fingers down under my hospital gown and feel a tiny dressing, like a Band-Aid.

The pianist waits with her hands folded in her lap. My head is clearing, and I remember her name now. She's Mrs. Pence, she's my old piano teacher, and she can sit still longer without speaking a word than anyone I've ever known, which always used to surprise me, considering what happened when she opened the piano and began to play.

I manage a question—"Are you still teaching the Debussy étude?"

"Sometimes. When I have a student with enough talent. How long were you listening?"

How long. I have no idea. Everything up to now is murky. Walking past the Alibi with Isaiah—no. I couldn't have been with Isaiah. Isaiah won't still be nineteen years old; he'll be close to thirty by now. I must have dreamed him. Walking, carrying my backpack—*what's become of my backpack?*—headlights streaming past me on the grade up to the Orchards. A piano being played in the early dawn, drawing me to the pianist's backyard and the shelter of the old blue spruce.

"What time is it now?"

She nods at the digital clock beside the water carafe. "A little after seven."

"In the morning?" It must be morning because the light in the window is clean and transparent. Then I realize it must be the *next* morning. I've lost a day.

"The paramedics had quite a struggle, getting you out from under that spruce. They tried to ease you out to the stretcher, but you were in such pain—the spruce boughs flailing and Jonathan running back and forth and barking—"

I've never heard her speak at length about anything but piano technique and interpretation. And I suppose the paramedics are still laughing with their buddies about finding a grown woman hiding under a tree. Did it happen? I do think I remember someone turning the pain into red lightning when he tried to straighten my legs. Did I scream?

"My dear. How long have you been in such anguish?"

A week. A month. Always. Telling myself it was just a stitch. "I kept thinking it would go away."

"Well." She stands and smooths her good gray linen skirt. "Your appendix was almost ruptured. It's a wonder you didn't die of it. But they've pumped you full of antibiotics, and the surgery was laparoscopic, so you'll be on your feet by this afternoon, and they'll probably discharge you this evening. I'll be back for you."

Why is she coming back for me? Another question with no answer. When I hear the door close behind her, I pull the sheet over my head, turn my face away from the window, and let myself sink under the dark currents to search for the elk. For some reason it's important to find my way back to the elk.

Instead, I go time traveling. Tonight, for once, the Alibi features live music in the lounge. Three young guys on the bandstand play while one or two couples leave their drinks to dance on the tiny dance floor. For all the live music it's a slow night in the restaurant, so in between carrying trays of dirty dishes to the kitchen, I can hang out in the archway between the restaurant and lounge and listen.

Not that I'm into their music. I'm a smart-ass sixteen-year-old, and I know everything worth knowing, and this summer I've been listening to Nirvana and Eminem. From these guys' clothes and their long hair, I hoped they'd be into rock, but no, they're playing covers of country songs, mostly popular shit like

"Unbroken," George Strait and that, the overly produced crap I hear blaring from other people's car radios, but occasionally something older and better. They're pretty good. The lead guitarist is damned good, in fact. At some point in the unforeseeable future, I'll learn that he's had classical training but turned his back on it to start his own garage band in Boise. Now the band's been all over the West, and they've got their name on a poster in front of the bandstand, *The Idaho Rivermen*, and they're headed for fame and fortune.

I can tell they love some of the older, crossover classics when the lead guitarist, also the vocalist, sings "Hickory Wind" in a sweet sad tenor. He's wearing blue jeans and a dark-blue satin shirt unbuttoned halfway down, and he's got long tawny hair and a jawline my fingers want to trace. I will hear the hickory wind in my head for a long time after tonight.

I'm too young to wait tables or serve cocktails, and there's an invisible line between the restaurant and the lounge I'm forbidden to cross. Dave the bartender doesn't have much to do on this slow night, and he's keeping an eye on me. He knows I'm underage and Brad Gilcannon, my policeman foster father, will give him hell if I'm late getting home. Brad's already unhappy with me. Brad hates that I've quit school, hates that I'm busing dishes in the Alibi two nights a week, hates that I spend so much time with my piano teacher, and he holds as strict a line on me as he can. Still, Dave may not realize how young I really am. Even at sixteen, I'm a tall girl.

When their set finishes, the guys in the band head for the men's room. The drummer and the rhythm guitarist come back and sprawl in a booth so close to my invisible line that I smell their sweat and beer fumes. Maybe that was their last set for the night because Dave the bartender wipes his hands on his pants and gives me a dirty look as he serves them a round of beers.

The lead guitarist brushes my shoulder on his way back from the men's room and looks down to see who he's bumped into.

Hey, darlin! He's a head taller than I am and so lean and rangy that his blue satin shirt hangs from his shoulders. He smiles, and I melt, and he puts an arm around me and leads me to the booth where the other two guys have started on their beers and are talking about breaking down their gear and loading it in the van. Dave looks up sharply and comes around the bar, wiping his mustache. He's had one or two himself on this slow night.

Ruby, you're outta line, you know you're not supposed to be in here!

Hey! She's fine!

Dave looks around at his last paying customers and then at the guys from the band who have paychecks to spend.

Just so you don't order nothing for her.

The boys tell me their names. Brazos Keene, the rhythm guitarist; Bill Jamison, who everybody calls Bill the Drummer; and Gall. Gall Margarus, the lead guitarist and vocalist. I tell them I'm Ruby. Gall keeps his arm around me, and I feel heaven in his warmth through his blue satin shirt.

Another round of beers, and then Bill the Drummer leaves the booth and starts striking the set on the bandstand, unplugging speakers and winding up electrical cords. Gall and Brazos watch him work and talk about learning to read music. For some reason Brazos is trying to learn, but he's finding it hard after years of picking everything up by ear.

Lazy, says Gall.

Oh hell! Easy for you to talk. You learned what, when you were about six?

I pipe up: I can read music.

They both seem to remember I'm there.

Do you know how to play?

Yes.

Aw, I bet you don't.

An old piano stands closed and battered at the back of the bandstand. I've never seen anybody touch it, but I slide out of the booth and run to the bandstand and open the lid of the piano. Even Bill the Drummer stops working to listen as I dash into *Tarantella*.

Holy shit, I guess you really can!

... ...

The nurse who comes to check me out of Versailles Memorial Hospital has a bristle of bright-red hair over an eroded face. "So you're Ruby Gervais," she says, pronouncing my name in the old Versailles way, *Jarvis*. *Szcher-vay*, Brazos had taught me to say.

"I always wondered what became of you," she adds. I know from her tight smile that she remembers all the old stories, and I suppose in returning to Versailles, population something under ten thousand, I'm bound to bump into others who remember. Brad Gilcannon for one. My mother for another.

She takes my blood pressure and checks my temperature while I sit on the edge of the bed. She makes quick chart notes with a pen that jabs the paper, and then she hands me my boots, which look as though the Alaska mud has been scrubbed off with a brush, and also a plastic bag.

"Your clothes. *She* washed them for you. Go ahead and get dressed. I'll walk you to the door. Hospital regulations."

My blue jeans, my shirt, my socks, and even my underpants, clean and neatly folded. I'm embarrassed at the thought of Mrs. Pence seeing the stained crotch of my underpants and laundering them; I can't look up or even slide off the bed to get dressed, although the nurse taps her clipboard with her pen while she waits for me to get on with it.

"Sorry."

Again the tight smile. "You ought to be. You have a lot to be sorry for."

Mrs. Pence waits in front of the gift shop, across from the admissions desk. Under the harsh overhead fluorescents, I see her face clearly and am shocked at how she has aged. In my young eyes she always was old, of course, but now her face is scored and drawn over her cheekbones, and her skin looks transparent.

"I've parked the Pontiac right by the curb," she says, while I try not to look at the potted flowers and grinning stuffed toys as she leads me past the gift shop's display window. Automatic plate glass doors open in front of us. "Are you all right? Can you walk?" she asks, and I nod, although I feel tottery.

Sure enough, there's the old green Pontiac with the chrome Indian head on its hood. It can't be the same car, or can it, after ten years? When I'm a month from turning twenty-seven? Or am I already twenty-seven? An old woman? My birthday is in late July, and surely this is late May, but I lost track of the seasons in Anchorage, where the only constant was the wind.

I've never seen the Pontiac moving, much less ridden in it. Mrs. Pence kept it parked in the little detached garage at the end of the driveway next to her house, where she grew a row of hollyhocks in summer—but how do I know that, when I've never been inside that garage?

Yet here is the Pontiac, and here is Mrs. Pence, behind the elegant steering wheel with the head of the Indian carved on the chrome horn button. The late afternoon sun through the windshield has turned the air stuffy and the upholstery hot. I take a deep breath and automatically reach for a seat belt, but of course the Pontiac is too old for such amenities, and so I lean back in the bench seat as we pull out of the hospital's parking lot and turn up the grade at a stately twenty miles an hour.

3

The foyer of Mrs. Pence's house looks exactly as I remember and yet disturbingly altered, as though disguised as its former self. Wallpaper in a dim damask stripe, a rack for coats, the first actual umbrella stand I ever saw, and the framed and faded photograph of the famous Ray Pence, the decorated American airman who met and married the young English pianist and brought her home to Versailles, Montana, with him. Ray Pence gazes toward the door in his uniform cap and jacket, handsome and impervious to time. His faint smile seems to expect goodness to walk through the door toward him. It's me, Ruby, I want to warn him.

Jonathan patters to greet us, wagging the stump of his tail. Like Ray Pence, Jonathan expects goodness, and I feel sad for them both.

"I'm sorry about the stairs," says Mrs. Pence.

The flight of uncarpeted stairs leads to a landing and the shadows of the second floor. During the years I walked through Mrs. Pence's front door with my backpack of music for my weekly lesson, right up until I turned sixteen and ran away with the Idaho Rivermen, I always continued down the hallway to the sunny room where the pianos waited, never up those stairs, although I used to imagine climbing them and sliding down the walnut bannister. But now I follow Mrs. Pence, who insists on carrying my backpack, while Jonathan runs back and forth in his excitement. My incision stings with each step, and I'm glad for the bannister rail.

Mrs. Pence sets down my backpack against a white-painted dresser. "The bathroom is next door, and you'll want to get some rest, dear. Come along, Jonathan."

I think of curling up on that bed and pulling the comforter over my head. But I turn and startle nearly out of my skin at a shape that glares at me through an uncombed mass of dark hair. It moves when I move, and I catch my breath and see the full-length mirror on the back of the door.

So it's come to this. I was sixteen years old, Gall held me in his strong warm arms, and the music he and Brazos and Bill the Drummer played was rich. The throb of guitars, the lyrics—*dream a dream . . . safe in his arms . . . until the end of time*—the length of a measure of music was all that mattered. Now, in a second-floor bedroom in my old piano teacher's house, I see a tall gaunt woman with tangled dark hair and a witch's face. If the sight of myself scares me, what will it do to everybody else?

·· ···

Isaiah must have been looking for me that night. I realize that now. No reason he would have wandered into the Alibi and just happened to spot me sitting in the booth with the guys from the band.

Ruby, get outta here. Brad's looking for you, says Isaiah.

Gall bristles up beside me. He's in Isaiah's face—And what's that to you?

Whoa, says Bill the Drummer, always the level head of the Rivermen, which I will learn later, of course. Bill reaches around me and lays a hand on Gall's shoulder.

Isaiah isn't having any peacemaking. You guys know how old she is?

And I'm telling you to back on outta here!

Dave is watching us from behind the bar. He sets down the glass he's been polishing and braces himself for trouble. I can make plenty of trouble for him, and Isaiah can too, for that matter. Dave can't have underage kids hanging out in the Alibi, and if I'm an underage sixteen, Isaiah's an underage nineteen, although he's been out on his own since he was younger than me, emancipated from foster care by a judge after yet another fight with Brad Gilcannon.

Isaiah bends over me to speak into my ear. Makes me look at him. Ruby. Brad's driving his prowl car around with his bubble on, checking all the streets. He'll have your ass if he spots you.

Gall's ready to fight—And who the hell is Brad?

I got a car parked in the alley. If you get in the back seat and lay down—

We can do a damn sight better than that for her, says Gall, and somehow I know what's going to happen next. Bill has the amps and instruments and other shit all packed and loaded, and now everybody is getting up, and Brazos is laying down bills to pay for the beers. And Gall hugs my shoulders, comforting me.

··· ···

The guys had been planning to leave Versailles the morning after they finished their gig at the Alibi. They would drive west over Lolo Pass to Lewiston, Idaho, where they had a week's contract. But they already had their amps and instruments packed in the van that night. Brazos had objected; there was a girl living in Versailles he'd once known in Boise, and he'd hoped to see her, although she told him she loved somebody else. But Gall had laughed at him—heartbroken!—and it took less than a minute of exchanged glances and few words for the guys to bundle me under their sleeping bags and head out of town. It was years before I realized what a chance they were taking, driving with a sixteen-year-old over a state line with her policeman foster father looking for her. But they hadn't been old enough themselves to worry overmuch.

Who, that girl that played the piano? No, I dunno where she went. Do you, Gall?

She said something about walking home, didn't she?

That's probably what she did.

The van rumbles around the sharp curves of Highway 12, making better time now that we're over the mountains and safe in

Idaho. Brazos hasn't said any more about the girl in Versailles. He's driving the van. Later I will learn that he always drives. Bill the Drummer has pulled an acoustic guitar from behind the second seat. He plays, and they all sing a song I've never heard, about a girl who ran away from her husband, whose big mistake had been buying her a Ford Econoline, although we're not in an Econoline but an old Volkswagen van, where I nestle with Gall in the sleeping bags and breathe in his sweet skin while he kisses me along my hairline.

I'm warm and contented and drowsy, and I drift in and out of sleep until suddenly the brakes screech and we've come to a halt.

Not Brad, don't let it be Brad, is my first thought.

Holy Christ, would you look at that!

And now we're all awake and sitting up and staring out the windshield at the giant in the headlights. Its head with its heavy, branching crown of antlers turns to stare back at us with eyes as fiery as though it were sending us a flaming message from the world of the wild: *My blessing on your way!*

Or so I perceive in the moment. Later Brazos will explain that the bull elk couldn't possible have seen us, couldn't have seen anything but the blinding headlights, but in the now Brazos cuts the headlights, and the beast makes its stately way across the highway, followed by another and another and another: huge shadowy beasts in no hurry.

Brazos finds his voice. That was the Selway elk herd. Glad I saw that. What a sight!

Bill the Drummer lets out his breath—I'm just glad the brakes were good.

We drive on toward Lewiston. In the hum from the heater, in the stink of male bodies and the comfort of close and sheltering arms, I feel blessed and safe, as though nothing bad can happen to me as long as Gall holds me and Brazos drives and Bill plays the guitar and sings softly about rain and snow and loss and love.

What did I think? That the Selway elk herd could save me? I have no answers. I kick off my boots, drop my blue jeans, drag the comforter over me, and shut my eyes against the light.

16

I wake to angry shouts below my window. At first, as I struggle out of the tangle of sheet and comforter, I think I'm in the motel in Anchorage, in the room with the wallpaper elk. *You bitch! You fucking whore!* But it isn't Gall who is shouting under my window. This is a woman's voice, hurtling words like nails being driven into a board. She's interrupted by a softer voice, but she breaks in with a furious rattle of words I can't make out but know are meant to hurt.

In my underpants and bare feet, I run to the window and look down over the shingled roof of the porch. The day has darkened. A streetlight illuminates the cottonwood leaves and the foreshortened figures of two women, one on either side of the gate in the picket fence. Mrs. Pence has her back to me, but I see the face of the dark-haired woman clearly, and I know who she is, although fury distorts her features, and I know she has reason to hate me but not why she would hate Mrs. Pence.

From her diatribe I pick out a single phrase—*You'll be sorry you took her in*—and I watch, naked and bereft, as the dark-haired woman turns and runs away, leaving the gate in the picket fence swinging behind her. She tears open the door of a car parked by the curb, gets in, and slams the door. Headlights burst on, tires squeal on gravel, and she's gone, although the gate still swings until Mrs. Pence reaches out and latches it.

My mother.

4

Rosalie, the latest one-name girl to sing at the festival, has a voice like a bell was what a columnist wrote about my mother's performance at the Monterey music festival. Not the famous festival, of course; she was born too late to have run away from Montana and sung with Jimi Hendrix and Janis and the Airplane and the other legendary names. But at some time in the late 1970s she sang in Monterey and was written about in the papers, and she saved the clippings in a cardboard box in a closet in the rented house where she lived after she came back to Versailles.

At the thought of my mother on some interminable Greyhound journey back to Montana, wounded and sick, with her feet leading her because her mind had given up on her, I'm stricken by the sense that, unknowingly, I've followed the same byways on the circular course that led her to that rental house on the north side of the Milk River and me to this second-floor bedroom in Mrs. Pence's house in the Orchards.

At least I haven't come back pregnant. Or with a new baby in my arms. I've never known whether I was born before she left California or after she came back to Montana.

··· ···

Time traveling. I am eight years old, and I should have gone to school today, but my mother has been gone for a long time, and I am lonely and hungry. The milk in the refrigerator tastes bad, but I have found some crackers to nibble while I wander out of the kitchen to find traces of her. In the living room, a couch and a tv on a tubular stand. In my little bedroom, a cot and a chest of

18

drawers that hold my school clothes. In my mother's bedroom, where I am not supposed to be, the tumbled bed and the guitar in its zipped black case. I open her closet door, where dust balls have found the corners but her few clothes still smell of her. On the shelf is a faded orange cardboard box with a picture of a cowboy hat on its side. Curious, I lift it down.

There is no hat in the box, only a bundle of clippings from newspapers. In the seamless space between past and present, I regret the hat, which I could have tried on and pretended I was my mother, although in that same seamless space I know that if there ever was a hat, it was long lost detritus along my mother's wandering byways.

Oh, well, I can always look at the clippings. They have softened over time and gone limp, and when I lift them out of the box, I tell myself they are probably very old. At eight I can read well enough to make out most of what is written there. *A voice like a bell.* And there is a picture of her holding her guitar, so beautiful, with her lush dark hair hanging down her back.

But she had come back to Versailles, Montana.

··· ···

The next time I wake, I know by the light falling through the window that it is early morning. My head feels thick with dreams I can't remember, but I see the room around me clearly enough. White walls, white curtains. A white-painted dresser, the door with the mirror. Except for what the mirror might reflect, there's an order in this room, a serenity. Surely Mrs. Pence hasn't given me her own bedroom?

At the thought I sit up and look around for clues. The bed I fell into last night has plenty of pillows and beside it a table with a small lamp for late-night reading. Above the bed is a picture of the English countryside, showing a big church with a steeple framed by huge trees and a stream in the foreground where cattle drink. The view seems peaceful and unchanging until I look more closely at the sky and see that it is pierced by the church steeple, which points toward an ominous dark blue overtaking the sunlit clouds of summer.

No. It does not seem to be a room that is used regularly. The sheets on the bed are freshly laundered, and the small white rug has been shaken out, but the paint on the iron bed frame is chipped, and dust has filtered over the surfaces of the table and dresser. When I lick a finger and draw it along the windowsill, it comes away gray, and when I pull out a drawer from the dresser, it's empty and stale smelling.

At the window I look past the porch shingles to Mrs. Pence's gate, where, last night, my mother screamed her rage. All seems calm this morning. The big cottonwoods droop their load of dust over Mrs. Pence's front yard and shade the old gingerbread houses on the other side of the graveled street. At the far end of the block, mailboxes wait in a row, some with flags raised for the post office truck. A couple of boys with bicycles loiter there, probably trying to think of ways to liven up their summer.

Then I turn from the window and catch my other self in the full-length mirror.

She's not as wild-eyed as she was last night, although her hair is a dark disheveled mess. Her face shows the Alaskan pallor, and she's naked except for the white cotton underpants that are torn at the elastic—how did that happen? Well, yes, I do remember how. In the bedroom with the elk wallpaper.

She's so thin that her ribs show. So thin she hardly needs a bra.

Does she look dangerous? Well, maybe.

I take a second look, though, and notice a narrow cream-colored edge between the mirror and the white-painted door. It takes me a minute or two with a fingernail to slide the old Polaroid out from behind the mirror.

A dark-haired young man, posed in front of a much smaller blue spruce in what clearly is Mrs. Pence's backyard. It's Ray Pence, is my first thought. But no, this is a sullen young man in blue jeans and a white T-shirt with a pack of cigarettes rolled in his sleeve above a muscled arm, and he looks to me as though he's likelier looking for trouble than expecting goodness.

Not Mrs. Pence's bedroom. But somebody's, once upon a time, who hid this Polaroid snapshot of trouble behind the mirror.

I use the toilet in the bathroom across the hall, and I smell my own reek before I pull the old-fashioned chain flush, so my senses must be returning. When I dig my comb from the bottom of my backpack and set to work on my hair, starting with the ends and working out snarls with my fingers and the comb, I can feel the tingles.

A little mound of dark combings has accumulated on the white coverlet by the time I've braided my hair back and tied it with a raveling, but at least my other self in the mirror no longer looks feral.

What next. Shirt and blue jeans. My de-mudded boots.

I can't stay here forever. And what next, I don't know, but as soon as my incision heals and my legs aren't so tottery, I suppose I could hitchhike over to Boise, see if any of the musicians Gall and Brazos used to know are still around, and try to pick up a keyboard gig or two or at least snag a couch for a few nights.

Music draws me downstairs.

In the piano room Mrs. Pence sits at the old Steinway grand with her back to the door. She's playing the Brahms F Minor Sonata that I was learning just before I left Versailles with Gall and Brazos. As I listen to the familiar notes, my fingers play a ghost version of the sonata along my thigh while the white plaster bust of Beethoven looks down from his niche. Mrs. Pence's framed diploma from the Royal Academy of Music hangs above Beethoven, where it always has. Her touch sounds as strong and nuanced as ever, and I wonder again how old she is. If she was in her seventies when I had my last piano lesson with her, she will be well past eighty now.

Her hearing seems fine because she turns briefly on the piano stool, aware of my presence in the doorway, then plays to the end of the sonata.

"Would you like to play?"

In front of her, after all these years? "No—no."

"Well, then."

She folds her music book, pushes back the piano stool, and opens the door to the kitchen, and I follow.

"Coffee?"

She doesn't wait for an answer but pours from the ready pot. From under the table Jonathan wakes, thumps his greeting, licks my ankle, and goes back to sleep, while I wonder all over again why he's glad to see me and why Mrs. Pence is being so good to me.

5

Bill the Drummer once asked me, How'd you happen to learn to play the piano, Ruby? To be classically trained and all?

Long story, Bill.

··· ···

My mother never really looked like Janis Joplin, although I love the picture of Janis on the album cover, and I like to pretend that she does. Actually, my mother is prettier than Janis ever was. My mother's hair is dark, like mine, but finer, and it lifts off her shoulders in a silvery nimbus as the streetlight at the end of the block begins to glow in the twilight. The odor of river mud rises from the Milk River, although the air has gone still with the end of the day. On the far side of the river will be nothing but empty prairie reaching into Canada, but I'm six years old, and emptiness is what I know.

My mother wears blue jeans and a soft cotton shirt with the sleeves rolled to her elbows. She leans back against the porch rail of the rented house on the north side of the Milk River and smokes a cigarette. From behind the screen door I watch the tiny red tip of the cigarette drift down from her lips until her hand rests on her thigh. I would like to open the screen door and sidle down the steps to her, but I know she would wave me away.

During the day I absorb the sounds and smells of summer in this seedy northern neighborhood. Somebody down the street uses an old-fashioned lawn mower that eats the grass with a gravelly whir that starts at one side of his lawn and pauses at the other side for him to turn around and start back. Farther down the street, somebody else is working on his motorcycle, which stinks of heated oil and barks when he tromps on the starter.

The neighbors directly across the street leave their windows open to catch a draft and relieve the heat, and music from the country station pours out of their radio. I catch my mother tapping her foot on the porch steps. She turns and sees that I'm watching her and asks what I want.

Are you hungry? Again?

No.

A car rumbles down the unpaved street. From the screen door I hear a throb of guitars through a rolled-down window and smell the dust rising from tires. The outline of my mother's back grows more and more indistinct in the gathering dusk. Does she raise her head, does she look for the twin red flash of brake lights as the car slows at the end of the block? The car turns at the corner and is gone, and my mother stubs out her cigarette on the porch steps, extinguishing the red spark.

At some point she must have arranged for my piano lessons.

Myself at six years old or eight or ten or twelve. Always tall for my age and way too thin. My hair in long dark braids. Arriving at Mrs. Pence's front door with my backpack of music. Sitting at the upright practice piano. Learning the major and minor scales.

··· ···

What do I remember about the day the woman from Child Protection Services came for me?

My screams.

I knew the cps woman. Or should have. Or so she told me. She had talked to me, and she had listened while the counselor questioned me about the bruising on my private parts and how the bruising happened. I said that the big boys did it, in the alley behind our house. At least that's what I was told I said because I didn't remember. And I didn't remember the boys. Maybe I remembered when I said it, maybe I didn't. Didn't matter because nobody believed me.

It's a goddamn lie! It's a goddamn lie!

That was my mother, screaming at the CPS woman. I didn't remember her face, only the pitch of her voice over my head. Years later I realized her rage was over the accusation that her man at the time had hurt me, not the boys in the alley. At the time I only knew something terrible had happened, and it was my fault, and I fought and grabbed at the legs of chairs and then the doorknob to keep from being taken away.

··· ···

That first foster family. Did the Mister really belt me one? I think I remember it. What I know I remember is the Mister's voice: *I never touched her! Never laid a finger on the little liar!*

People believed strange things in those days. What happened? What didn't happen? What could I, what could anyone, know was true?

That first foster family lived in one of the old frame houses on the north side of the Milk River, on a street a couple of blocks from the gypsum plant. I remember trivial things, like the high ceilings and the dun-colored cabinets in the kitchen and the doorways to the bedrooms, which had curtains instead of doors, but I can't remember the people's names. She was slab-sided and freckled and smelled of stale sweat that permeated the polyester pants and shirts she bought at yard sales. He had retired from the gypsum plant with a bad cough and spent a lot of time on the couch, staring at the television. I used to hear him at night, hack, hack, through my bedroom curtain. She called him "the Mister." They must have badly needed the pittance the state paid them for fostering children because the first Tuesday I stayed with them, I threw an awful fit.

"It's my piano lesson day! It's my piano lesson day!"

"Whoever heard of a kid crying to take a piano lesson?" asked the Mister. Then, fed up when I wouldn't stop screaming, "Cool it, kid! Or I'll give you something to howl about!"

"No! No! They'll take her away," she shouted, and he shouted something back.

The next Tuesday, instead of walking home from school, I hiked up to the Orchards for my piano lesson. I remember Mrs. Pence's surprise when she came to the door and saw me standing there, but she let me in and gave me my lesson. But either she made a phone call or the freckled foster mother did, because the CPS woman paid a visit after dinner that evening. I eavesdropped from behind the curtain in my bedroom doorway, hating them all.

"Maybe the easiest would be to let her keep taking lessons."

"Where's the money coming from?" the Mister wanted to know.

"I'll talk to Mrs. Pence, see what we can work out."

What was worked out or how long it took, I don't know, but every Tuesday after school I climbed up the grade to Mrs. Pence's house for my piano lesson, and I lived and breathed for an hour within an elegant web of musical tones and progressions, and every Tuesday after the lesson I went back to another fracas at my foster home. They threatened, and I threw wingding fits, screaming and beating my head on the floor and scratching long welts up and down my arms and legs. Finally, the Mister, as he promised, gave me something to howl about by belting me one, and the CPS woman took me away that very night.

··· ···

And that, Bill, was how I came to be fostered with the policeman, Brad Gilcannon, while still taking classical piano lessons from Mrs. Pence.

6

I look around a kitchen where I've never been and yet I seem to know: the trellised wallpaper, the elderly gas stove, the sink that wears a curtain like a skirt to hide the dish detergent and scouring powder. The plumbing may not be as old as the house, but it's old enough.

Mrs. Pence sets coffee and a bowl of cold cereal and milk in front of me. She's wearing a gray corduroy skirt and a gray cotton sweater this morning, and yes, even in the rising heat of summer, stockings and shoes with low heels. Of course! She's dressed for a day of piano lessons.

"How are you feeling this morning?"

I shrug; I don't know how to explain that I'm defenseless without the physical pain or that I have blank spaces of memory. In the morning light that falls through the kitchen windows, her hawk's eyes are as sharp as I remember, but her face wears a new web of wrinkles. Her fragility frightens me. She doesn't know me. I'm a stranger now. I might be up to anything. Why doesn't she seem to be afraid of me?

"You may be feeling the anesthetic leaving your body," she suggests, and I nod. Her coffee tastes thin. *Typical English slop*, a voice sneers. Whose voice? My mother's? I can't remember Mrs. Pence and my mother ever speaking to each other. My mother screaming at her, yes.

"Do you have plans, Ruth?"

Plans. Something other people have, as Gall would say when Brazos or Bill the Drummer tried to nail him down for a gig. The husky texture of Gall's voice as clear as if he's sitting next to me at Mrs. Pence's kitchen table. I don't know what has happened to Gall, I didn't leave so much as a note for Brazos and Bill after I stole Gall's money, and here I am, in this town where everybody who remembers me hates me, in my old piano teacher's house. Eating her cereal in her kitchen. I feel a burn of tears and then anger. Out of the snarl I've made of my life, how could I have a plan?

Hitchhiking to Boise.

"No. No plans."

Her hawk's eyes search my face. I know that if she ever hears a false note, she won't rest until it's corrected.

"Well." She uses one hand to help herself rise from the table. She sweeps my cup and bowl into the sink and adds, with her back turned, "Of course you'll need to heal."

The doorbell rings.

Mrs. Pence goes to answer it, and I glimpse a little girl in blue jeans with a backpack hitched to her shoulders. She gives me a shy, curious look as Mrs. Pence leads her into the piano room and I escape out the kitchen's back door.

Bright sunlight illuminates the signs of a property run down. The sagging steps, the flaking paint on the picket fence behind the big spruce, where I'd somehow known to hide. The backyard lawn already has gone brown from unseasonable heat, although it's been mowed and trimmed. I smell grass clippings and coffee grounds on a neat compost heap, and I think I remember a neighbor boy who once mowed Mrs. Pence's lawns. Maybe he also kept up the flowerbeds, because I don't remember Mrs. Pence ever gardening.

But somebody is gardening back here now. Where the hollyhocks used to grow along the garage is a narrow spaded bed with a couple rows of something with fluffy tops, carrots maybe, and some green spikes that might grow into onions and something else green that might be leaf lettuce. Somebody has started a salad garden. With the sun warm on my shoulders, I follow the rows of carrot tops and onion sprouts around the corner of the garage and find, flourishing where they would be found only by accident, by someone wandering like me, several green plants with the familiar fivefold serrated leaves.

I pause for a time by the garage in the warm afternoon shade. Somewhere nearby a lawn is being watered. I can hear the swish-swish of the automatic sprinkler. It's the wrong time of day to be watering a lawn; the droplets will evaporate in the heat almost before they hit the grass. Also it's illegal. Mrs. Pence remarked that it has not rained in the Orchards for weeks and that there are watering restrictions. Somebody's going to be in trouble. Otherwise, all is unremarkable: a car passing slowly on the gravel street and fading into distance, the air permeated with the scent of spruce needles, the scent of honeysuckle growing over a neighbor's porch. A child shouts in a high-pitched treble, *No! Not yet! I'm still playing!* And someone answers, farther away and indistinct.

A patch of bud behind Mrs. Pence's garage. Who is the gardener?

··· ···

"Are you thinking of rejoining your band? Are they still in Alaska?"

This evening, after her day of piano lessons, Mrs. Pence has set the table in her dining room for two. Like an emblem of past affluence, the table is a carved dark wood with a matching breakfront that holds china, and the room is dim behind drawn shades. Dinner is a gray meatloaf, lukewarm. Mrs. Pence watches until I try a little salt to see if it helps and take a second bite of meatloaf. How had she known I'd been in Alaska? Had I talked while I was under the anesthesia, or had she found my passenger receipt in my backpack when she took out my clothes to wash?

"No. I won't go back to Alaska."

Compared with going back to Anchorage, hitchhiking to Boise is a great option.

"They won't be missing you? What will they do for keyboard and vocals?"

At my look of surprise, she explains, "We used to see posters for Ruby Red and the Idaho Rivermen."

I nod. That would have been after I turned eighteen and it was safe to play in Montana again.

But her question makes me wonder about Brazos and Bill the Drummer, who is the ordinary working guy the two rich Boise kids recruited for their band because he's so damned good on drums. Had Brazos and Bill tried to keep the gig going at the Kodiak Club after Gall's meltdown? Did they wonder where I'd gone? If they found out I'd stolen Gall's money, they might have called the police, and the police might have checked with the airport and discovered that I'd bought the ticket to Spokane.

No. The last I'd seen of Brazos and Bill, they had been too enraged with each other to worry about me.

"You never finished high school, Ruth?"

"No. But I—"

The equivalency exam. Getting me ready for it, prodding me to do it, was another of Brazos's projects—Come on, Ruby. You can do this. This math ain't that hard. Bill? You remember enough geometry to help her with it?

"Oh!" says Mrs. Pence, when I explained. "With the high school equivalency, you can apply for work."

"A job?"

"Unless you're thinking of starting another band? Going on the road again?"

She is right. A plan. A job. An even better idea than hitchhiking to Boise. One foot in front of the other for as long as I can stay awake and keep moving.

"A dear friend of mine is advertising for a data entry position at the college," says Mrs. Pence. "You can type, can't you?"

7

So, at seven-thirty on Monday morning, I drive Mrs. Pence's Pontiac down the grade to turn on Main and then on College Way. Cloud shadows drift eastward across the low bluffs over the Milk River, and the brown grass on both sides of the street smells of roasted seeds and road oil. The air is parched and headed for 110 degrees before noon.

The Pontiac must be nearly as old as I am. I'm having trouble with the unfamiliar standard gear shift, forgetting to step on the clutch and stalling out at traffic lights and having to restart. But I make a major discovery: the Pontiac's radio still works, and when I fiddle with the clumsy old knob, I find a retro country station playing James McMurtry's "Fire Line Road," and I almost pull over to listen.

Instead, I turn into the lot behind the administration building and park the Pontiac where the Indianhead hood ornament with his streaming hair can keep watch in the shade of the firs along the baseball field and where I can listen to the end of "Fire Line Road," lock the Pontiac, and take a deep breath. I'm early.

I've been on the Versailles State campus once before, for a job fair while I was still going to high school, where I stood around pretending to read brochures from the rows of tables while people who knew where they were going dodged around me and hurried on their way. I didn't belong here then, and I don't belong here now. The brick buildings with their luxuriant ivy and their inscrutable windows, the walkways, the banks of flowerbeds, speak of profound thoughts and privilege.

No watering restrictions on campus, for example. In the Orchards lawns may have turned brown and gardens are shriveling, but on campus the underground sprinklers fling glittering arcs of plenty through the shadows of trees and the sunlit grass.

Mrs. Pence got out a campus map and showed me where to find the Office of Student Accounting. The college is in summer session, she explained. Many of the faculty will be off for the summer, and only a few students will be taking classes, so you won't see many people. In fact, the shaded sidewalks are mostly empty. But when I enter through the plate glass doors of the administration building, the clatter of women's voices and women's shoes rushing across granite toward their offices makes me think I've come to the country of women.

I know the office I want is on the third floor, but I pretend to check the directory to give myself a moment to breathe. Then up a flight of stairs, up another flight and up another, while the air grows steadily warmer and stuffier. And there it is: an oak door with an opaque glass window lettered in gold. OFFICE OF STUDENT ACCOUNTING.

The lesson learned on the road. Always look as though you know where you're going, even when you don't. Especially when you don't. I close my eyes for a count of three, pretend I'm about to hit an opening chord on the keyboard at Brazos's nod, and walk in.

A narrow waiting area with a couple of chairs beside the door is divided by a counter from a larger work space with a closed and polished door at each end. Green plants hang in the windows and framed travel posters of Paris and London and Madrid on the walls, but all else is gray. Gray walls, gray metal file cabinets, and gray desks holding computers shrouded in gray vinyl covers.

No one seems to be around, so I sit down to wait and then nearly jump out of my skin when someone says, "Can I help you?"

A woman straightens from a coffee maker where she had been pouring water. No wonder I didn't see her bending down on the other side of the counter; she can't be five feet tall. But she is shaped like a fireplug, stout and formidable, and her tone makes clear that she's in charge of this gray space.

"I'm Ruth Gervais." *Szcher-vay.* "I'm here to apply for the data entry job?"

She doesn't react to my name. "Oh, okay. Most people apply online. But you can fill these out," and she hands me a clipboard with some forms. "The coffee takes about fifteen minutes. We need to get a new coffee maker up here."

She has short clipped hair and a child's round-cheeked face, but her eyes are dark brown and cautious, and I'm put in mind of Mrs. Pence's hawk's eyes. I don't suppose this woman ever misses a false note either. But I take the clipboard and forms and the ballpoint she gives me, and I print my name and Mrs. Pence's address. My social security number, my date of birth, my level of education. I'm pondering how to answer the question on work experience when a very young woman bursts through the door in an aura of citrusy perfume and a blaze of color, orange jeans and a yellow T-shirt and a cascade of maroon ringlets.

"Oh, Jamie!" she gasps. "I'm sorry! I'm so frickin frickin late!"

"You'd better start doing something about it," says the short woman. "Coffee?"

"I'm *dying* for coffee! Dustin wouldn't let me stop at the Mocha Bar this morning."

She turns and stares at me as I write *vocalist and keyboard player in a country-western band* on the form, add some dates, and hand the clipboard back to the woman called Jamie, who glances through it, pauses on my final answer, and lays the form in a wire basket.

"Can you type?"

"Yes."

"Come back here and show me."

She opens a swinging door in the counter and leads me to a desk, where she uncovers a computer. "Here you go. Can you enter these names and numbers?"

At the computer keyboard I flex my fingers. I've got big piano-playing hands with a broad reach, just like Mrs. Pence's, and while I haven't done any typing since I dropped out of high school, Mrs. Pence had me practice on her laptop keyboard last night, and I know I'll be okay. Accuracy and speed on a computer keyboard are a treat for a pianist.

The names and numbers on Jamie's pages require just enough attention to keep my mind on track while my hands and fingers take over. The computer screen fills, and I hit SAVE in the file Jamie indicates and tap-tap-tap through the next page and the next in a rhythm that lulls me. If this is the most that is asked of me, I might be able to do this work. If *vocalist and keyboard player in a country-western band* doesn't sink me.

"Stop!" Jamie shouts. "That's good! Stop!"

I hit SAVE one last time, fold my hands in my lap, and surface back into the gray world. Jamie and the girl with the maroon ringlets are staring at me.

"Wow! I never *saw* anybody type that fast."

"You're hired. Catina, get her a cup of coffee."

"You can do that? Hire her, just like that?"

"Dr. Brenner *said*—"

"Yes, but—"

While they argue about a search process and temporary hiring and somebody they call the Queen, I'm thinking that with this job, I'd just have to breathe and type. I could drive down from the Orchards and walk across campus every morning and take the cover off a computer and let myself dissolve into rows of names and numbers that might as well be random for all they mean to me.

"Here's coffee," says Catina, offering me a cup.

The outer door opens to let in a tall gaunt man in a gray suit with a close gray crew cut and a face as blank as a robot that has been assigned to oversee this gray office.

"Dr. Brenner! We've just hired Ruth Gervais, here."

He sets down his briefcase and takes the cup of coffee from Catina. A ghost of a smile lights the bones of his face and fades. "Ruth?" His voice is a robot's hollow baritone. "You're Mrs. Pence's—" He interrupts himself to taste the coffee. "I've known Mrs. Pence for many years—yes, thanks, Catina. And I keep telling you. I can pour my own coffee. But it's very good coffee. So. Ruth."

I wait. He says no more, but his eyes travel over me. Brad Gilcannon used to say that people with college degrees were educated fools, but I don't think Dr. Brenner is a fool. He's thinking about something that matters to me—I just don't know what.

At last he nods and carries his briefcase and coffee through the door with his name on it. The door shuts behind him.

"He never says much," explains Catina.

"Go ahead and finish the batch you were working on," says Jamie. "We take a half-hour lunch in the summer so we can leave a half-hour early in the afternoon. Do you always dress like that?"

I look down at myself. You'll need a decent outfit to get started, Mrs. Pence had said. She went over her checkbook register and pursed her lips and finally decided she could manage the black skirt and black heeled shoes and hose and what she called blouses, one in black and one in a subdued blue, that I could alternate.

Until your payday, she said, as she combed back my hair and pinned it in a knot.

"We're pretty informal here in the summer," says Jamie.

8

At four thirty the clatter of women's voices and women's shoes on granite stairs and hallways is a noisy river out the doors and into the afternoon heat. They are the women of the classified staff, I have learned, and in the summer, with most of the faculty gone and the big administrators on vacation, they pretty much own the campus.

I save my files and help Jamie cover the computers and tidy away the coffee mugs and the clutter of papers on the counter. Catina is long gone, a departing flash of orange and yellow and a scent of citrus.

"That damned Dustin," explains Jamie. "He throws a shit fit if she's a minute late."

She and I walk out of the administration building with a cluster of women and a few men in suits. Everyone seems to know Jamie, and they stare openly at me.

"Good night, Jamie."

"Good night, Jamie."

"Good night," she says to everyone, and to me, "See you tomorrow."

As I unlock the Pontiac, I watch her small sturdy figure trudge through the shade of the line of firs, which lies like a mirage across the parking lot. She's a woman who knows where she's going. When she disappears behind the firs, I climb into the oven of the Pontiac, thinking *See you tomorrow*. And tomorrow and the next day in this strange new world.

··· ···

Just as I pull the Pontiac into Mrs. Pence's driveway, with the cottonwoods and maples and ash trees of the Orchards hanging their dusty load of leaves overhead, the retro radio station begins "Fire Line Road" again, and I kill the motor and rest my forehead on the steering wheel.

We were playing "Fire Line Road" at the Kodiak Club that night, or trying to play it, when Gall spun out of control and Brazos and Bill the Drummer chased him all over Anchorage while my head vibrated with that hard-driving drumbeat and the hard-bitten lyrics and my pain screamed. Yes, yes, Gall promised when Brazos and Bill the Drummer finally caught him. I'll fly home, I'll go into treatment, whatever. Brazos caught my arm on his way out of the motel room.

I never thought he'd care if I balled you, Ruby.

Brazos and Bill the Drummer shout at each other outside the door of the motel room where the elk roam the wallpaper.

You're quitting us? Now?

Brazos, for god's sake! There's no *us* anymore! I should have left a long time ago. Only reason I stayed was because of her. And now this crap! To Ruby? What the fuck was in your head?

Yeah, well, I never thought—

No, you never think! Gall's a lunatic, but you should have had brains enough not to do what you did to her.

She never said not to. Anyway, why do you care about Ruby?

You stupid bastard, why do you think I care?

... ...

I raise my head from the steering wheel and get out of the Pontiac just as one of Mrs. Pence's piano students hurries down the porch steps with her backpack of music. She's about fifteen, with pretty blonde hair that floats around her face. Blue jeans, sandals, a lacy top. I wonder if she rates the Debussy étude. Probably not. I've been hearing a lot of "Für Elise" in various stages.

"Hi!" she says. "You're Ruth, right? You're staying with your gramma for a while?"

"I'm staying with Mrs. Pence. She's not my grandmother. She used to be my piano teacher."

"Oh." She studies me, thinking complicated thoughts, while I feel scathed and suspect. Living with the old lady, spending her money, is probably what people are saying about me.

"Oh, well," she says. "G'night then."

She rights her bike from the sidewalk, mounts it with her satchel over her shoulder, and wheels off. The two boys doing wheelies by the mailboxes must have been waiting for her because they fall in behind her.

Mrs. Pence's next student is murdering "The Happy Farmer" as I pass through the foyer on my way to the stairs, where Ray Pence smiles at me from his frame, still expecting good news.

"I got the job," I tell him.

Safe in the white bedroom, I nod to the sullen young man in the Polaroid, step out of my shoes and ease off my sticky hose, hang up the skirt and blouse, and think about a shower but settle for passing a cold washcloth over my face and arms. Flat on my back on the bed, my breathing shallow in the warm air of the second story, I listen to the faint starts and stumbles through "The Happy Farmer" from downstairs.

What I can remember about my first piano lesson. I might have been five or six, and I have no memory of before or after the lesson, but I know I sat on the oak bench in the piano room, the same bench where the "Für Elise" student sat this afternoon and the "Happy Farmer" girl sits now. Mrs. Pence smelled of what I later knew was English lavender soap. Still does.

Do I really remember her arranging my fingers in the curved position and showing me which key was middle C?

The air in the white bedroom is heavy from the heat on the shingled roof. Sweat trickles through my hair and sticks to the sheet. I run my fingers along my thigh and find the sweet spot between my legs, thinking of rubbing myself until I reach relief, the way Sharyn the Screamer showed me. Then I stop.

Gall.

My memory is clear enough of that last night at the Kodiak Club, Gall laughing like a maniac and playing "Fire Line Road" faster and faster on his wild out-of-control guitar, faster than any of us had ever played, until I stopped singing and Brazos and Bill the Drummer struggled to drag the beat back down.

Gall, you gotta get help.

Gall promising yes, yes, then running down the freeway through the middle of town and spooking the goddamn moose that used to clatter across the median and hold up traffic. That was Anchorage for you, a moose in the middle of traffic. And then Gall. When Brazos and Bill finally caught him, he was Yes, hell yes, I'll fly home, get help, whatever you say. But something terrible must have happened after they took him to the Anchorage airport because they came back shouting and swearing at each other outside my motel room door.

No. Better not to think about the Rivermen or Bill the Drummer or Gall, even if I never feel pleasure again or even relief. Better to think about the mindless job. If I can keep the job and earn a paycheck, I can repay Mrs. Pence for the clothes she bought me and perhaps buy a little fan to set on the windowsill and get me through the rest of the summer.

Get through the rest of the summer. There's a goal. Anything might happen by the end of summer.

Downstairs the pianos wait for me. I feel their silent hum through the floor. The upright Kimball grand with the oak-leaf design carved on its front, the little walnut spinet where Mrs. Pence sometimes accompanies her students, the long and gleaming Steinway that no one touches but Mrs. Pence. They all will be in perfect tune. Mrs. Pence would go hungry before she allowed her pianos to go untuned.

Moonlight falls through the curtains as I turn back the sheet and slide out of bed, wearing nothing but the ragged T-shirt that has lost the scent of Gall. The floor of the white bedroom holds the warmth of the day as, barefoot and silent, I feel my way down the stairs, past Ray Pence's smiling face, and along the hallway to the piano room.

Even on the dark side of the house, light from the moon illuminates the black and white keys of the upright grand and the spinet. The Steinway, of course, is a closed and shadowed bulk.

Beethoven keeps a pale presence in the dark. The familiar oak bench in front of the upright grand waits for me. Automatically, I slide it several inches away from the piano—my legs are longer than the legs of the pupil who last sat here—to play. I could turn on the music light clipped to the front of the piano, but I don't. I touch middle C and listen to the lovely tone rising from the soundboard until it fades.

My hands must recall the stumbling attempts of the student this afternoon—*Just get it right!*—because they lift themselves to the keys and begin the rippling eighth notes of "Für Elise." As long as I don't think about how many years it's been since I played a real piano or whether I will remember the next measure or where to place the accidentals, my hands need only to be set free to play through the first movements and find the long chromatic descent that leads to the reprise and the conclusion. Mindless, my hands seek the piano, and the piano answers with the beauty of the sad A minor.

When I tiptoe out of the piano room, I see the narrow strip of light under Mrs. Pence's bedroom door and know she has been awake and listening.

9

Friday. Payday. At the little grilled window in the foyer of the administration building, I stop to ask for my check, and the woman behind the grill rummages through a file until she finds mine.

"Ruth Jarvis, right? With a G? How do you like working for Old Stone Face?"

"Okay."

"Better you than me. Do you want to sign up for direct deposit?" she asks, and I realize I'm going to have to open a checking account.

With my check in hand, I push open the plate glass door at the end of the corridor and catch up with Jamie on the stone steps.

"Look at that, will you?" says Jamie.

Across the street from the administration building, on the strip of lawn by the firs, a young man in a red T-shirt and a baseball cap, a golf club in his hands, leans over a little white ball.

"Who is he? What's he doing?"

"He's practicing his putting. At least that's what he wants us to think he's doing."

He glances up, sees we're watching him, and gives the bill of his cap a sharp tug. Then he hunches over the ball and gives it a mild tap with his putter. The ball rolls about fifteen feet, and he gives us another furtive look as he goes to retrieve it.

"That's Dustin."

"Catina's Dustin?"

"The boy himself."

Jamie and I watch as he lines up his ball again and putts it in our direction. Something is self-conscious about his abrupt movements and the looks he sneaks in our direction. I don't know much about golf, but I know I'm seeing a performance.

"What he's really doing is watching for Catina. He's making sure she isn't stopping to talk to any other guys."

We watch while he putts the ball once more. I can't see much of his face under the bill of his cap, but he has a nice ass. And Catina really is late. Up until today she had shot out of the office ahead of Jamie and me at four thirty.

"Well—" Jamie shrugs. "Enjoy your weekend."

On my way home from campus I stop at the branch bank in the Orchards and open an account and deposit my check. It's a small one because I've only worked five days, but it's enough for now. After I set aside the money to repay Mrs. Pence for my clothes, I can buy the little fan at the hardware store in the shopping strip and also a few things at the Safeway, including tampons, which I had dreaded having to ask Mrs. Pence to purchase for me.

I hear a piano as I open the front door. Another lesson in progress, another pupil trying to play "The Happy Farmer" but missing the B flat and having to start over. *Finish it!* I want to scream, and wonder how Mrs. Pence stands it.

I set my bag from Safeway on the kitchen table and look around for utensils. With a cutting board and a fairly decent knife, I slice chicken breasts and dice the celery and onion. Mrs. Pence doesn't possess a wok, of course, but I've often watched Bill the Drummer improvise. One time he scrubbed out a hubcap and cooked stir-fry at the side of a highway. I'll sauté the chicken and vegetables and then scramble an egg or two into leftover rice from the refrigerator. White rice and beans obviously are Mrs. Pence's staples, meatloaf a splurge, and I don't want to face another week of the bland and tasteless.

"The Happy Farmer" player blunders away in the piano room—*ta-dah, ta dah, ta-dah-ta-dah-ta-dah* and another missed

42

flat and a restart—while I lace my fried rice with soy sauce. By the time Mrs. Pence dismisses the student and comes to find out what's happening in her kitchen, my stir-fry smells as good to me as anything Bill the Drummer ever cooked.

Mrs. Pence looks from me to the skillet, then rummages in a cupboard, brings out a bottle of white wine, and uses a dish towel to wipe the dust out of two glasses.

"A bit of a celebration!"

We toast each other with wine that's warm and flat.

"It was a present from a student," Mrs. Pence explains, "some years ago."

She looks too thin to me, and too pale, as though she hasn't been getting outside the house enough. Her plates look like the survivors of several sets of china, her assortment of tarnished sterling silver knives and forks a medley of unmatched patterns. I pick up an oversized fork in an ornate floral design and am surprised as always by its weight and the way it holds the heat of the food. Had she brought the sterling from England with her? Why all the odd patterns? I've seldom heard her speak of England and then only in a sidelong way, right after she adopted the puppy, which was not long before I left with the Rivermen: *His name is Jonathan because he is an American dog.*

She picks at the fried rice, and I worry that the soy sauce has too much tang for her after all her bland food. But she eats a little of the chicken and then folds her napkin.

"So, the job turns out to be—well, *not unsuitable?*"

What to tell her. That the work isn't difficult. And the campus isn't the place of lofty vision I always feared. Maybe the great ones are thinking their thoughts at some high level where the air has thinned, but the corridors and stairs and front offices belong to the secretaries and clerks.

But working in the Office of Student Accounting is like waking up and finding myself in the middle of an animated cartoon. That remote third-floor space, inhabited by a fireplug woman and a glad girl of ringlets and bright colors, overseen by a gray robot and haunted by someone they call the Queen—and I suppose I'm as strange as any of them in my cheap black clothes chosen by Mrs. Pence—that office is also a safe space where information seems to float up to the third floor like warm air.

By the end of the first week I've learned that Dr. Brenner—*Old Stone Face*—frightens people but is a decent boss; that a woman in computer services wears long sleeves to hide the needle tracks on her arms; and that everybody but Catina believes Dustin the Golfer is a jerk, although a really cute jerk. I'm sure the news that Dr. Brenner has hired Ruby Jarvis, of all people, already has filtered through the corridors.

"Don't musicians in bands gossip about each other?" asks Mrs. Pence.

I think about that. "They're mostly guys. They know things about each other, but they don't talk as much."

Of course, in the case of the Rivermen, Gall and Brazos had known each other since high school in Boise and Bill the Drummer almost as long. I used to listen to them reminisce. There was one story they told about a big Samoan who hung around the basement where they practiced. I never understood what was so hilarious about the Samoan, but they would laugh so hard that Gall once spilled his beer down the front of his shirt and they all laughed harder.

"The job is all right," I assure Mrs. Pence. "It's going to be okay."

The truth is, I feel removed. Like something has been removed from me. Well, the appendix, yes, the useless bit of flesh, and maybe the surgical incision stands for some deeper removal. A fragment of a familiar song—*let it rain, and let the rain heal my heart*—from the speakers of a passing car still wrenches me. I have to guard my thoughts by cutting off any stray creepers that lead back to the bad places. But here in Versailles, so far removed from Gall and where time has looped back into scenes pretending to be their former selves, I walk through the days. I rattle my data into my computer, come back to Mrs. Pence's house and wake from dreams I can't remember, and I prowl downstairs to play the piano in the dead of night. Something has been removed all right. Nothing has been added.

On Monday morning I climb the three flights of stairs to the Office of Student Accounting and, even as I open the door, sense a storm so strong I think I've wandered into an alternate time zone. The coffee has been brewed and the plants watered, but Jamie stares into her computer screen without glancing in my direction.

"The Queen's back from her vacation," she whispers when I'm near enough to hear. "I hope the hell Catina gets to work on time, for once in her life."

I uncover my computer and look around the long room where Jamie and Catina and I work. At each end of the room is a polished walnut door. One door is Dr. Brenner's. We see him coming and going, silent and skeletal and gray, and once in a while he sticks his head out to speak to Jamie, but otherwise he stays in his office and minds his own business.

Whose is the other office? I've never bothered to read the nameplate on the door, just as I've never been curious about the identity of the Queen Jamie and Catina whisper about, and now it's too late because a woman is walking through the outer doorway, and I recognize her just as she recognizes me.

Anne Roscovitch.

At first I think Anne hasn't aged a day—the same big blue eyes, the long pointed nose, the blonde hair down to her shoulders—but of course she's aged. Anne was in her teens when I was eight, and now her cheekbones have sharpened and lines have etched her lips, and she's dressed in a way I've seen none of the women on campus dress, in an expensive blue silk suit and blue stiletto heels. Her eyes lock mine, and I feel as though I'm looking through sunspots.

Catina picks that moment to sidle in. She looks from one to the other of us with apprehensive eyes.

"What are *you* doing here?" says Anne.

I'm still holding the cover to my computer. I can't speak.

"She's the new data entry," says Jamie.

"She's *what?*"

"The data entry position? The temp hire? Dr. Brenner said to get somebody in who could type and was accurate—"

"*Dr. Brenner* did this? Do you know who she *is?*"

"Ruth Gervais?"

"She's *Ruby Jarvis!*"

Anne turns on her five-inch heels, marches to Dr. Brenner's door, raps twice, lets herself in without waiting, and closes the door behind her.

The silence is so profound that I hear Catina breathing through her mouth. I sit down because I have to. I lay the computer cover on the desk. I look at the desk. Gray metal surface, gray metal sides. Three small drawers that hold nothing. I imagine myself crawling under the desk, down on the industrial-grade carpeting among the dust rolls and lost paper clips and forgotten ballpoint pens. On my computer the screen saver pattern expands and contracts.

I've always known I'd eventually run into someone in Versailles who remembers me and hates me. I just never thought it would be Anne Roscovitch.

Jamie leans over my desk. "Better drink your coffee," she says, and sets a cup in front of me. But the coffee sloshes when I try to lift the cup to my mouth.

"Are you okay?"

No, I'm not. But I'm not eight years old either, and I raise my head and will my hands to stop shaking.

"Catina, you've got the phone. Ruth, you come with me."

Jamie leads me down the polished granite corridor, past the open doors of serene offices where women bend over their work, where a telephone is answered mid-ring and conversation is low and discreet. She stops at a locked door, which she opens with a key from the bunch she carries.

"Private restroom for staff. That's us," she says, and relocks the door behind us.

Someone has gone to a lot of trouble to make this space pleasant. White wicker furniture with flowered cushions, an ornamental mirror over the sink, and a vase of plastic tulips at a window that overlooks a sidewalk and a slice of lawn. I drop down on the settee and look at the floor of discolored octagonal tiles that wicker and plastic flowers can't disguise. My feet look foreign to me in the black heeled shoes and black hose selected by Mrs. Pence. Somebody else's feet.

Jamie sits beside me. She's so short that her feet dangle. I take a deep breath and listen to the silence and the small sounds, pipes gurgling from a flushed toilet somewhere and voices from the sidewalk under the window, as indistinct as the chatter of birds.

"I take it you know Anne Albert."

"Anne *Albert*?"

"She's just staff like us but a high grade, a twelve or thirteen. Look, I don't know what the problem is, but don't worry—she can't get you fired."

I hadn't thought that far ahead.

But Jamie exudes calm, and I will myself to listen to what she's telling me about Anne.

"She's from Boise. Rotten childhood and so forth. Ended up in foster care here in Versailles."

"That's how I knew her. We were in foster care together."

Jamie gives me a sharp look. "I don't know the whole story, I grew up in Bozeman myself, didn't move up here until a few years ago. But give her credit—she got her act together and graduated from this college. She started working on campus as a clerk, and then Dr. Brenner hired her as his administrative assistant, which is what they call a secretary now. Don't worry about her. She's just pissed because Dr. Brenner went out and hired you without asking her permission. She'll get over it or she won't, but either way it won't matter."

Maybe it matters, and maybe it doesn't, but I'm soothed by Jamie's certainty. No holes in Jamie's mind, no fears.

"She's married to a rich doctor here in town. Francis Albert. That's why she can buy the kind of clothes she does. Are you okay now? We need to get back and see how Catina's doing. And—we need to get you out of those goddamn Walmart black clothes. You look like you're wearing stuff your grandmother picked out for you. How old are you anyway?

10

Catina ducked out at four fifteen while Jamie was in Dr. Brenner's office, conferring with him about something. I'm entering my last few rows of student data and keeping myself from time traveling by trying to think what I might pick up at Safeway for dinner when I catch a whiff of sharp scent and turn on my swivel chair to see Anne in her five-inch heels, towering over me in my chair. When she speaks, it's in a shaky whisper.

"Don't think I don't know why you're here!"

I hear the ratchet of one of the printers shutting down.

"Don't think that you can hurt me now! Because you can't! You can't! You can't!"

Her hands are trembling as badly as her voice. "I'm not afraid of you, Ruby Jarvis! You liar! You liar!"

Her blazing blue gaze holds mine, but her face is working, and suddenly she turns on her stilettos and runs out the door.

··· ···

The Chopin Prelude in E Minor is more difficult than "Für Elise," and I finally resort to clicking on the piano light and turning the pages of the Schirmer book until I find the music. Even then, the sad chords resist me until I work out the right hand and then the left at a tempo too slow to call a tempo. After all the years playing an electronic keyboard and then typing at a computer keyboard, the piano keys are asking my fingers for a force they've lost.

But line by line I find my way. How long have I been playing? I don't know. Line by line, over and over, until my heartbeat slows and my breathing slows and whatever I had dreamed about has faded. I'm mindless, lost not in sound alone but in the weaving of sound into a web that contains me above a bottomless chasm. And then I come to the end, and my mind switches back on.

It had been a long day. When Jamie and I came back from the staff restroom, I tried to concentrate on my rows of names and numbers even with Anne seething behind her closed door. She hadn't talked long with Dr. Brenner, Catina whispered. She walked out of his office and into her own and closed the door and hadn't come back out.

I tell myself to think about something else. Think about music. Think about a tenor voice that, once heard, is hard to forget. Gall sings that it's a hard way—take a deep breath while the instrumental line fills in—to find out. No, don't think about that. Don't think about the hickory wind and trouble that's real.

And don't think about Anne or her strange words. The way her voice shook. Why would she be afraid of me?

··· ···

I'm sitting cross-legged in one corner of Brad Gilcannon's TV-watching room, as they call the living room at his house. Isaiah and the other big boys in Brad's fosterage are somewhere, maybe shooting hoops in the driveway. Brad's own little boys are sitting on the floor watching cartoons. Brad, out of uniform, has stretched out in his recliner, and Anne is cuddled up beside him. A father and his pretty teenaged daughter, anyone watching from outside the window might think. I'm only eight years old, and I haven't been fostered with Brad for long but long enough to know that Anne is special. She makes straight As in high school, and she has medication she must take at exact times without fail. Her blonde hair tickles Brad's face when she bends toward him, and he brushes it away and laughs. She traces the outline of his top shirt button with her finger, and then they both look up and see that I'm watching them.

Ruby's got truth issues, says the tweed jacket woman when she leads me into Brad's living room. We can't get her to tell the truth about her bruises.

We'll take care of that, says Brad. The heat in Brad's house is turned up higher than the heat in my mother's house or the Mister's house ever was, and the lights are so bright that I squint against them. Brad's wife stands in the kitchen door. She has faded brown hair clipped short in a cap around her face, and she holds her hands cupped like a basket in front of her stomach, and I wonder if her stomach hurts. I know, or maybe I learn later, that the two little boys playing with action figures on the floor belong to her and Brad, but the others are foster kids like I'm going to be.

The tweed jacket woman bends down to speak into my face. You don't have to worry here. Mr. Gilcannon is a policeman. It's his job to protect little girls like you.

Have her step in here so she can meet the other kids, he says.

In the living room four boys, one of them a black boy, watch television while an older girl keeps her book open and takes notes on what she is reading. Her long blonde hair falls over her face like a curtain.

This is Ruth Jarvis, but everyone calls her Ruby.

The girl glances up. She has a long pointed nose, but her eyes are large and blue and beautiful. I can tell she's not interested in me. She shrugs and goes back to writing in her notebook.

Is this really what happened the first time I saw Anne? Was she writing in a notebook? In the thinning of the light that soon will be morning, I think I may have woven the whole scene out of fragments gathered over the eight years I lived at Brad's house.

Fragments perhaps, but I'm certain of one thing. Anne hadn't been afraid of me then.

··· ···

After a night mostly spent relearning the Chopin E Minor Prelude, I'm blear-eyed when my alarm goes off. Bathing my eyes in cold water helps a little. I shower and pull on my office clothes and feel my way downstairs, hoping not to meet Mrs. Pence and worry her with my obvious lack of sleep. At least I'm in luck there—she's already warming up with scales in the piano room with the door shut, and I go through the kitchen and out the back door to unlock the Pontiac.

The early sun hits me in the face, and I shut my eyes and watch red and purple blotches swim under my eyelids. When I can open my eyes again, I'm looking down at the little garden of carrots and onions that somebody tends along the side of the garage. The little plants have been freshly watered this morning, a thriving green border along the shriveled backyard grass. On impulse I follow the rows around the garage to check on the contraband and find the marijuana plants also well watered and burgeoning.

Somebody in the neighborhood, thinking no one would ever look behind Mrs. Pence's garage for an illicit crop? A somebody who also grows carrots and lettuce and onions?

I shake my head and instantly regret it. When I unlock the Pontiac, the sun blinds me. I can stop at the shopping mall on my way home and buy sunglasses, but meanwhile I'll have to squint my way down from the Orchards to campus. Being half-sightless and brain clouded from lack of sleep isn't blotting out Anne Roscovitch. Anne Albert, as she is now.

Catina comes to work in worse shape than I'm in. When she takes off her dark glasses, it's clear that her liquid makeup isn't enough to hide her black eye. She flounces over to her station and drops her shoulder bag and glares around the office to warn off Jamie and me from asking, but I see from the set of Jamie's shoulders as she reaches up to water the hanging philodendrons that we're in for another storm.

Even for her, Catina blazes with color: a bright-green silk shirt with brilliant turquoise pants and turquoise sandals and a rose silk scarf wrapped around her waist. I have a vision of myself on a bandstand in fringed red leather, but my bandstand days are over, and Catina is young and beautiful, even with a black eye.

I drop my eyes to my computer keyboard before Catina catches me looking at her, and just then the outer door opens and Anne walks in.

Anne Roscovitch Albert.

Her eyes fall on me, and I straighten from my keyboard as I promised myself to do, and I look back at her until her eyes move on to Jamie with her watering can and Catina in her defiant colors.

"Jamie. I'll see you in my office."

She's wearing the blue stiletto heels that attack the carpet as she strides to her door and unlocks it.

Jamie shrugs, taps on Anne's door, and disappears after her.

I find my place in yesterday's lists and search for my numbing rhythm, but my fingers seem only to draw static from the keyboard. Something's about to be torn apart. Anne has always known how to protect herself. Always. She can't fire Catina for having a black eye or Jamie for—whatever she might dream up—because they're classified staff and can be fired, as Jamie has explained, only after a lengthy documentation of cause. But I think it's likely she'll make Dr. Brenner so miserable that he'll do anything for peace, just the way Brad did, to get Anne to cuddle with him and charm him all over again.

Not that I can picture Dr. Brenner cuddling with Anne. But maybe she can get him to fire me.

A small sound behind me, a muffled sob.

"Catina?"

"Just never mind! Just never mind!"

She has buried her face in her computer screen. I try to concentrate on mine, but it is filled with blurred letters and numbers. For nearly a month I've been keying numbers and letters into the database with no idea what they mean, but now, in this gray office where the shadows of hanging plants fall across gray desks and computers and carpet, I'm no longer safe.

Anne's voice, indistinct and savage, rises from behind her closed door.

My eyes meet Catina's. Her mouth has dropped open.

Jamie walks out of Anne's office. Before the door closes behind her, I get a glimpse over her shoulder of Anne's office walls in decorator blue, blue curtains at the window, blue armchairs, and a framed painting of flowers over Anne's desk.

Jamie sits at her computer, studies her screen for a moment, riffles through the pages of a manual on her desk, and underlines something without looking up.

Anne's door wrenches open a second time, and Anne runs out on her killer heels. She blunders into a file cabinet in her haste, slips, and catches herself.

The outer door closes behind her.

"What is going *on*?" Catina breathes, but no one answers.

Nothing for Catina or me to do but go back to work. Jamie's rigid shoulders make it clear she'll allow nothing else.

Just before twelve Dr. Brenner opens his office door, and we all look up from covering our computers.

"Jamie. Catina. Ruth."

He pauses to look out the window. The strong light picks out the outlines of his skull and the granite furrows of his face.

"Mrs. Albert. She's getting a divorce. It's a hard time for her."

Another pause. "Jamie? Your hearing is set for tomorrow?"

Jamie nods. "I'll need the morning off."

"Take the day off."

He nods and is gone.

"The way I heard the story yesterday," says Jamie into the silence, "he's the one divorcing her. Francis Albert, I mean. Maybe he finally got sick of her and found a new friend."

She closes her manual and pushes back her chair. "Ruth and Catina, go to lunch. I have an appointment to keep."

11

The shortened summer lunch break means we either bring a sandwich to work or we walk across the courtyard to the campus food court, where we can get quick salads or pizza slices or burgers. I dislike the food court for its noise and its echoing enormity of a hundred plastic tables, each with its set of four chairs, spread across a tiled floor under a thirty-foot ceiling. But today any distraction will do.

The various grills and pizza counters and salad bars run along one side of the food court, and a freestanding cement staircase rises toward the skylights and a railed balcony. Only a few of the tables are occupied today, mostly by classified staff women with voices that rise and echo as shrill as birds.

Between the air-conditioning and all this space, I always shiver here. I hadn't slept, and I'm not hungry, but I take a tray and a bowl and go through the motions. Once I'm seated with my back against a solid wall and Catina sitting opposite me like a friendly shield, it's hard not to slip into time traveling. I look down at the bowl of salad I scooped from one of the salad bars and see chopped iceberg lettuce. I'd forgotten to pour dressing on the lettuce, but I'm not going to walk back through the tables of chattering women to the salad bar.

"I know," says Catina. "All this noise. But just wait until you hear the noise the students make when they come back in the fall. It's sort of quiet now, believe it or not. It's just staff like us and a few schoolteachers come back to grab some credits."

I stab a chunk of dry lettuce and put it in my mouth and chew. I need to act like a normal person and stay in the present and not embarrass Catina, but I don't know if I can pull it off.

"I don't mind having no Jamie for once."

Catina lowers her voice and glances around, even though we're twenty feet from the nearest occupied table. "It's just that she's at me about Dustin all the time. I can enjoy a little peace and quiet."

"In our office?"

"Well—not recently."

She takes a large bite of pizza. With her cascade of maroon hair and her piercings and her fading black eye, she looks like an unhappy teenager.

I try another bite of lettuce and watch two guys who have just come in through the big glass doors. Guys are a rare sight in this enclave of women, and these two are dressed like students in hoodies and jeans, but they're my age or a little older.

Something about the dark man draws my eyes, something loose limbed in the way he walks, something familiar. He's laughing about something his friend said as they passed our table, when suddenly he stops.

He turns, stares at me.

Skin the color of cocoa, hair a silky black mass of curls.

Isaiah.

"*Ruby?*"

Isaiah. Not a face from my dream nor from my fever-borne hallucination but Isaiah's actual face, where surprise is changing to pleasure. Why is Isaiah glad to see me? Why is Isaiah pulling out a chair and sitting down beside me?

"How long have you been back in town, Ruby? What are you doing on campus?"

Isaiah's eyes, so warm and familiar that I can barely meet them. Catina stares with her mouth full of pizza, and I know I need to say something, I need to act like a normal person, but the best I can do is mutter something about *Not all that long* and *I've got a job on campus.*

Isaiah seems hardly to hear me. He reaches over and takes my hand. My pale hand in his dark hand.

"Same old piano-playing hands. You still play?"

"Sometimes."

"So do I."

His big-knuckled hands, dark and battered and pale palmed. His square-tipped fingers lace around mine, the way he took my hand in my hallucination, if that was what it was, outside the Alibi the night I came back to Versailles.

Catina swallows her pizza and recovers herself. "Her name is Ruth. Why do you call her Ruby?"

"Doesn't everybody?"

"Well, *no!*"

He's still holding my hand as he takes in Catina's piercings and the makeup over her fading black eye. She knows it too, knows what he's seeing, and she's obviously getting riled.

"So who *are* you?"

"I'm her brother," says Isaiah. At my sharp breath he adds, "Well—foster brother anyway."

... ...

After I've been fostered with Brad Gilcannon for a few days, I learn that Isaiah is almost exactly three years older than I am. That first night I only know he is bigger than me and skinny and scary, with cocoa skin and a mop of black curls. He gets up from the floor, grins at me, and does a complicated spin and slam dunk with an imaginary basketball.

You've got truth issues!

Ruby, don't you pay any attention to that ornery little devil. Isaiah, if you can't act like a stand-up white kid, you can go and turn the TV off. Ruby, you come over here and talk to me, says Brad.

When I obey, Brad smiles and pulls me onto his lap as Anne looks up from her notebook. I think she's going to object, but she doesn't, not this time. Brad has a thin lined face with a brush of brown hair and brown eyes behind dark-rimmed glasses. He's not in uniform tonight. I would have been frightened of the uniform. Tonight he's wearing ordinary blue Levi's and a blue denim shirt with a faint peppermint scent. Later I'll know that the scent comes from the sugar-free gum he carries in his pocket. Tonight he gives me a stick of the gum and puts his arm around me and asks me what my favorite songs are and whether I ever play them on the piano. After a while I snuggle into his warmth and stop shaking.

That's what my bones tell me happened that first night at Brad's. His face and Isaiah's and Anne's shine as though from a strip of color film with darkness at both ends. Did he give me a stick of sugar-free gum that night? Never mind. The scent of peppermint. His warm arms. It happened.

Three children in fosterage with Brad. Anne, Isaiah, Ruby. It happened. Something is happening again.

··· ···

Old houses gossip at night. I can hear them. Up and down the darkened streets, on currents more subtle than the stir of air, past the shadows of lilac hedges and the curbs where cats keep watch from under parked cars, around the circles of light cast by the streetlights, from one house to another, travel the creak of floorboards, the settling of attic joists, the whisper of leaves brushing against shingles: *We've got her! Her! She's here!*

I'm awake in Mrs. Pence's second-floor bedroom. The walls have settled back where they belong. A dark rectangle on the mirror where I stuck him is the sullen young man in his Polaroid. Was he in my dream? The sheet hangs halfway off the bed, crumpled from my throes. The window's faint glow is from the streetlight at the other end of the block. I'm hearing the ordinary sounds of the summer night, an air current moving through the front yard cottonwoods, a touch of leaves on the glass panes, a sigh of old shingles. The lighted numerals on my digital alarm shows 4:45 a.m., still a couple hours until I need to shower and dress for another day of work. But I can't sleep.

Finally, I pour a little water from the carafe into a glass and carry it to the cushioned bench under the window, where I look down through the cottonwood leaves and the patterns of their shadows on the silent street and try an old ruse on myself, imagining that I have merged with the shadows of the leaves. I'm erased, with nothing to feel, nothing to fear, as flattened as the glass between me and the shadows. Sometimes the ruse tricks me into going back to sleep, but not tonight, not this very early morning with the light just beginning to turn transparent, not with my mind busy with then and now.

"We got to get together, Ruby," Isaiah had said in the food court. "Now you're back, we got to catch up. I've got a little band going. You'll have to sit in with us. Play some keyboard with us, okay?"

And I noted his fingernails, a guitarist's nails.

Three kids in fosterage, Anne and Isaiah and Ruby, and now here we are in Versailles again.

Seeing Isaiah in the food court today must have set off my dream, spinning it and casting off broken bits of memory and invention. So. Easy explanation. Wouldn't happen again. If I ran into him again, it would be: Hey, Isaiah. How's it going?

Good, and you?

Good.

But I still can't sleep, and finally I steal down to the piano room and take up the Chopin Prelude in E Minor again. My fingers are getting stronger and more certain, but for some reason the E minor key is transposing itself to a plangent G major.

He promised to love me and call me his flower—and I have floated out of the piano room to a retaining wall outside an Anchorage motel, where a man sits beside me with his guitar and plays "Wildwood Flower."

  ... ...

It's a warm evening for Anchorage, and I'm grateful there's no drizzle. The concrete retaining wall along the courtyard of the motel has stored a little of the day's weak sunshine, and I can sit on the wall and bear the pain in my side and wait until the door to the room with the elk wallpaper finally opens and I am let in. After a while a door does open, and I look up, but it's not my door—it's Bill the Drummer's.

Bill's got his acoustic guitar slung over his shoulder, and he'll have to walk past me to reach the van where it's parked, so I look down at the sidewalk, but he stops.

Waits until I raise my head.

Bill glances from me to the door of my room, and I know that he knows what's happening there and why I'm sitting on the retaining wall, but he says nothing, and I'm grateful. Instead, he unslings his guitar and sits down beside me, not touching but close enough that I can smell something lemony in his freshly laundered shirt. Bill does his own laundry, never asks me to do it for him.

A lock of dark hair falls over his forehead as he tunes his guitar, cocking his head to listen to the pings and adjusting the pegs. Maybe he's not as good on his guitar as on his drums, but he's good enough, and there's something real and solid in the warmth of his heavily muscled drummer's forearm that occasionally brushes my shoulder as he searches out the chords he wants.

After a minute or two I realize that he's playing the old Carter Family tune "Wildwood Flower." Not singing, not speaking, just playing. He sits by me as the evening settles, and "Wildwood Flower" wends its plangent way and contains me in it until, at last, the door to my room opens.

What Bill the Drummer might ask if he were sitting beside me in this second-floor bedroom: Why do you think your memories are coming back, Ruby?

I don't know, Bill.

12

In the morning I've turned into the parking lot behind the administration building before I realize I've driven all the way to campus with my mind in another time and place. I pull Mrs. Pence's Pontiac into a slot in the shade of the firs and start to shake. If I don't stay in the here and now, I'm likely to run over somebody.

I rest my head on the steering wheel and concentrate on details. The scratch of upholstery, the faint ping of the Pontiac's motor shutting down, the Indian on the horn button cutting into my forehead. The glitter of sunlight shafting through the boughs of firs and hitting the windshield. When I finally look up, I see neat bungalows on the other side of the street, student rentals for the most part. On a lawn, a child's swing set, the kind with a ladder and a slide at one end. A sidewalk and steps lead to a green-painted door, all so normal, and yet who knows the thoughts, the fears, behind the closed door.

··· ···

At a police-sponsored conference Brad Gilcannon learned all about satanic rituals and how to ferret out the Satanists who were living among us in plain sight, and his investigation is making newspaper headlines. He's a local hero for the work he does. Now he leans forward as he drives, peering at street addresses. His car smells of the pine refresher that hangs from his rear-view mirror and sways on its little green string whenever he hits the brakes. Anne sits beside him in the front seat and tells him where to look. From where I've been stuck in the back seat, I can't see her face, only her blonde ponytail that sways like the pine refresher when Brad brakes at the next house.

Here?

No.

Here?

No.

Here?

Yes!

Brad jots down the street address in his notebook. Anne's ponytail is twitching from the excitement of the hunt, but I can't concentrate. I'm carsick from riding in the back seat, and I hold my stomach and swallow back the bitter taste that roils up to my mouth.

Brad drives up to the rental house on the north side of the Milk River and slows.

What about this house here, Anne?

Yes, that's one of them.

Ruby?

When I don't answer, Brad barks at me. *Ruby!*

Yes, I mumble through my clenched fingers over my mouth, and Brad parks by the curb and jots down the address.

We'll get to the bottom of this horror, he says. I promise.

··• ···

I was eight years old that summer. Anne was going to be a junior in high school in the fall. At the police seminar where Brad learned how to uncover and root out satanic cults and detect child abuse, he also learned that children never lie about abuse. My truth issues were why we were driving through the streets on the north side of the Milk River in Brad's car, and I was the problem. Just want to get to the truth, said Brad. I promise! We're gonna get to the bottom of this.

The really perplexing question had to do with the accusations and the confessions, all later recanted. Forty-eight people signed statements that they'd either witnessed or taken part in the sacrifice of babies and the rape of small children on altars, and they named the names of others who'd done the sacrificing and raping.

And I had done the same. Named my own mother. Yes. I have a lot to be sorry for.

Truth issues! Anne is screaming at me. Ruby, I'll pinch you if you don't tell the truth! I told you the truth! Now you tell it! Anne's fears. Brad's fears. What had possessed Brad and otherwise sane adults to believe in the scenes they imagined were being enacted behind their backs, just outside the edges of their vision? I once asked Brazos, who read a lot and had theories, why people seemed to *want* to believe in the cults and the satanic rituals. *Wanted* to believe in the dead babies, *wanted* still more vacant lots dug up, whole fields dug up to find the bones they were sure were buried somewhere.

Brazos shook his head and talked about the Salem witch trials, which didn't answer my question. Now I wonder if people in Versailles enjoyed the fear, if the panic was pleasurable, like living in their very own horror movie.

A cult!

The scene unfurls in red and orange flames that leap and spread and crackle and fill my imagination. Before such a conflagration I'm doomed; we're all doomed. Oh, the thrill of it, the rush of panic, the surging heartbeat! Run! Run for your lives! Or gather here in the temple of despair!

The flames rise from a brazier that has been set before the altar. Flames redden the faces of the watchers and reflect from the walls, the stained glass, the paintings of saints hung upside down. But who is the figure behind the altar, why is he hooded in black, and what is he waiting for? His eyes move behind the slits in his hood, gauging his audience, watching for—yes, now they approach the altar—his acolytes in black robes and hoods. Between them they carry the limp child. Her hair and the hem of her white dress brush the floor as they carry her. Her eyes are closed. Perhaps she has been drugged. *Or is she dead?* No, at least not yet.

The acolytes lift the child to the altar and back away. And now the hooded black priest lifts the hem of her dress and folds it back, exposing her naked white legs, her hairless pubic fold—

Stop! In the name of decency, stop!

Except they didn't stop. Brad and the others asked Anne and me over and over, keeping at us, insisting on details. What had we seen? How did we get the bruises on our private parts? It wasn't really the big boys in the alley, was it! It was the Mister! Or it was what's-his-face, my mother's current man! Are they all a part of it? A part of the cult?

In particular they wanted to hear about the dead babies. Where were the dead babies? *Tell us where the babies are buried!* Eventually, as they pieced together the stories wrung from Anne and then from me and from other frightened foster children, they dug up the vacant lot behind a church and sifted for bones, but not a dead baby did they uncover.

··· ···

I can't sit here in the parking lot forever, in the shade of dusty birches and firs, where the only shadows are those dappled by early sunlight that forecasts another scorching day, so I drag myself out of the Pontiac and up the flights of stairs to the Office of Student Accounting, where I find the outer door locked.

I dig out my key and unlock the door and set my backpack down by my computer station. The office feels empty. No Jamie, of course. Dr. Brenner's office door still closed, Anne's door closed. No sign of Catina, no coffee started. Even the spider plants and philodendrons in the window look wilted and shadowy, and I try to remember if this is one of Jamie's plant-watering days.

After I turn on the overhead fluorescents and click the START button on my computer, I go to fetch water for coffee. Dr. Brenner arrives as I'm measuring coffee into the filter. He looks more grim and gray than ever, and his eyes linger on the empty pot.

I shake my head. "It takes about fifteen minutes to perk."

He bends down, making me think of a skeleton folding at the waist, and studies the coffee maker as though to discover some flaw in its design. "Maybe we should invest in one of those Canadian velocity brewers."

When the door opens behind us, we both look up, but it's Catina with her black eye plastered over with makeup and her hair a cascade of wet ringlets.

"No Jamie, huh," she says.

But at least Catina is a bright presence, with her scent of citrus and this morning's orange shirt and cropped pink pants like a sunrise lighting up the office. She sips her soda through a straw and sets her go-cup beside her computer, in no hurry to get to work.

"I wish she had let one of you go with her," says Dr. Brenner.

We had tried. No, no, Jamie said. They won't let you into the room. It's just me and the lawyers and the CPS people.

What are CPS people? asked Catina.

Child Protective Services. It's about my little girl, Jamie explained. My ex in Bozeman has custody of her. I'm trying to get custody back. Or at least visitation.

Dr. Brenner lingers by the coffee maker with his empty mug. *He's decent*, I remember Jamie saying on my first day in the student services office. This morning he seems less like an automaton, almost human, as he studies his mug as though he expects it to fill magically on its own. Fortunately, at that moment the coffee maker emits its deep climactic gurgle, and I take the pot off the burner and pour for him.

This is also the moment, of course, that Anne Albert appears. Navy-blue silk suit this morning, navy stiletto heels, and enraged blue glare. Her clothes! If Dr. Brenner is the robot assigned to this animated cartoon office, Anne is its fashion runway model.

Anne takes in the three of us, standing around the office coffee pot with our heads together like three conspirators against her: me in my black crow clothes, Catina in her flamboyant colors, and Dr. Brenner towering over us, a rack of bones in a gray suit. She says nothing but flicks an angry glance over us, unlocks her office door, walks in, and closes the door behind her.

"Well," says Dr. Brenner. He lifts his coffee mug to me, like a toast, and takes himself off to his own office.

Catina sucks on her straw. "She never even said good morning."

"Does she ever?"

"No."

"Nothing new then."

"Oh, there's something new coming down. You just wait."

The morning rolls on.

The light in the window gradually strengthens, and Jamie's hanging plants get their color back. Catina plops herself into her chair and uncovers her computer, talking to herself in a whisper. I've been assigned a new set of student numbers to enter, and after a few minutes, thankfully, I find my rhythm on my keyboard and let it lull me. No point in trying to decipher Anne Roscovitch's—*Anne Albert's*—strange behavior. I stop hearing Catina's whisper or the clacking of a printer. Only, when someone walks down the corridor outside the office, I hear a trailing thread of song that must be playing on an electronic gadget tuned to the golden oldie country station I listen to in the Pontiac. A rich voice singing about kissing an angel good morning. The song fades with the footsteps.

13

Another morning. More of the same. Seven thirty, and already the air in the admin foyer is warm and stale. By afternoon we'll all be sweltering.

I lock the Pontiac and walk under the birches in the patterns of sun and shadows, counting sidewalk cracks to try to stay in the present. Other women, mostly classified staff, hurry toward the administration building in a rat-a-tat of heeled shoes on cement and high-pitched voices, a clamor of pointless noise.

On the third floor I smell the coffee as soon as I open the door to the Office of Student Accounting. This is a good sign. Jamie's back, and the coffee maker is bubbling, just the way it's supposed to do, and Dr. Brenner is waiting with his mug. He gives me his robot's faint smile, but I have the feeling I've interrupted something between him and Jamie.

Maybe she's been telling him what happened at her hearing. I want to know too, but I'm not going to ask. When the coffee maker utters its last gurgle and Jamie pours for all of us, her eyes meet mine, deep and brown but expressionless.

And then Catina bursts in— "Oh, I'm late, I'm late, I'm so fricking late"—in bright yellow pants and a yellow T that looks brand new and her black eye almost completely faded. She looks me a question as Jamie turns back to her computer, and I shrug.

"So. The first half-session is almost over," says Dr. Brenner.

We all know that. We're well into June now, and we nod, and he retreats to his own office with his coffee, looking stonier and bonier than ever. He's never told us more about Anne or her divorce, although we know Anne is planning some leave.

We work steadily through the morning. With the half-session only a few days from being over, we're getting student records to update. Plenty to do. But ten o'clock is time for our first coffee break, and Catina and I glance at each other, but Jamie pushes her chair back and slips out of the office by herself.

"It must have been *bad*," Catina hisses, and I nod. I'm wondering just how bad the outcome of Jamie's hearing was and what she might have been telling Dr. Brenner, with the result that I've been having trouble finding my rhythm, losing my place in the lines of numbers and striking the wrong keys. The whole office feels wrong with Jamie in a mood.

But Jamie comes back almost immediately. Perhaps she walked down to the women's room and washed her face. Her eyes are bright, but otherwise she is her sturdy fireplug self.

"If we skip the break, we can take a little longer lunch," she says, and so we all go back to work.

The heat bears down when we leave the office at noon and walk across the courtyard to the food court. The leaves hang limp and unmoving above us, and the pavement shimmers with mirages. I feel trickles of sweat through my hair, the damp tendrils pulling out of my braid, the weight of the air, the sunlight of the here and now.

It's easier to stay in the here and now when I'm with Jamie. Jamie stands for no nonsense, none of the mind floating and memory trolling that comes over me, and I'm thankful she's back, even in a mood.

The frigid air-conditioning in the food court hits like a blow for the first few minutes, until our startled pores shrink back in our skins—"Whew," says Catina, and I know what she means. We pick up our trays and go our separate ways, Jamie for the burger bar, Catina for pizza, and me for salad, to meet at our usual table near the stairs.

Jamie sets down her cola, takes a long draw through her straw, and studies her burger. "Ought to give these up."

"Why?" says Catina.

Jamie shrugs. Something's on her mind, though, and I think she might be ready to tell us what happened in court.

But no.

"Ruth, you were in foster care when you were a kid, right?"

"Yes," I say, surprised.

She takes a bite of her burger and chews for a moment.

"How old were you when they took you?"

"When cps took me away? The first time I was six. The second time? I was eight."

Another long pause. Catina, wide-eyed, has forgotten the slice of pizza that's halfway to her mouth.

"How long were you in care?"

A trickier question. I think about an answer and come up with the truth as far as it goes. "I guess—until I was old enough to, well, take off on my own."

"So you never went back to your mother."

"No."

But Jamie never asks her next question because here's Isaiah with his sloping walk and his smile. He pulls out a chair for himself at our table as though he's been invited.

We all stare at him. And what Isaiah must be seeing—Catina with her mouth open for her forgotten pizza, Jamie edgy and glaring at his interruption, and me with my messy memories probably written all over my face.

But his eyes are on me, and I don't know what to do. I don't know what he wants. All I know is that he's fractured the shell I thought I'd grown and let the old memories of Versailles crawl out in their ugly larval shapes. *Act like a normal person* isn't going to do it for me.

Okay, so at least act like a grown-up.

I lay down my fork among the chunks of tomato I've been pushing around my plate and look Isaiah in the face. His thick black lashes, his brown eyes that are fixed on me. The unfamiliar crow's-feet web that spreads to his cheekbones and reminds me that years have passed, years Isaiah spent doing what? I have no idea. I feel a weight at the thought of the years. A few more years and I'll be thirty myself.

"What are you doing here, Isaiah?"

He answers me literally. "I'm picking up certification credits. What, you don't believe it? That I'm a teacher?"

His eyes slide around me to take in Jamie and Catina. "I'm the wrestling coach at Mike Mansfield High School, and I teach history and physical education."

Mike Mansfield High School, where the corridors seem to stretch forever and turn dark corners, and the long overhead fluorescent bulbs burn out so regularly that there were rumors of electrical shorts. Anne Roscovitch had graduated by the time I started at Mike Mansfield as a freshman, but I still sensed the older girls whispering about me as I passed their lockers. Too many stories were still too fresh.

"You ever think I'd turn out to be a history teacher, Ruby?"

"No."

"So you teach history," said Jamie. She's bristling at this stranger who has interrupted our precious lunch break, while other classified staff women stare at us with open curiosity as they walk past our table on their way to the recycling bins. Jamie will have her fill of droppers-by and gossip seekers to chase out of our office this afternoon. I can just hear them: *Who's the black guy?*

Isaiah looks completely at ease. But then he has always looked at ease. By now he's probably used to people staring at the only black guy in the room, maybe the only black guy on campus except for some basketball players. But in the middle of the cafeteria, as voices chatter and plates and forks clatter their way along the conveyor belt to the dishwasher, Brad Gilcannon is pounding his fist into his hand and threatening Isaiah—God damn you, I swear I'll kick your ass from here to the courthouse if you don't tell me the truth—while the rest of us kids cower, thinking Isaiah will surely get killed this time.

Ain't gonna tell you no nevermind that never happened!

One of Isaiah's favorite tactics to drive Brad crazy was pretending to be a badass black city street kid, when the only streets he'd ever seen of a town bigger than Versailles were on television.

"We've got to get back to the office," Jamie says, and pushes away her plate. "Look at the time!"

"Where you living these days, Ruby?"

"With—" I hesitate. "My old piano teacher. She has a spare room, and I can—well, help out."

"Mrs. Pence?"

"You know her?"

I can't think how, and Isaiah doesn't get a chance to answer, because Catina has already carried off her tray and Jamie is impatient, waiting for me. As I lay down my fork, Isaiah reaches across the table and touches my fingers. "Big piano-playing hands," he murmurs as Jamie pulls me away.

"Who the *hell* was that?" she says, more to Catina than to me.

"He's cute," says Catina.

··· ···

Brad's fights with Isaiah are getting worse.

Isaiah and I are the only foster kids still living with Brad. After the appeals and then the exonerations began, one by one the other three boys were taken away, and we're never told where they went or why. No Curtis one day. No T.J. a few days later. Then no Paul. Then Anne turned eighteen and moved into a dormitory at Versailles State, although Brad tried to talk her out of the move and was grumpy for days afterward.

After they're gone, Isaiah and I get along better. Just the two of us, after all, except for the little Gilcannon boys.

Brad is testy and drawn into himself and not just because of Anne. He goes to work on his shift, and then he comes home and takes his plate and leaves the dinner table to eat by himself in front of the six o'clock news on the TV, and then he watches it all over again on the nine o'clock news. The abuse convictions and then the appeals and exonerations in Versailles, Montana, are making national headlines, and Brad is eating more and drinking more.

Isaiah comes home late from high school football practice. Brad looks up sharply at the sound of the front door opening and closing. Pulls himself out of his TV-watching recliner, confronts Isaiah on his way to the kitchen.

Practice was over an hour ago.

Coach kept us late.

Like hell!

I catch a glimpse of Brad's wife's face in the kitchen door before she turns back to where she's supervising her boys and their homework at the table. Something bad is going to happen, and I hover, as if I could wish that bad something out of the house and into the night. Or wish it wouldn't happen. Wish that Brad would be Brad again and like to hold me on his lap. You're too big for that, he said the last time he pushed me away.

Brad grabs Isaiah by the upper arm and turns him so he can smell his breath. Isaiah's had a growth spurt during the past summer, and I see that he's as tall as Brad, although not so heavy. For an awful few seconds I'm afraid Isaiah will try to twist out of Brad's grip and throw a punch, but he doesn't. He just stands there and looks right at Brad, and not a muscle of his face moves.

You can ask Coach.

That goddamn football coach! *Coach!* Thinks he's a big shot! He thinks he knows it all, and he don't know a goddamn thing!

He knows I was at practice.

Brad snarls and shakes Isaiah, and when he still can't get a reaction from him, he shoves him against the wall between the living room and the kitchen, so hard that one of Brad's wife's ornamental plates falls off its bracket and clatters and breaks. Brad's wife peers around the door, white-faced. Brad's wife has a name, Nona, but no one calls her by it.

Pride! Don't think I don't know what you've been up to! Swilling my food and stealing my beer and out there in the dark chasing them goddamn chippies as bad or worse than your lowlife mother was! You know they let her out of prison today, don't you? So she can go back on the street like a goddamn bitch in heat! You ever wonder which one of her customers planted you? And that poor damn fool of a lawyer thinks he can turn her around. Isaiah Pride! Your name oughta be goddamn Isaiah Shame! You black bastard!

Isaiah makes no attempt to break away from Brad, but something changes in his face, something like contempt. Growling, Brad jerks him away from the wall and flings him so hard he has to catch his balance.

Get the fuck outta my sight. Go downstairs and go to bed.

Brad turns, sees me. Ruby, you get to bed. Nothing going on here that's any of your business.

The last I see, Brad's wife is sweeping shards of china into a dustpan. But much later I wake and hear the faint sounds of Isaiah's guitar through the floor of my room, an old tune I think I recognize, "Silver Threads and Golden Needles," which I heard long ago on an old Janis Joplin album in my mother's house north of the river. Even though I am afraid, I slip out of bed and down the basement stairs to the room Isaiah used to share with Curtis and T.J. and Paul. The guitar pauses at my scratch on the door, and then Isaiah opens it and looks down at me.

Hey, he says, and he puts his arm around me and leads me inside, where I sit beside him on the bed while he plays the tune about silver threads and golden needles. Eventually, he sends me back upstairs before I get in trouble with Brad.

14

At four thirty on the dot, Jamie covers her computer, drags her fanny pack from under her desk, and she's out the door and gone. Anne's door is closed, as it has been all day.

"Wow," says Catina. "And to think it used to be pretty normal around here."

It's never seemed normal to me, but I don't say so.

Dr. Brenner comes out of his office with his briefcase. He takes in Catina and me and lingers on Jamie's shrouded computer.

"Did you girls get a chance to talk?"

When Catina seems tongue-tied—*Dr. Brenner, actually talking to us!*—I speak up. "No, not really, sir."

"Hmm."

He sets his briefcase on the nearest desk and seems to ponder. Then he looks directly at me, and I see that his eyes are magnified and alive behind the black-rimmed glasses he occasionally wears.

"She—well, she hoped to get custody of her daughter yesterday. Instead, the judge set another three-month probation period. Anything you two can do—well, to ease things—if you can think of anything."

"Of course!"

"Of course!"

He nods, takes up his briefcase, and nods again. "Good night."

"Good night," we chorus.

"Wow," says Catina as the door closes behind him. It's getting to be her favorite word.

"That must be what she was asking you about," she goes on. "About foster care and what it was like and whether you ever went back to live with your mother."

I nod.

"Did you miss your mother a lot?"

The office suddenly feels deserted, with only the two of us. Even the corridor has fallen silent. The voices and footsteps of departing secretaries and clerks have passed us by. The overhead fluorescent lights flicker. Catina's new yellow shirt and slacks are the only bright spots in a room of gray filing cabinets and gray desks and computer covers. She looks so young to me, with her piercings and her eyes so large and shadowed by her ringlets, and I realize that she, too, is asking me something I don't quite understand.

"Yeah. I missed her a lot. Even though I started to love Brad—my foster dad. It was awful, especially at first."

"But you can remember her?"

"Yes."

"My mother died when I was five. I don't really remember much about her."

"I'm so sorry." I feel the absurdity of the words. "Who took care of you after that?"

"My father and my grandmother. And it was fine. They were kind of old-fashioned. I just wish I could remember more about her."

I can't think of anything else to say. We sit in silence for a few long moments while the shadows of computer stations stretch farther into the room.

Finally, Catina rises and straightens her slacks. "Well! Let's get the flock outta here."

"The what?"

"Oh, the flock? Something my dad said the old sheepherders used to say. My dad's Basque."

"What's Basque?"

"Who knows? Some old-country thing. They had lots of sheep-herders." Catina shrugs. "There's been enough fricking excitement around here for one day. I'm going home to peace and quiet."

"Peace and quiet with Dustin?"

"Oh, Dustin! He's cool! He felt so bad about my eye that he bought me this outfit." Catina grins, clearly pleased with herself.

... ...

How much I missed my mother.

After I've lived in Brad's house a week, I slip out through a basement window and sniff the night air, the pungency from the gypsum plant that I've known all my life, the grit and dust left over from the afternoon. What time is it? I don't know, I've been huddled in bed listening to the sounds of the other kids settling down for the night, somebody thrashing under the sheet, somebody farting, somebody giggling. The long summer dusk has taken its own sweet time to darken. Now I edge along the neighbor's bloomed-out lilac hedge, keeping to the lawn, because a streetlight illuminates the pavement, and when a dark shape darts out of the lilacs, runs across the street, and disappears into the darker shadows under a parked car, I nearly jump out of my skin. For a long minute I crouch down in the lilac roots and wait for trouble. But it was just a cat. Just a cat.

And not that I don't love the safe feeling of sitting on Brad's lap, the sharp-sweet scent of the gum he keeps in his pocket, the rough texture of his work shirt against my cheek. What leads me down this street by dead of night is the thread that reaches all the way from me to my mother. Her outline at the screen door as she watches the last streaks of sunset. The heavy softness of her hair when she lets me touch it.

I know the way, more or less. I've been strapped in the back seat of Brad's wife's car with some of the other kids when she drove to Safeway, and from the Safeway parking lot I could see the highway bridge over the Milk River that I'll have to cross. It's a long walk, farther than from the Mister's house. And I'm not

76

easy about crossing the river on the narrow pedestrian bridge, where even at this time of night the cars will roar by with blazing headlights and the deep secret current will flow almost under my feet and there will be no lilac hedges or even the shadows of parked cars to hide a small scampering girl from anyone's eyes.

I decide I won't think about being afraid until I get to the bridge.

I walk and walk. My legs ache, my feet ache from the slap on concrete. I need to pee. All that keeps me going is the image in my mind of the screen door at the rented house north of the river, on the far side of the fearsome bridge, and in the screen door the outline of my mother growing more and more indistinct as the sunset in my memory fades.

A car draws up even with me, slows. I keep my head down, I won't look, but I'm aware that it's a black-and-white with a cherry bubble light on its roof.

A window slides down.

Ruby?

··· ···

"How did you learn the old music?" Isaiah asked me when we both were teenagers.

"I heard my mother singing. And I listened to her records."

She had real records. And now I'm time traveling; I'm lifting the album out of its box and opening its cover where brown paper sleeves hold the gleaming black records with their red and gold centers, like hidden royalty. My fingers shake with the excitement of touching the records, though I'm barely old enough to read the labels. The Carter Family, "Wildwood Flower." Vernon Dalhart, "The Prisoner's Song"—*if I had the wings of an angel.* Jimmie Rodgers. Where'd she ever find those records?

Damn it, kid, keep out of my stuff!

"She had a real turntable," I said.

"What became of it?"

"No idea. Probably trashed."

No, I have no idea what became of the records. Yes, probably trashed. The rented house north of the river hadn't had nooks and crannies where belongings could be stowed away, and my mother's closet shelf I knew well, and there had been only the box with the picture of a hat and the clippings.

What was she waiting for, that woman who sat and smoked on the porch steps and listened to music from a neighbor's radio? What did she long for? What became of her?

Was she alone and listening to music when the car slowed and the off-duty policeman, foster father of frightened children, turned to the blonde teenager beside him in the front seat and said, Was this one of the houses? And when she nodded, he said, Ruby?

When the child in the back seat doesn't answer, he barks her name again. Ruby!

Yes, the child whispers through the fingers she has laced over her mouth.

15

"What is it like for you to remember?" I ask Mrs. Pence on Saturday morning.

She looks up from the sheet music she's reading over her breakfast bowl, surprised. Strands of hair float from her usually neat coif, creating an insubstantial halo in the morning light and giving her the illusion not of youth but of innocence.

"Remember what?"

"Anything."

I see that I'm perplexing her. "What it's like to remember? To *do* it." I'm not finding the right words, and I start over.

"Do you ever feel like you're time traveling? That you can be somewhere, doing anything—having breakfast, for example—when, flash, you're somewhere else for a moment? At some other time?"

"Time travel," she muses. "That's one way to put it."

She spoons up a bite of oatmeal and sips her sorry coffee. *Typical English slop.* But her gaze has softened.

"At my age? My mind is a magpie's nest."

I've never seen a magpie's nest, as far as I know, but the image evokes a messy basket of sticks and twigs that contains, besides the magpie, oddments scavenged from here and there. A spoon, a bone, a lock of hair, a key without a lock. If I, who am about to turn twenty-seven, live to be Mrs. Pence's age—I try and fail at a mental subtraction of twenty-seven from eighty-something—how many more spoons and bones will I have collected in my nest? The sugarless gum that Brad chewed incessantly, the notebook

Anne wrote in, the imaginary basketball Isaiah slam-dunked through an imaginary hoop?

"The hardest part for me was the trees," says Mrs. Pence.

"Trees?"

"I stayed in London with my mother through the whole war, you know. There was talk of evacuating me, I was only ten, but my mother was too sick to do without me, so I stayed. By '41 the Royal Academy reopened, and we thought it was safe for me to go back. One day there would be a girl in my form missing, and someone would say, She lives in such and such a road, doesn't she? And nothing more would be said. But we all knew that such and such a road had gotten the worst of the bombings the night before and that the girl might turn up the next morning, or we might never see her again and never know whether she lived or died."

Her eyes drift off. "We went on with our lessons. We got almost accustomed to the empty chairs. But walking home in the evenings, after I got off the tube, I would see the bomb craters, the burned tree trunks, and sometimes the stumps and splinters of those lovely old trees, limes and oaks that had been growing for hundreds of years—such beautiful trees that I would never see again. Poor shattered trees."

I wait for her to say more, but she doesn't, and so I ask, "How old were you when you left England?"

It takes her such a long time to answer that I think she must be time traveling herself, sorting through who knew what scraps and spoons and keys that don't open locks. Finally, she seems to return.

"I was twenty-two. I had my BMus, and I had been teaching after my mother died. She had cancer, you know, and it had been so difficult to get treatment during the war. Every time she was scheduled, there would be a siren, and they would have to take the radium back down to the underground vault."

So much I don't know. "Did you miss England?"

A sad smile. "Mr. Pence tried to describe Montana for me. We'll be east of the Rockies, he said. Where we'll live is rolling hill country with lots of sky, he said. I remember the names as he spoke them, wonderful names. The Highline. The Marias River. The Judith River. The White Cliffs of the Missouri. I imagined having a home in a place like the moors of Yorkshire or Lancashire. But when Mr. Pence met my plane in Great Falls and drove me up to Versailles, I thought I'd come to the end of the world."

So much I want to ask. But already she's gathering up the sheet music she'd been going over and heading for the piano room.

I pause in the hallway with grocery sacks in my arms, listening. In the piano room, behind the closed door, Mrs. Pence has just struck the big opening chords of the *Polonaise-fantaisie* and is rippling up the long elegiac arpeggio that nearly spans the keyboard. Her fingers sound as strong on the keys as they ever have, and I have time to think *big piano-playing hands* before the music sweeps over me and I nearly sob with the power of the yearning. The *Fantaisie* winds its intricate, deceptive way, sometimes rhythmic, almost playful, but always yielding to the undertow of melancholy. Where does the power of her playing come from, what does Mrs. Pence long for, what can she possibly regret?

What do you long for, Ruby? whispers Bill the Drummer in my head.

"What happened with your friend and her daughter?" Mrs. Pence had asked me at breakfast. "How did her custody case turn out?"

"Jamie? She got another probationary postponement. She didn't get to see her little girl."

"So hard to lose a child," she mused. Then she gave herself a small shake, like a reminder. "Mustn't dawdle," she said, more to herself than to me as she rose and carried her cereal bowl and her cup and saucer to the sink. "I have a full slate of lessons today."

Of course she did.

Now I listen until the *Fantaisie* comes to the end and the beautiful tones fade and fall silent. I imagine Mrs. Pence lifting her hands off the keys in the same formal motion she had taught to me, then folding her hands in her lap and bowing her head to listen to the last reverberations from deep inside the concert grand.

The grocery sacks in my arms are heavy, and the kitchen waits, so reluctantly I continue down the hall and set down my purchases on the scrubbed table. Jonathan, asleep under the table, thumps his tail to say hello and goes on sleeping.

Mrs. Pence had picked at my stir-fry, so I'd tried to remember what she cooked for herself in the old days and finally settled on a nice piece of fresh salmon and new potatoes to go with the garden peas one of her neighbors had left for us. Without the din of the campus food court in my ears, I feel hungry myself, so I wash my hands at the sink and settle down to shell peas.

The simple, repetitive motion, the snapping open of pods and the rattle of shelled peas into the saucepan lulls me, while the sharp garden scent of the discarded pods lingers on my hands and limns my fingernails with a pulpy green stain. I don't know a thing about gardening, but probably it's peaceful. Maybe I can learn how, and next summer I can take over from the mystery gardener, spade up a few new rows in the backyard and plant some seeds. More carrots maybe. And peas.

Wherever I'll be next summer.

When the doorbell sounds from the other end of the hallway, I push back my chair to get up and answer it, but then I hear Mrs. Pence's footsteps, followed by the creak of the heavy front door. Jonathan hears it too, scrambles out from under the table, and trots off to see what's going on. Probably a late piano student. I go on shelling peas.

Sounds of voices in the hallway, Mrs. Pence's voice high and pleased, the other voice a man's, baritone—and I turn from my pile of peapods to see Isaiah with an arm over Mrs. Pence's shoulders and Mrs. Pence with her arm around Isaiah's waist and Jonathan sniffing his shoes and wagging frantically.

"Ruby," Isaiah says, and corrects himself. "*Ruth*."

"Ruth," Mrs. Pence agrees.

I'm too surprised to speak. My thumb has stuck in the peapod I just split open, the peas going nowhere.

"It's a pity we don't keep chickens," says Mrs. Pence. "They'd eat those fresh pods."

"Don't look at me. I ain't hassling chickens."

Mrs. Pence makes a little face of comic regret over the chickens, and she and Isaiah both laugh. I can't believe what I'm seeing.

"Never mind chickens," says Isaiah. "Ruth, are you planning to cook those peas for dinner tonight?"

He's wearing a white T-shirt and jeans, and he's brimming with enjoyment at my surprise. When I can't find words to answer him, he pulls out a chair for himself and reaches for a pod and shells it into the pan.

Mrs. Pence sits beside him, smiling fondly. Flirtatiously even. How had she met Isaiah, of all people? How long has she known him? Beside his dark male vibrancy she looks more fragile than ever. The unshaded bulb that hangs from its cord over the kitchen table has bleached her face and deepened her cruel wrinkles and her softening skin. What does Isaiah want from her? I feel a protective surge of anger and realize I've twisted a peapod into a squashed mess.

Isaiah glances at the leaking green pod in my hands and then at my face. "Ruby," he says. "Ruth. I can't get around that name, you know. You've always been Ruby to me."

His dark eyes soften when he looks at me, but he's wary in a way I don't remember, and I wonder what his life has been like. I saw him so seldom since childhood—once or twice, downtown at night, before I left Versailles—and I remember that that night in the Alibi was the last time, and I shudder with the memory.

He reaches across the table for another pod. "Tell you what. Let's finish shelling these mothers, and then I'll cook dinner for us."

"Yes!" says Mrs. Pence, who has been looking from one to the other of us and smiling. Now she reaches for a peapod herself. For a moment our three pairs of hands lie in the circle of light from the unshaded bulb: Mrs. Pence's pale and arch tendoned and brown spotted with age; mine spare and limber now that I've been practicing the piano again; and Isaiah's hands brown and supple, pale on the palms and darker around the knuckles. Big piano-playing hands with long, strong fingers and oversized knuckles, all three of us.

Isaiah, who had come looking for me that night in the Alibi. Isaiah, who had hated Brazos and Gall on sight. But I wasn't in the Alibi now, even though it felt like it for a moment, the walls of smoke-darkened fake leather and the booths that were upholstered in cracked red vinyl and the TV that hung above the bar and was tuned to whatever, probably some sports analysis program that nobody listened to, and the shelter of Gall's arms, and my last sight of Isaiah.

In Mrs. Pence's kitchen, where the unshaded light bares the flaws of flaking wallpaper, chipped enamel sink, fraying old curtains, and my wandering thoughts—one thing I should do with my next paycheck is buy a shade for that light bulb—Isaiah remains. We've finished shelling the peas, and now he's heating a skillet. I go to scrub potatoes at the sink, where I'm pretty sure Mrs. Pence can't hear me over the running water.

"What are you doing here, Isaiah?"

I expect him to be evasive or to try to turn me away with a joke, but he turns from the stove and looks at me for a long moment and doesn't speak, so I plunge in.

"I don't want her hurt."

"Coming from you—" He doesn't finish. He doesn't have to finish. I'm burning with equal parts anger and shame at what he hasn't said. I was the out-of-control, acting-out teenager who'd run off without leaving word with anybody, hadn't gotten in touch with anybody, left my mother anguished by my betrayal, left Brad Gilcannon to pick up his life as best he could after the humiliation of the abuse acquittals, and left Mrs. Pence to trace my whereabouts from the Idaho Rivermen's posters that had started cropping up around the West. From the anger and shame I speak the truth.

"I didn't think anybody cared."

Except Brad maybe, but that was another story.

Isaiah just looks at me for another long moment. If he feels any anger, he's keeping it well hidden. What I see in his face is more like weariness, and I suppose it costs him something to keep up the laughing vigor he usually shows.

"I've been trying to keep an eye on her," he says.

We both glance back at Mrs. Pence at the kitchen table with the cup of tea Isaiah had made her. She yawns, recovers, and sips a little tea, her eyes soft and her mind elsewhere.

"She still got all her piano students?"

"I think so. I see them coming and going—and hear them."

He grins.

"Seriously," he says, "I've got a good little combo together. Come and listen one night. Play some keyboard with us."

"Maybe."

"And sing."

A voice like a bell. "I'm no Rosalie. You'd be disappointed."

He's turning the salmon filets in the skillet and doesn't answer right away. Then he says, "You been in touch with Rosalie?"

"No," I say, surprised.

"Hmm."

I wait, but he's busy with his cooking, and he says no more about my mother.

16

I think at least I'll be able to sleep this night. It'd been how long since I slept more than an hour or two? After the dinner dishes are washed and Isaiah has said good night and taken himself off, I come upstairs and go to the window, where, by the glow of the distant streetlight and the rising moon, l see Isaiah's dark head and white T-shirt growing smaller as he walks farther away. I watch him for a few minutes until he disappears around somebody's shadowed veranda at the end of the block, and then I drop the curtain and go across the hall to the bathroom to brush my teeth and my hair and rinse out the hose I'd worn to work. And sleep.

But no. What seems like the next minute, I'm wide awake, and the numbers on the digital alarm are 2:30. Oh hell. Just like the old nights of the damned.

The nights of the damned. It's the awakening that signals the onset. I'm oblivious in deep sleep, then *snap*, I realize I'm wide awake. *Where's Gall?* Not in bed beside me. Now my eyes are open, neck and arms and legs tense under the sheets. Not an unfamiliar sound in the room, not a light or a sensation or a secret movement by the sullen young man in the Polaroid that might have stirred me from sleep. But I'm as alert as a hunted deer, ready to leap out of bed and run.

A branch taps the window, a faraway car accelerates on the avenue, but there's nothing in this room but shadows and me. The heap of my clothes on a chair, the closet door ominously ajar. The red glowing numerals on the digital alarm clock now read 2:31 a.m.

What seems like an hour later the clock reads 2:32 a.m., and I'm sweating, my panic growing. Will the clock never move? Will it never be morning? If only I could sleep. All the time knowing that by daylight I would be able to sleep, sleep all day in blessed, blessed obliteration until five or six in the afternoon. So why can't I sleep now?

Toss. Turn. The clock reads 2:33 a.m. By now I'm shaking, holding onto myself, my arms wrapped around my knees, my face buried in my arms, my own body odors as sharp as fear. Fecal, disgusting. If I don't hang on, I'll be torn apart. Bits and pieces of me, disintegrating molecules spinning out of reach. No safety net, no rope, nothing to grab for, nothing that will hold. The black hole yawns. And all I want to do is scream, scream and run down the street, tearing off my clothing, tearing off my skin. *I want out of my skin!*

Not quite like those nights, not as bad. For one thing I'm not worried about Gall, at least not in the same way. Wherever Gall is—whatever he's become—he's not in the Screamer's bed or some other girl's bed. And so I lie still, thinking I might go back to sleep, but it's no use.

So, walk somewhere. Wear myself out. Then come back and try to sleep.

I pull on jeans and flip-flops, steal down the stairs, and ease open the front door, where I listen for a moment, not wanting to wake or worry Mrs. Pence.

The three-quarters moon is on its descent by now, riding low behind the trees and edging the leaves and silvering the ancient shingles on the houses on the other side of the street. Dark clouds race aloft, creating the impression that the moon itself is racing for the horizon, but not a breath of breeze stirs the leaves down here at street level. Everyone on the street prays for rain to succor the lawns and save the gardens, but rain doesn't look likely tonight.

I wish it would rain—wash my tears away . . .

I've come to think in song lyrics.

I close the gate in the picket fence behind me and follow my indistinct shadow down the street in the direction I had seen Isaiah walking. It's a way I have walked before. Beyond the residences of the Orchards, the street narrows into a graveled lane that dips down into a gulch, where the heat of the day lies in the grass. The distant light to my left is from the airport, and the darkness in the gulch is too deep for me to make out my feet or know where I'm walking except for the feel of the gravel under the thin soles of my flip-flops. The lane follows the gulch for a few yards and then climbs back to even ground on a winding grade scraped out of the side of the gulch. Soon I'm breathing hard from the exertion of the climb. Sitting at a computer all day long has left me out of shape for night walking.

When I come to the pasture where the horses sleep on their hoofs in a corner of the fence, I sit down in the grass to rest, get my breath back, and listen to the night sounds. The grass smells of baked seeds and dust, and somewhere is a rustling of some small animal hunting or being hunted. Far away a dog barks and one of the horses lifts his head, stamps, and goes back to sleep. Far away the airport lights burn, far away traffic rumbles, but here, for now, I'm the only watcher and listener.

I'm thinking of curling up and sleeping in the warm grass when something large and dark swooshes over my head on wings that slice the air and disappears on the other side of the gulch before I can dodge or gasp.

I'm clutching handfuls of grass. The night world around me has changed. The odor of road dust and horses, the bulk of trees and distant houses against a horizon imperceptibly lightening with the dawn of the longest day of the year. All the same and all changed by the watcher and listener.

I'd seen an owl on the hunt, I suppose, going after whatever frightened thing huddles in the grass.

James McMurtry on the radio, singing about bear tracks *coming after me.*

I rise and brush off my jeans and look around to get my bearings. Another few yards, and I will stand on the edge of the bluff above the Milk River.

The lane, little more than a trail by now, opens upon a flattish space of thin soil and weeds on the brink of the gorge. The pale line of light in the east is enough to pick out crumpled trash and the glint of beer bottles and the darker verge where the road, as I remember, angles down to the residences along the river. Teenagers used to drive up here and park. From the litter, apparently they still do.

What looks like a thin dead branch lies in my way, and I reach down to toss it aside. When it crackles in my hand, I realize I'm holding no dead branch but a desiccated snakeskin, and I fling it away and wipe my hands on the thighs of my jeans. This is no place to be wandering around alone in the dark. I should go home.

But from here I see streetlights and rooftops that look close enough to hit by throwing a handful of gravel. It's farther than it looks, though.

My mother lived down there after she was exonerated and freed from prison and married to her public defender. Drawn by some thread, I walked past her house one night after my shift at the Alibi, on a street called Lila Drive. It must have been just a week or two before I left Versailles with the Rivermen. My mother could never have known that I watched her bedroom light until it went dark.

··· ···

Isaiah is the brave one.

He's defiant: I ain't seen no dead babies, and I ain't gonna say I did!

Anne screams at him—You did too!

I did not!

You're nothing but a dirty little black mistake! I made Ruby tell, and I'll make you tell!

Anne usually ignores us younger kids, but I can tell she's really angry at Isaiah, angry enough to kill him. Her just-washed hair straggles down, and she tosses it back, too angry even to care that her high forehead shows. Isaiah's on the balls of his feet with his knees flexed, nothing warm about his grin now. He's just waiting for her to give him the excuse to deck her one.

Anne! Isaiah!

Brad's wife is drying her hands on a towel as she runs from the kitchen. One of her little boys, looking scared, grabs at her skirt.

Isaiah, you go downstairs right now! And stay there! Or I'll tell Brad!

Did Isaiah do as he was told? Why the blank spaces between the flashes of what I remember? Are they really getting to be fewer?

··· ···

When I open the gate in the picket fence, I hear Mrs. Pence playing the piano downstairs, but I push back the impulse to linger and listen, and I enter the house as silently as I can. Climb the stairs as silently as I can, not to disturb her, and close my bedroom door.

But I wonder. Does Mrs. Pence have nights of the damned that drive her to the piano?

17

Monday begins quietly. Jamie arrived early as usual and started the coffee and watered her plants before the rest of us came in, although she now seems withdrawn, thinking deep thoughts of her own. Dr. Brenner gives her a sharp look when she pours his coffee, which he keeps telling her not to do, but she says nothing. Anne goes straight to her own office and closes her door behind her. The hands of the office clock make their slow rounds, and we work through the morning.

At eleven-thirty Jamie turns off her computer and slings her bag over her shoulder. "I've got an appointment, and I may be a little late getting back."

I look at Catina, who shrugs, and so we return to our computer screens and our columns of names and numbers.

A new silence wakes me from the trance of keyboarding, and I look up. Travel posters, spider plants, sunlight falling through the window. Catina bent over her work, her ringlets in spirals down her back. Jamie's desk bare, her computer shrouded.

Anne stands over me.

"I know what you're doing! I know it was you!"

Over her shoulder I watch the second hand of the office clock continue its imperturbable circle. Better to watch the second hand than Anne's face, although I can't *not* see her lips drawn back from her teeth in a rictus, her eyes hot enough to burn, her high forehead broken into red blotches. This isn't just Anne being Anne. Something is seriously wrong, and I push back my chair, rise, and turn to her.

"Are you okay? Do you need help?"

In her five-inch stilettos she's as tall as me and swaying. "I don't want help from you!"

"Is there somebody I can call?"

Drawn by trouble, Dr. Brenner sticks his head out of his office. "What's going on?"

Anne whirls around. "Her! She's what's wrong! *Ruby Jarvis!* Sneaking around at night and throwing eggs at my house!"

"Anne," says Dr. Brenner in a tone I've never heard him use, "what makes you think Ruth would do such a thing?"

"Because she did! Eggs dripping down my front door! Dripping down my windows! Cooking on the glass! This heat is—is—" Suddenly she throws herself at him.

He catches her awkwardly and pats her shoulder. "Anne," he says, more gently. "I'm so sorry. When did this happen? Last night? Have you called the police?"

"—the heat is killing me! The stench! And eggshells all over my walk!"

"Have you called the police?" Dr. Brenner repeats.

"What would the police do? I know who did it! She's the only one who hates me enough to hurt me!"

"Anne, Anne. Have you been taking your medication?"

On the periphery I catch sight of Catina, cowering behind her computer screen.

"Anne, get your things together. Would you like me to drive you home?"

And she nods like a child.

Dr. Brenner guides a still-weeping Anne to the door and glances back. "This office is falling apart," he says, more to himself than to us, and closes the door behind him and Anne.

"Wow."

I'm remembering a sobbing Anne flinging herself into Brad Gilcannon's arms. Had she forgotten her meds that day?

I pull myself from—where? Brad Gilcannon's tv-watching room?—back into the Office of Student Accounting, where Catina and I sit and look at each other until Catina pulls out her phone. She wakes the screen, pushes some buttons, shakes her head.

"When was this supposed to have happened? Last night? Here we go."

She studies the screen. "Here's the police blotter for yesterday and so far today. A domestic dispute—that wouldn't be it—minor in possession, traffic collision on First and Main. Well, she said she didn't report it. If it happened."

I'm trying to decide which is worse, really getting her house egged or pretending her house has been egged.

"Why is she so *against* you? I mean, she doesn't like any of us, but it's like she hates *you*." Catina gives me a sudden sharp look. "You didn't sleep with her husband or anything, did you?"

"I don't even know who he is."

"Well, it's got to be something. It's like she's afraid of something."

It's nearly noon before Dr. Brenner turns up with yellow stains on the knees of his gray trousers. "I helped her with the mess. She's going to take some sick days. I don't think she's been taking her medication as she should. A friend is coming to stay with her."

··· ···

How long since it has rained in Versailles? Even in the hours before dawn, the air smells parched, and the wild grass beneath my feet is so brittle that it snaps with every step I take. And yes, I'm making my way by touch down the road that leads off the bluff into the upscale housing development, drawn like a sleepwalker by who knows what invisible thread.

Below the roofs of sleeping houses and a filigree of willows that lines its banks, the Milk River is a silver thread flowing east to merge with the Missouri. The water I'm watching began its flow near Montana's border with Canada, two hundred miles to the west of Versailles, flowed east and then northeast into Alberta, and now flows below me on its way southeast to join the Missouri and continue to the Mississippi and the Gulf of Mexico.

What passes for cool air rises from the water on invisible air currents like a wave of farewell.

I'm Ruby the watcher, floating on my own current.

It's easy enough to locate Lila Drive. The trees that were newly planted the night I walked here from the Alibi have grown much taller, and they shadow the pavement with their foliage.

The house, on the other hand, is smaller than I remember, a split-level with an attached garage and a wide front lawn with a clump of birches and a mailbox on a post beside the driveway. No name on the mailbox, only the house number. No car parked in the driveway, no crack of light falling through the drawn curtains, no details to remind me of my mother. Even the paint on the siding is reduced to some obscure pale color by the glow from the streetlight at the end of the block.

It's possible she no longer lives here. It's been ten years, after all. In ten years she could have divorced her public defender. Maybe she went back to singing in bars. Or maybe she stayed with her public defender and they used her fat cut of the wrongful imprisonment money to buy a mansion elsewhere in Versailles. Or a country estate. Or, or, or. No silhouette of a woman in a screen door is here.

Suddenly the pavement is flooded with the headlights of a car on Lila Drive. I freeze in the shadows of the birches. The car turns, however, not into the driveway that might be my mother's but into a driveway across the street.

Some automatic device activates a security light near the roof and sends a garage door rumbling open. The car pulls into the garage, and a woman gets out of the driver's door. For a moment she's illuminated in the security light: sharp features, halo of golden hair.

So this is Anne's house.

I don't think she saw me. Surely the security light blinded her to any movement of mine in the shadows under the birches. And yet something halts her in the act of dropping her car keys into her handbag. For what seems a long moment but probably is an extenuated couple of seconds, she stares in my direction, while I kneel as petrified as the owl's prey in the dappling of leaves.

Nightwalker, lurker under trees—exactly the wrong place for me to be. If I'm seen and recognized, I'll be thought damaged and dangerous and a thrower of eggs. She'll likely report me as a stalker.

The moment passes. Anne drops the keys into her handbag and turns with no sign of hurry or alarm and disappears. I have just time to register a man getting out of the passenger side of her car, a glimpse of his shoulders and leather jacket and a blond head as he, too, disappears and the garage door rumbles closed.

Francis Albert, the rich doctor, returning to her? Or a new man for Anne? Or the friend who has come to stay with her? I don't know, I don't care, I only care about stilling my heartbeat and waiting until I'm sure no one watches from a shrouded window as I slip out from the protection of the birches and steal away.

18

My eyes are gritty on Saturday morning, and I have nothing much to do but wash up the breakfast things. Maybe I'll take a nap. I never have trouble sleeping during the day. The trick would be to force myself awake before it's time for lunch, and then what? No. I tell myself I've forgotten, but I haven't. Isaiah and his guys are practicing in a barn somewhere, and I half-promised him I'd sit in.

After a while I get up from the kitchen table—I'd persuaded Mrs. Pence to stop setting the dining room table—and set the oatmeal pan to soak and run water in the sink to wash two plates and bowls and Mrs. Pence's cup and saucer. Never a coffee mug for her, always the porcelain cup with its tracery of vines and roses and its matching saucer. That done, I stack the dishes to dry themselves in the drain and slip out the kitchen door, as I've taken to doing, to check on the little backyard garden.

The carrots and onion spikes thrive in the reflected heat from the garage wall. I kneel and probe the soil around the rows with my fingers and find it soft and moist.

It's early enough that the sun still feels pleasant on my back and shoulders when I stand and brush the crumbs of soil off my fingers. Jonathan, who followed me from the kitchen, curious about what interests me, sniffs at the edge of the tilled soil where it meets the scorched lawn. He glances in the direction of the driveway and then at me. It occurs to me that Jonathan knows the mystery gardener and sees him often on his weeding and watering visits.

The marijuana plants behind the garage are bushy and luxuriant. When I look closer, I see fresh stubs where some of the leaves have been clipped.

"So, Jonathan."

He gazes up at me with soulful eyes.

I walk back through the house on my way to the stairs just in time to meet the blonde "Für Elise" teenager coming out of the piano room with her backpack of music.

"You're Ruth, right?" she greets me. "Still staying here, I see."

I nod while she takes in my height and careless braid and dirty hands. It doesn't seem possible that any girl can be quite that young and that sure of herself.

"I'm Madison Albert," she says, "in case you were wondering."

I'm so surprised that I'm speechless—"You're *Anne's* daughter?"

"God, no!" she says, and then she giggles, not a teenager's giggle of embarrassment but a gleeful giggle at my embarrassment. I can't think of a thing to say.

She shoulders her backpack. "See ya!" she sings, and disappears through the front door.

I go upstairs to my bedroom, and when I glance out the window, I see she's walked past the street corner, and the two kids who have been hanging around the mailboxes all summer have swung out on their bicycles and followed her again. She looks back and scolds them, and they shout some grief back at her and keep following her.

··· ···

Isaiah's barn turns out to be a half-hour's drive into the countryside, near the Rocky Boy Indian Reservation. I park the Pontiac in a weedy lot next to a newish white Ford pickup and a minivan with a crumpled rear fender. Late afternoon sunlight slants through a stand of quaking aspen, glints along a wire fence, and sheens the barn's weathered siding. The barn itself lists off-center like a drunk trying to keep his balance. When I get out of the Pontiac, I hear not exactly music throbbing through the cracks but more of a vibration that threatens the poor old barn and spreads across the sparse gravel until I feel it through the soles of my boots.

A pair of llamas, alert for trouble, swivel their heads on their long necks and study me from their pasture as I walk up to the door of the barn. No trouble here, llamas. Go back to your grass. I open the barn door, and for a moment I'm blind in the gloom. Then my eyes adjust, and I see a concrete floor, a row of what once must have been stalls, and a board half-ceiling holding up a loft where a few bales of hay still are stacked. Light from an upper window falls across a small bandstand where Isaiah and his guys have set up their drums and guitars and amps with what looks like miles of extension cord. Does the place actually have electricity? The extension cords must be plugged in somewhere.

They're pounding away at a tune I don't recognize, with a sluggish bass line and a fiddle-dee-dee treble. Then Isaiah lays down his guitar and shades his eyes with his hand.

"Ruby, that you? Come on over here!"

He introduces us—Terry on drums, Brian on steel, Stu on bass. Isaiah and three white guys in their thirties, practicing in a barn like teenagers. The white guys eye me.

"I told them you play keyboard."

"You've got a keyboard out here?"

Isaiah pulls away a vinyl cover. "Right here. You gonna play some for us?"

Isaiah's keyboard is a little Yamaha. I sit on the folding stool and touch a key. When was the last time I played keyboard? It must have been that last night at the Kodiak Club. The tone of Isaiah's Yamaha is a little tinny, but oh well, and before I think what I'm doing, I move into the sad slow chords of "Hickory Wind."

After the first few bars I'm weightless and uncaring, in a space out of mind where I've been before but have forgotten. Sunlight burns through the high window; the chinks in the barn's siding glows; the dust motes turn to gold and float around me. The only time that counts is 3/4 time.

I come to the end.

"Damn," says Isaiah. "Start again."

He starts a soft backup on his guitar, and soon the echoing high notes from Brian's steel rise behind us. I'm aware of Terry and Stu beginning an underpinning of rhythm, and what can I do but sing about the wind making me feel better each time it begins?

And if my voice never was bell-like, it by god can hold its own in a falling-down barn with a half-assed group that practices on weekends, and I lean back and let the lyrics lift from my throat and soar through the sun and shadows into the rafters. Yes, I remember the trees, the pines and the oak. Poor shattered trees. Long ago. Not so long ago. I sing to the end and listen to the last wistful notes from the steel.

A silence that rolls on and on.

In that wide quietness, as I come back to the ordinary, the amps and extension cords and the dirty corners, I turn and find Isaiah beside me, and I see that he's crying.

"Damn," he says, and swipes his forearm across his eyes.

"We got a gig at the Three Hundred Club this weekend," he says when his voice steadies. "Will you come and sing with us?"

I hardly hear him. Playing "Hickory Wind," singing it, hadn't killed me. I had been so deep into the lingering pain behind those chords and those lyrics that I hadn't even thought about pain of my own.

I'm not the woman I was. Not the angry sixteen-year-old nor the Ruby who stood up to sing with the Rivermen in the fringed red suede skirt and vest that Gall bought for her in Jackson Hole, Wyoming, nor the Ruby who saw Gall leave her bed for the Screamer or whichever cute teenager had been hanging around the back door of the club. No, and not the Ruby who crawled, burning in anguish, back to Versailles to hide. First I'd had my appendix carved out, and then I shed a skin. The question is what next.

Bill the Drummer whispers in my head again. *What do you long for Ruby?*

"Ruby?"

"I might come and listen to you and the guys."

"Listen, hell. I want to hear you sing."

"Does this band of yours have a name?"

"We're the Working Poor."

... ...

I don't know why I let Isaiah think I'll sing with the Working Poor, and I don't know what I'll wear if I do. The red fringed suede skirt and vest I wore when I sang with the Rivermen I abandoned in Anchorage.

The odors of Jackson Hole were sharp. The main street smelled of money, I now realize, or more exactly, it smelled of the expensive things money could buy. The silversmith shops, for example, with window displays spilling over with hammered silver, the silver concho belts and Navajo pearls and the glitter of liquid silver necklaces and squash blossom necklaces. Silver rings, silver bracelets set with turquoise.

Next door the saddlery shop smelling of leather and exotic oils and displaying silver-mounted saddles and bridles of tooled leather and heavily ornate spurs. And then the leatherwear shop, heady with the scent of something raw, something wild, in all the beautiful dyed colors. Here Gall led me through the welcoming glass door that stood open to the sidewalk, and he rifled through the racks of clothing until he found the red fringed suede skirt and vest.

Go try these on, Ruby Red.

In the lighted triple mirror of the changing room, I saw a girl I'd never seen before, a girl with dark eyes and long dark hair and a glowing face, dressed in the expensive red leather. And I saw her again in Gall's eyes when I stepped out from behind the changing room door.

There was a side of Jackson Hole I understood a long time later, behind the shops and the elk horns around the square and the RVs parked in front of the expensive shops and the bars where the music spilled out into the street. But when I was sixteen and knew everything, I thought I was walking on newly swept and burnished streets, far removed from the dust and stockyard stench and muddy river currents of Versailles, Montana. Jackson Hole was a town where Gall laid hundred-dollar bills on the counter to buy me the red fringed suede.

Gall. Brazos. I thought the names were made up, to make the guys seem more western in their country-western band, and I wondered how poor old Bill the Drummer got stuck with his plain name. But no, Brazos explained, it really was his name, after a character in a western novel that his mother admired—an awful novel, he said, he'd tried to read it once—and Gall really was Gall, after some ancestor who had been a big man among the Lakota. Gall shrugged off the ancestor. I've never been on the rez, he said. Never wanted to.

The red suede skirt and vest that I left behind in Anchorage likely ended up in a thrift shop somewhere, and even if I still had that outfit, it would look dated as well as being a killer to wear in this heat. But I've saved a little cash since I repaid Mrs. Pence for my crow clothes, and I think I might buy a red T-shirt to wear with jeans.

After all, the Working Poor aren't all that bad. Isaiah might be truly good if he practiced more, and when he and I harmonize, we've got a sound. Terry, the drummer, is probably the weakest link. He's a little tentative, a little too fearful of making a mistake. It took me time, listening to the Rivermen and other bands, to hear the amazing difference a truly fine percussionist makes— Bill the Drummer, for example, who probably has found another band by now.

Bill the Drummer. When I wash my hair and comb it out, I see it's grown past my waist, with ends that haven't been trimmed since Bill the Drummer last trimmed them. The thought takes me back to—oh, god, McCall, Idaho.

Bill the Drummer keeps a pair of barber scissors in the tray of his toolbox, where he also keeps pliers and screwdrivers and some other small tools he probably knows the names of. Yesterday he used the scissors to trim Brazos's hair and trim his own hair, and now he wipes the blades with a handkerchief while I sit astraddle a chair I've carried out of the McCall motel room. The late-afternoon sun balances on the smoky haze over the tips of pines along the horizon and streaks the little motel courtyard with a dirty gold that fills the cracks in the concrete where weeds have sprung. The air smells of smoke. I hand Bill my comb.

How much do you want off, Ruby?

Just the ends.

He runs his fingers along the back of my head, lifts up most of my hair and twists it and pins it out of the way with my barrette. My hair reaches my waist, falls to within a couple feet of the concrete when I'm sitting down, and Bill has to drop to one knee to comb out the remaining strands and start his snipping.

If your hair grows any longer, I'll have to grow a longer arm.

Gall lurches out of the motel room, shirtless and carrying his can of beer—Fucking fires. Now they've closed Highway 55.

The hell they did, says Bill, and combs out another layer of my hair to trim. A stir of air carries a dark wisp of hair past my bare feet and a few yards across the concrete.

It was on the news.

Bill snips, snips again. The sun is warm, and the sensation of his fingers in my hair is vaguely pleasant. The cloud of smoke over the tips of pines is the only sign of flames.

Gall watches us for a moment and takes another swig of beer. Next they'll evacuate this fucking town. And there goes our gig.

That was on the news? We're going to evacuate?

It's not official yet. I'm just saying.

There are fires in the summer, always fires. This summer we had packed up and left Joseph, Oregon, and driven across Idaho to McCall for what promised to be a two-week top-of-the-tourist-season gig and has turned out to be a limping, day-to-day proposition as fires to the south and east grow and spread and hotel reservations are canceled and vacations cut short. Gall wants to park the van in his parents' garage in Boise and fly up to Anchorage, where nothing is burning, at least that he's heard of. To hear him, anybody would think Anchorage is the country music capital of the world—the Nashville of the Northwest maybe—and he thinks we have a shot at the top there. But Brazos wants to hang on as long as we can here in McCall and hope we can at least save enough to pay for airline tickets if we don't drive the van.

Brazos, yawning, comes out of the room on the other side of the courtyard that he and Bill share and walks across to us.

What have you heard? Fires getting any closer?

It's not good.

Fucking forest service, Brazos says.

It's an old grievance with Brazos. Yesterday when the TV news was full of the deaths by flames of the two smoke jumpers in the Malheur River fire, Brazos fumed about mismanagement and how the deaths were just the same as murder.

Yeah, well, and I think we oughta get the fuck outta here, Gall had said.

Bill lifts the last layer of my hair and fans it across my shoulders and back, and I feel the weight settle as it leaves his hands. Watching, Gall drains the last of his beer and crumples the can. Bill, you 'bout finished with her now?

Just about.

If they'd left the little fires to burn, but no, Brazos complains, they—

We're killing time here, man. Do we have to wait until they throw us out and lock the doors?

—year after year, all that underbrush and trash timber growing up and drying out, and then they wonder why the fires explode—

The hell with your goddamn underbrush! I want to get outta here, man! Christ, I need another beer. Wash the goddamn taste of smoke outta my mouth.

You better go easy on the beer. We got a gig to play.

Fuck! I'm good! I'm always good!

Gall throws his empty can in the direction of the dumpster and jerks a lock of my hair so hard it hurts. You're not touching my hair with your goddamn scissors, Bill.

Bill the Drummer wipes his scissors and lays them in the tray of his toolbox, but he watches Gall pull me off my chair by my lock of hair, and I know he doesn't like it, but what it tells me is how much Gall needs me. Gall pulls me all the way back to our room by my lock of hair, and I'm thinking it can't be any worse in Anchorage. It will be our first time there, and we're booked in good clubs, and we're going to cut a CD. It will probably be much better in Anchorage than in McCall.

19

In the morning I drive to work with all the windows of the Pontiac rolled up to keep out the haze of smoke in the air. June is sliding into July, and the old stockyard west of town stinks. Flags hang from porches, and smoke from a grass fire near Cutbank, miles to the west, has settled over Versailles. Soon it will be my birthday. The heat is a constant weight, even in the early mornings, and it still hasn't rained. Finally, stifling, I roll my window down and feel some relief in the side currents pulling at my hair whenever the Pontiac isn't slowed to a crawl in the morning rush or stalled altogether at traffic lights.

I'm not ready to go to the Three Hundred Club by myself and sit like an overage groupie at a table near the bandstand, much less get up and sing. I remember the club, of course, a big barn of a place with a bowling alley behind the bar and the dance floor. Maybe by now it's in better repair than Isaiah's barn.

The heat is even worse on the third floor of the administration building. I step over a blitz of paper on the floor as I open the door to Student Accounting. Jamie has all the windows open, although the office smells of smoke, and she's redirecting an electric fan that has blown all the forms and charts off the counter.

Dr. Brenner hangs his suit coat on the back of a chair and loosens his necktie and glares at Jamie and me.

"We're going to have to get some air-conditioning up here! Next thing these computers are going to crash from this heat!"

"Yes," says Jamie, turning her fan back on and coming around the counter to help me gather up the scattered sheets of paper.

With her hands full of general information forms, application forms for student loans, data summaries, and college policy statements, forms that no one ever uses because all the students fill them out online, she hisses at me, "We need a girls' night out!"

"Where's Catina?" I whisper back.

Jamie purses her lips and shakes her head.

Dr. Brenner still fumes in the main office where Jamie's fan whirs and makes his shirt billow around him.

"This is ridiculous. Turn off those computers before we have a meltdown. You're pretty well caught up, aren't you? Don't you have work you could carry over to the food court, where at least it's cool enough to breathe?"

"I think I can find some work," says Jamie with a neutral face.

"Do it then." He slings his jacket and tie over his shoulder, picks up his briefcase, and is gone.

I look at Jamie, and Jamie looks at me.

"You heard him," she said.

We gather stacks of paperwork. Jamie's arms are so full that she doesn't have a hand free to open the door, so she bumps it with her rear end. It half-opens, stuck against something. Over Jamie's shoulder I see that Dr. Brenner has paused at the top of the stairs and turned to look back at whatever obstructs the door.

"What the hell?" says Jamie.

She gives the door a full-footed kick, and somebody on the other side yelps.

"What do you think you're doing?" says Dr. Brenner.

A young man crouches in front of the door, rubbing his ass. He must have seen his chance when Dr. Brenner left the office to sit down with his back against the door. When Jamie kicked the door, it pinched him. Now he scrambles to his feet and looks around wildly, but Dr. Brenner looms between him and the stairs, and Jamie with her arms full of paperwork cuts him off from the corridor.

"Yeah, Dustin, what are you doing here?" says Jamie.

I recognize the golfer now, with his tight-fitting jeans and his backwards cap. He's got a shag of dark-blond hair and dark brows that meet at the bridge of his nose and give him a sulky look.

"Where's Catina?"

No one answers.

"Is she still back there in the office?"

Dustin turns to Dr. Brenner but gets the full force of robot impenetrability. His eyes slide, fugitive like, toward the stairs.

"Young man, I think you'd better leave," says Dr. Brenner. He steps aside, and Dustin shoots off. We listen to his trainers pounding on the composite stairs, all the way down the three flights.

Dr. Brenner shakes his head, but he's grinning to himself as he gathers up his suit jacket and briefcase and makes his own way down the stairs. So—the robot has a sense of humor. Who knew?

"Ain't love amazing," says Jamie.

Well, yes. Amazing. How Brazos still held a torch for a girl he'd known years ago in Boise. And how I loved Gall, who screwed every ass he could get his hands on.

Of the two rich kids from Boise, Brazos was the dreamer of the Rivermen and Gall the crazy talent. Bill the Drummer was the workhorse, but there had been a time when Bill had taken up with a girl in Albuquerque and fallen in love. I don't remember much about the girl, but I clearly remember Bill's rage when she started seeing somebody else behind his back.

I'm gonna kill her! I'm gonna kill her!

Calm down. She ain't worth it, Brazos advised him, which of course had no effect upon Bill. He stormed around the bar, drinking straight shots until the bouncers threw us all out, and, once we got back to the motel, yanked off a boot and threw it at the television, where a late-night news anchor was reporting on the war in Iraq. Maybe Bill hoped to smash the screen, but the boot bounced off the screen and lay inert on the green motel carpeting, while the TV anchor placidly went on talking about IEDs and car bombs. Bill started to cry. He picked up his boot, one of the pair of Justins he'd bought in Jackson Hole, and left for his own room on one stockinged foot and one booted foot. The next day he was himself again, his face swollen from his tears and all the whiskey he had drunk, but he was steady as he helped to strike our set from the bandstand and roll up the extension cords and load the amps into the van for wherever we were going next.

Love is amazing all right.

······

The smoke doesn't seem as bad after work, so I mow Mrs. Pence's front lawn and watch her piano students come and go. The second "Happy Farmer" girl is late, but she scurries inside, and soon I hear the familiar blunders, interrupted by occasional stumbles. Will she never get it right?

The grass is so sparse and brown from the drought that it doesn't need mowing, but I like the peaceable ratcheting sound of the old hand mower, which I found clean and freshly oiled when I dragged it out from the garage. When I finish mowing in front, I start on the backyard. The sun scorches my head, and I pause in the shade of the blue spruce and lift my braid off my neck and look back at the tracks of the mower marking where I've been. A robin flies down from the spruce and perches on the picket fence that separates the yard from the alley, cocking his head to get a better look at me. Maybe he's wondering what I'm doing in his territory, or maybe he hopes I'll get out the hose and sprinkler and water the lawn and bring up some worms.

"Sorry," I tell him, and he flies off.

Warm sun, the sounds from a block away of children at play, and the scent of spruce needles. I don't know what I'm feeling, but it bubbles through me even as the old spruce speaks to me. I leave the mower and bend down to part the branches that shelter the warm dim space around the trunk of the tree. Where I crawled, in pain, in the dawn after the night that brought me back to Versailles.

Where I had crawled—

No. I never had hidden here as a child.

Yes, I had.

Kneeling on the cushion of spruce needles, I close my eyes and let my mind drift. Telling me what I know. That I played here as a child. That I had hidden under the spruce boughs from the sharp, quarreling voices of women.

She's mine! I'm taking her with me, and I'm keeping her!

Like you kept the other one?

I hate you!

I stand up slowly and brush the spruce needles off the knees of my blue jeans. The sounds of the neighborhood drift back. A car passing on the street, getting farther away. The creak of a porch swing. The children, their voices raised now in a spat. The voices from Mrs. Pence's porch are those of one "Happy Farmer" girl leaving and another "Happy Farmer" girl arriving.

I grip the handle of the lawn mower, lean into it, and finish mowing the backyard.

The kitchen feels cool after the backyard. I pour myself a glass of milk, set the carton back in the refrigerator, turn, and nearly drop my glass. Standing behind me, rocking on the balls of his feet, is Dustin Murray.

He must have eased open the front door and sneaked down the hall past the blundering rendition of "The Happy Farmer." It takes me a moment to remember my glass of milk and set it down. Something's wrong with him. The muscles around his mouth twitch, and his eyes are unfocused.

"Where's Catina?"

"She's not here."

"I gotta know where she is. I gotta."

He looks wildly around the kitchen as though he expects Catina to materialize in the patch of empty sunlight that falls through the window on the scrubbed linoleum. I think of Mrs. Pence in the piano room, giving a lesson in happy oblivion.

"Sit down and tell me what's going on."

To my surprise, he sits. I sit opposite him. His hands have taken a prayerful position.

"Would you like a glass of milk?"

He shakes his head, but the offer seems to bring him back to the daytime world of kitchen table and kitchen sink. "I thought for sure she'd be here."

Tick, tock, from the old windup clock over the refrigerator. I find myself counting with it. Tick, tock. Tick, tock.

"What I tried to tell her." Tears run down his face, and he scrubs a hand across his eyes. "I tried to explain to her. I was *careful* to explain she wasn't going to make it in some big grad program. I told her, I *told* her, okay, maybe she graduated from this rinky-dink college, but that didn't mean shit."

He sits there bereft in his baseball cap. I can find no words.

"She's all I ever wanted. To marry her. I dream about it! How she can go on working in Student Accounting, that'll be okay with me. How she'll come home from work and cook supper for me, and we'll be so happy."

I wonder what in the world to say to him. "Dustin. Maybe she's just not ready to settle down."

"Not ready? She's twenty-three!"

"How old are you?"

"I'm twenty-four! And I graduated high school!"

His voice rises, and I put a finger to my lips.

"Mrs.—my grandmother—is giving a piano lesson just down the hall." *Grandmother.* Easier than explaining.

"Oh. Sorry."

His eyes dart around the kitchen, seeking answers to the unfairness of it all in walls and curtains and hanging pots and pans. He really is very good-looking. The thick thatch of dark-blond hair under the baseball cap, the regular features and cleft chin. Is that why he has the idea the world owes him a pretty wife?

He sighs. "How old are *you?*"

"Twenty-seven in a couple weeks."

"Um. And you never went to college?"

"No."

"And you've done fine. You got a boyfriend?"

"Not anymore."

"Why not?"

"He had a—breakdown. A drug overdose."

"Oh. Not much you can do about one a them. But you shoulda stood by him. And here I thought you was going out with the blackie."

Something in my face makes him sheer off. "I thought you was okay, though. Even if you was on her side. I never saw you acting like you was better than other people. It's a good thing you aren't going out with the blackie, though, because he woulda been cheating on you. With her."

"You'd better leave."

I'm too angry to care if he's a threat or not, which maybe he senses, because he gets up from the table and heads for the front door. I follow him out and watch until he has crossed the street and climbed into a black Mustang.

Dustin has always looked so ridiculous, with his golf putter and his golf ball and his cute ass that got pinched in the office door when Jamie kicked it open, that I've never thought of being afraid of him. But when I close the door behind him, I lock it. In the kitchen I lock the back door, taste my glass of milk, and find it lukewarm.

Is there anything I should be doing about Dustin and his grievances? Like calling the police? And telling them what? Or calling Catina and warning her? I know she has a cell phone, but I don't know the number.

When I can't think of anything else to do, I finish my milk and go upstairs to shower.

20

"Iced tea maybe?" says Jamie.

In the racket of the food court, we stand in line until we each get a glass of tea with wedges of lemon and make our way to a table, where we spread out our stacks of papers. The papers are camouflage. There's no real work in them. Dr. Brenner is right—we have caught up with the backlog of data entry and won't have a lot more to do until the flood of student records at the start of the second half-session hits us, so we may as well waste another day sheltering in the food court from the heat and the smoke.

"Where do you think Catina went?"

Jamie shrugs. "That's something she's not talking about."

"We know Dustin doesn't know where she is."

"Dustin! The little bastard. You know what he told her?"

"What?"

"He said if she ever dumped him, she'd never catch herself another guy. And she believed him."

The sulky young face, the thrust of Dustin's brows. "Did he mean—" I pause, trying to remember some fragment from my magpie's nest.

"He's trying to convince her she isn't pretty enough to catch herself another guy. Or sexy enough. However his pea brain thinks."

I remember a moment a week ago. The new fall catalog for the college had come out online, and several times I noticed Catina scrolling through it when she was supposed to be entering data.

Finally, carrying my empty coffee cup for a refill as an excuse, I paused and looked over her shoulder to find her studying a virtual page with a picture of a young woman with an armful of books, smiling up at the doors of the business administration building.

Catina glanced around, caught me looking, and hastily brought up a screen saver.

"Sorry," I said, and continued to the coffeepot.

An older fragment. Something about a fiddle player in another Boise band that Gall and Brazos and Bill knew. What the fiddle player had done. Said if his girlfriend ever dumped him, she'd never get another guy. She dumped him anyway, and he took a shot at her. Maybe actually shot her? I can't remember.

"We need a girls' night out," Jamie repeats, and I nod.

She sips her third refill of iced tea and makes a face. "God, I hate tea without sugar."

I push the plastic sugar dispenser across the table to her, but she shakes her head and slaps her stomach. "I've got to get this flab off somehow."

She pokes at her lemon wedge with her straw. Finally, she reaches for her fanny pack and digs out her billfold.

"I've been meaning to show this to you."

I take the little photo she hands me. It's one of those colored headshots taken at school and sent home in sheets to be cut apart with scissors and distributed to—who?—grandparents or aunts, I suppose. For children who have grandparents and aunts. A little girl with brown eyes, a high forehead, and wispy brown hair smiles from this photo.

"That's her. Prairie Rose."

I realize I'm looking at a picture of Jamie's daughter. I look more closely and think the little girl's smile looks tentative.

"She's pretty."

"It's been two years since I've seen her. But at the hearing they did make him give me her school picture."

"I'm sorry."

"My own fault. Booze."

She takes back the picture and stows it in her billfold. "She's eight now. The same as you were when they took you. And you said you missed your mother."

"I did."

Jamie's eyes are on her billfold, which lies there on the table in front of her, a double fold of blue fabric, worn to threadbare gray at the corners and held shut with a loop of dark elastic. Jamie's face looks slack in a way I never noticed before, and I think of Mrs. Pence's face, the grief there, the yearning she draws from her piano when she plays.

From the time I started working in the Office of Student Accounting, Jamie has been staunch. She listens to Dr. Brenner and faces down the Queen and lectures Catina and lectures me. Now I'm seeing her, really seeing her, and I'm shaken. What does Dr. Brenner see in Jamie's face that I haven't seen? For that matter, what does he see in mine? I remember my sense, the first time I met him, of deep thoughts unfolding in his skull.

I'm not living in an animated cartoon, and I need to start paying better attention.

Jamie lays her hand on her billfold for a moment, as though feeling its pulse. Then she seems to snap back into the present moment and stows the billfold in her fanny pack.

"So a girls' night out. Maybe this Saturday?"

"Not Saturday."

"No?"

"I'm singing at the Three Hundred Club on Saturday."

Jamie's eyes widen. "You sing?"

"I used to."

"That's right. You wrote it on your application. Has this got anything to do with your flashy friend what's-his-name?"

"Isaiah."

"Right. Isaiah. Saturday night. I'll tell Catina when I see her."

Another morning, and the wind carries smoke from a timber fire somewhere in southern Montana to join the smoke out of the west. But Dr. Brenner's new water-cooled air unit is spewing some relief into the office, and the coffee maker is groaning into action when I come in. Jamie is watering her hanging plants, but the stiff angle of her shoulders speaks of trouble.

"Catina called in sick again. At least somebody did. Some guy."

I take the cover off my computer. Some guy. The reason for Dustin Murray's suspicions.

Jamie pours her cup and mine and sits at Catina's station, next to mine.

"She's been looking at that new business degree program. The way it works, you sign up and take evening and weekend courses, so it doesn't get in the way of your job, and if you're a college employee, you don't pay fees, and after a few years you have a master's degree in business."

"She could do that?"

"Sure. She's already got a degree, you know. In sociology. She's bright, even if she doesn't act like it. With the master's degree she can get a grade three or four levels higher than what she's got, and she can get out of data processing."

"And she'd earn more?"

"Oh yes. Quite a bit more."

"Dustin came by my house. He was looking for her."

"The little shit. I wish she'd unload him."

"I wish I'd tried harder to find her and tell her about him."

"Ahh, don't worry. He's a nothing."

I think of poor Dustin with his desperate eyes and his fine taut body, all six feet of him. A good-looking couple, people would say about him and Catina. If only she didn't want to move up three or four grades and make more money. Why wouldn't she rather have Dustin? Poor Dustin, I catch myself thinking. He's like the song lyrics that want so badly what they can't have. Somebody should write him a new *I can't get what I want* song.

"Don't," says Jamie, reading my mind. "The way they hang onto us is making us think they need us."

21

On the way home from campus, I stop at the big mall on the edge of the Orchards and find it crowded with summer sales racks.

The air-conditioning blows full blast, and a few tired-looking women poke around among the outsized bathing suits and dusty sundresses nobody wanted to buy when they first arrived in the shops last spring. I look at a table of limp T-shirts in pastel colors like leftover Easter eggs and feel depressed.

I had kept the red skirt and vest in a big canvas carryall, folded in newspapers to keep the suede from creasing, and whenever we'd checked into motels, I shook it out and hung it up. The canvas carryall was gone too. Strange, when I can feel its drag on my shoulder and the way its strap bit down when I had to carry it too far. There must have been a day when I saw the red suede for the last time, but there had been too much bad shit coming down for me to notice.

... ...

I knew where Gall had hidden his cash. I still had the key to his room—*our* room—and I felt behind the panel under the bathroom sink until I got my fingers around the roll of bills and pulled them out and stuck them into my brassiere. I came out of the bathroom and knew I was seeing our room for the last time: wallpaper printed with elk walking through fir trees, a couple of enlarged photographs of mountain peaks capped with snow, and a bedspread and sheet pulled most of the way on the floor, stinking of Gall and the Screamer, stinking of Brazos and me.

I kept doubling over, I felt so bad. The digital clock on the bed stand showed 5:00 a.m. in red. I must have—well, I must have known I could catch a flight from the Anchorage airport down to the Lower 48 because I called for a taxi and stuffed what I could find of my clothes into my backpack, along with Gall's T-shirt that I found tangled in the bedsheets. I couldn't have managed the carryall even if I'd remembered it. I threw the room key on the stand beside the clock. When my taxi, with me in the back seat, pulled past the lighted motel coffee shop, I caught sight of Brazos and Bill the Drummer in a window booth. From the way their heads jerked and hands gestured, they probably still were shouting at each other about the wild night and whatever they'd had to do with Gall and whether Bill really was bailing from the band. They never saw me. I was too sick to care.

··· ···

"Ruth!"

I nearly jump out of my skin. I've been far away, and now I'm back in the Versailles mall, where the air-conditioning is brutal and the lighting so diffuse that it casts no shadows, where something resembling music plays over a sound system, where shoppers pick over racks and tables of faded goods, where I'm Ruth, not Ruby.

It's Catina, of course, sucking through a straw on something thick and green in a clear plastic container. For once she's wearing ordinary jeans and slides, and she hasn't bothered with eye makeup, which in a strange way makes her look both older and younger, but she's smiling, and she smells of her favorite citrusy perfume.

"You didn't come to work today."

"I called in sick."

I don't believe her, either that she was sick or that she called in, because it would have been Jamie who took the call, but I suppose it doesn't matter. Something is coming down. I can feel it, like thunder waiting to break over the bluffs beyond the river.

"So, what are you doing here?" Catina asks, and I explain Jamie's idea of a girls' night out and the Three Hundred Club and the Working Poor and needing something to wear.

Catina glances around at the sales racks. "You don't want any of this crap."

"No, I already decided that."

"You got your car here? I'll show you a place."

As we leave the mall, I notice Catina's quick sweeping look across the parking lot, checking the entrances, and I wonder if she knows Dustin has been looking for her.

"Drive up the grade and turn right on Fifteenth," she directs me. "There's a great little shop next to the liquor store."

The right turn at the top of the grade leads into a neighborhood of rental houses and strip malls, and I can't think what kind of a great little shop would open its doors there. It turns out to be a Goodwill, and Catina is out of the car and taking a quick look in each direction before I can turn the key in the Pontiac.

"You have to get here at the right time," she explains when I catch up with her. "The stuff gets picked over pretty fast. We might have to come back."

A woman seated at the back of the store glances up as we enter and goes back to whatever she's reading. One good thing about the Goodwill, nobody follows you around asking if they can help you. I've visited my share, and this Goodwill has the same dusty, musty smell that makes me think of stale popcorn and the dregs in soda cans. The bare floorboards creak with all the depressed things people have gotten rid of. Racks and racks of clothes. Shelves of paperback books lining the walls. On the far side of the store, a household goods section with stacks of cups and dishes and toasters and griddles. I wander over and spot a wok that can be purchased for fifty cents and think I might take it home to Mrs. Pence's.

"Over here!" hisses Catina, and I leave the wok and join her at a rack of shoes and boots.

"Red cowboy boots?"

"What size are you?"

"Those look pretty small."

She reluctantly sets the boots back on the rack. "Let's look through the shirts," she says. "Sometimes you can find a bargain. I got my turquoise shirt here, real silk, for five dollars."

As she riffles through the shirts, I try to remember the last time, or any time, I'd gone shopping with a girlfriend. Not in high school, after all the convictions had been appealed and the sentences overturned and Brad's investigation was under suspicion and I was an outcast. Later, with the band, I didn't have friends who were girls.

What about the Screamer, whose real name was Sharyn? Was there a time I would have called her a friend?

Why is Catina my friend? True, she's part of the united front at the Office of Student Accounting, her and me and Jamie and to some extent Dr. Brenner against the Queen and the various campus tittle-tattlers and stuffed suits. But when have I spent time with her out of the office before today? Is Catina a nice girl who has a bad thing going with Dustin? Could Sharyn have been seen as a nice girl who had a bad thing going with Gall?

A hunter-green shirt with a dull sheen catches my eye, and I pull it off the rack.

"Yes!" breathes Catina. She takes it away from me and holds it at arm's length with her head cocked to consider. "Great color for you. You're so pretty, Ruth. You just need to smile more."

"Twenty dollars!"

"It's real silk."

"You paid five dollars for yours."

"Yes, but that was then. It all depends on the day you find it."

The sleeves look a bit short, but I can always turn back the cuffs. With my blue jeans and a coat of polish on my old boots, I'll look good enough for the Three Hundred Club.

"Okay," I agree and carry the green shirt back to the counter, where the woman lays down her book, rings up the sale, and folds the shirt into a secondhand paper bag.

"Do you need a ride home?" I ask Catina on our way to the door. I have some idea she and Dustin live in one of the big apartment complexes overlooking the shopping mall, and I think she probably had walked down to the mall when I ran into her.

"I'd appreciate it. I'm staying with my dad and grandma. They live over in the South Orchards. I just had to get out of the house for a while, so my dad dropped me off at the mall. I was super glad to spot you."

After the dust and must of the Goodwill, the parking lot feels fresh, even in the heat and the lingering traces of smoke. We climb into the oven that is the Pontiac after being parked in the sun, and I toss my new shirt into the back seat. I can always come back for the wok if I want it. It didn't look as though it was going anywhere.

I put the Pontiac into reverse and am backing out of the parking slot when Catina throws herself down on the floor under the passenger seat.

"Don't look down! Don't look around! Just drive normally!"

"Drive normally where? To your dad's house?"

"No! What you'd *normally* do! Drive home!"

"To Mrs. Pence's?"

"Wherever!"

I wheel the Pontiac around and drive past the liquor store and out of the parking lot with the hair on the back of my neck tingling with the effort not to look anywhere but straight ahead.

"What's going on?"

"Don't look down!"

Don't look down, don't look around, don't look back. But as the Pontiac carries us up the avenue at its stately pace, I do steal a look into the rearview mirror and see the black Mustang pull out from the curb by the liquor store and fall in behind us. Its windows are too heavily tinted for me to distinguish the driver. I can't help it—I glance down at Catina and see that her face is tear streaked.

I drive along the avenue with the broad Pontiac taking up more than its half of the traffic lane and its sporty black tail following at a discreet half a block. When I signal to turn into Mrs. Pence's neighborhood, I see the Mustang signal for the same turn. Down the dip where the side street turns into little more than a graveled lane, down into the gully and through the horse pasture and up again, and then another turn on Mrs. Pence's peaceful street, where nothing ever happens, except for the cottonwood leaves that meet overhead and whisper among themselves and the boys who hang around the mailboxes doing wheelies on their bikes.

I start to pull up beside the picket fence but change my mind and instead turn into the two-track gravel driveway that leads to Mrs. Pence's detached garage. The garage door, of course, is closed.

Now what. I risk a glance and see the Mustang has paused by the mailboxes, where the bicycle kids observe it with interest. On the floor on the passenger side, Catina has rolled herself into a ball with her arms wrapped around her head.

I get out of the Pontiac and go to open the garage door, which is a heavy rough-carpentered wooden door that moves, if enough effort is put into it, on an iron slide. I'm putting my shoulder to the door to force it along its slide when Isaiah comes around the side of the garage. His mouth drops.

"Ruby! What are you doing?"

I'm too surprised to reflect that I could just as well have asked him the same question. As to his question, I have no ready answer. I give the garage door a heave, and it moves a few grudging inches, and Isaiah leans against it and shoves it the rest of the way open for me. As though on signal, the Mustang eases away from the mailboxes and draws even with Mrs. Pence's driveway, where it idles until Isaiah gives the invisible driver a two-finger wave. The Mustang accelerates in a spin of gravel up the street, where it turns at the next corner and disappears.

Isaiah opens the door on the Pontiac's passenger side, and Catina falls out.

"Hey!" He gives her a hand up, and she throws her arms around him.

I watch as the sun beats down and Catina sobs in Isaiah's arms while he strokes her shoulders.

"How about we take you to your dad's house?" he says after a minute or two, and she nods.

Isaiah turns to me. "I walked over here. You think—"

And I hand him the keys to the Pontiac.

When they're gone, I walk around the garage and find the little garden freshly tended. A handful of wilting weeds has been left on the grass. I kneel and pull two or three maple seedlings that the gardener missed and gather up the handful to toss on the compost heap.

What have I seen? A truly frightened Catina? Or Catina, the princess of drama?

22

Catina doesn't come to work the next morning or the next, and no one calls her in sick.

"When did you see her last?" asks Jamie, and I tell her about the trip Catina had taken with me through the Goodwill, the green silk shirt I'd bought, and Catina's fear when we left the Goodwill.

"God. I wonder if her father knows where she is."

Her voice trails off with her thoughts.

And just then Dr. Brenner arrives, and he doesn't head for coffee and his office as usual.

"What's going on?"

Jamie takes a deep breath, lets it out, and glances around as though she hopes Catina will materialize where she belongs on a weekday at 8:00 a.m. I know Jamie is torn between her loyalty to Dr. Brenner and her loyalty to Catina, but what can I do—

"We don't know what's become of Catina," I admit.

Dr. Brenner's face is expressionless, as always, the robot turning thoughts through the nuts and bolts and cogwheels in his head. "I wonder if Jim Belasco knows where she is," he says after a moment.

He goes into his office, and we see his telephone line light up. Soon he's back at his door.

"Jim doesn't know where she is either. She hasn't been home for two nights. I told him to call the police."

I should have called Isaiah.

··· ···

Someone, maybe the mother of a piano student, had given Mrs. Pence a loaf of homemade bread, a braided loaf with a crusting of poppy seeds that would trouble her dentures. Rather than waste the loaf and the thought, she wanted to pass the gift on to Isaiah, and she asked me to take it over to him that evening.

Isaiah's apartment was on the second floor of one of the old gingerbread mansions a few blocks from Mrs. Pence's house. When the mansion had been converted to apartments, an exterior staircase had been attached to the siding. The staircase led to a smallish landing and a window that had been cut down to the floor to make a door. That first door, Mrs. Pence had said, would be unlocked and open onto a corridor, where Isaiah's door would be No. 2. I dutifully carried the loaf of bread up the unlighted stairs, grumbling to myself about breaking my neck in the dark, opened the door on a corridor lit by a forty-watt bulb, and knocked on No. 2.

It took a long time to open. I was pretty sure Isaiah was home because his white pickup was parked along the side street, but I was about to leave and take the loaf of bread back to Mrs. Pence when a crack widened and he peered out.

Seeing me, he opened it a little wider. He was barefoot and clad only in boxer shorts, and he looked a little dazed. Had I wakened him?

"Ruby, what's up?"

I explained about the bread, and he took the loaf as gingerly as though it might do something unpredictable. "Uh—tell her thanks," he said and shut the door, leaving me shaking my head in the dim corridor, cursing the damned loaf of bread and cursing myself for invading his privacy.

I knew what I had smelled on him. Citrus and semen.

··· ···

On Saturday nights Mrs. Pence likes to settle down by her radio with her eyes closed and listen to whatever musical performance is featured on the classics station. Since I've taken over most of the cooking and washing up, her radio sessions begin earlier, and sometimes she naps through the andante movements with her head against the side of her old rose velvet wing chair and her breathing hardly discernible. It's her way of making up for some of her middle-of-the-night assignations with the Steinway grand.

I wait until I'm sure she's asleep before I slip upstairs to change clothes for the Three Hundred Club. As I feared, the hunter-green shirt is too short in the sleeves, but with the cuffs rolled back, it doesn't matter. I brush my hair and from force of habit start to twist it into its workday bun, then let it fall over my shoulders. When I look in the mirror, I see a tall woman with long dark hair, a green silk shirt and blue jeans and boots with scuff marks the polish doesn't quite cover.

Good enough for the Three Hundred Club, though, where the lights will be dim. Even with the thought, I'm seeing myself in another mirror, in the leather wear shop in Jackson Hole, and then in the mirror of Gall's eyes, and what I see is a girl who matters, who is cared about, a girl whose name is Ruby Red. There was a time, when that reflection faded from Gall's eyes, I would have done anything to get it back.

His tenderness for me lasted quite a while. His featherlight kisses, never on my mouth but on my throat and my eyelids and especially around my hairline. His arms around me, also featherlight but with the hard-clenched muscles always just behind the embrace. And it was enough for me to sleep curled in his arms, absorbing his warmth and the scent of his body. It was months after Versailles and Lewiston, months after Jackson Hole, maybe even after Spokane and Bellingham, maybe during the first tour in Anchorage, that I began to wonder why he never went further with me.

Anchorage, it must have been, because that's when Sharyn the Screamer lingered near me in the filthy laundry room back of the motel where I was washing Gall's and Brazos's underwear and she was folding shirts. Gall and Brazos had walked past the window on their way to the van, and of course my eyes had followed Gall, the slope of his shoulders and the way the wind lifted his hair.

"He can be a real bastard in the sack," Sharyn murmured. I supposed she was bragging, and I shrugged. I'd known he slept with her, after all. Much later I wondered if she was trying to warn me.

But what happened after her remark was that I stopped being his kitten in bed, warm and content to be held and stroked. Started wanting more of him. Wondering why he didn't want to have sex with me. I began kissing him, aiming for his mouth but settling for his neck and collarbone and working my way down until he stopped me. A time or two he got out of bed and pulled on his pants and sweatshirt and left in his bare feet, so I knew he wouldn't be going far. Maybe to Sharyn? Finally, he returned, unsteady on his feet and reeking of bourbon through his pores.

I had nearly been asleep and roused to see him looming over me and unbuckling his belt. He threw back the blanket and sheet and grabbed the neck of my nightgown and ripped it all the way down the front. There was enough light from the motel neon through the window that I could see he was up and he was hard, so if he'd been with Sharyn, he'd recovered pretty fast, but that was all I had time to think. His right hand was under me, and he was gripping my buttocks so hard that my legs opened, and then he was between my legs, cursing me under his breath. Nothing tender about him now, just *plunge, plunge, plunge*, to the tune of *damn, damn, damn*. And then I felt his contraction and ejection, and he lifted his head and upper body as if searching the ceiling for something, an answer maybe, and then he rolled off me and was asleep or maybe passed out, almost at once, leaving me to wipe myself with my ruined nightgown and wonder.

What I didn't know was that we had come not to a beginning but to something bad.

But he had wakened something in me I hadn't known I had. Desire, I guessed it was. Wanting him and wanting him, yearning for the *plunge, plunge, plunge* punishment that didn't bring relief but frantic yearning for more. I became hard to get along with, snapping at people for flatted notes or missed beats or maybe just looking at me the wrong way. Bill and Brazos started keeping their distance from me.

Again it was Sharyn who sidled up to me. Looking back, I realize I always misjudged her. She was a tall, skinny girl with freckles and almost-white eyelashes and hair that tried to be red but had faded, and she'd never been "Outside," as they said in Alaska about the rest of the United States. I always thought she looked up to me and the Rivermen and supposed we were sophisticated outsiders, but there again I misjudged her. She was the one who knew things I didn't.

"He can be real stingy," she said.

I stared at her. What could she mean? Gall, stingy, who had laid down ten hundred-dollar bills for my red fringed suede?

"You can do it for yourself," she said. "Bring yourself off, I mean. It helps a lot."

And then she whispered, "I could show you how."

23

So, the Three Hundred Club.

It had begun as a bowling alley on the east fringe of the Orchards, a long, low, wooden building that had been painted gray at some distant time. Since then it had changed hands several times, and one of the owners had added a bar and a dance floor.

The long summer twilight has faded by the time I pull into the parking lot after I put off leaving Mrs. Pence's, maybe reluctant to leave her alone and asleep in her wing chair but more likely because I didn't really want to sing with the Working Poor. I told myself she had been just fine by herself for years and she knew where I was going. Told myself to get a grip and stop finding excuses.

Lighted neon over the club door advertises summer league bowling and the weekend's featuring of the Working Poor. They aren't playing when I walk in, although their equipment is set up on the small bandstand. In the dim lighting I make out a smallish audience grouped around the dance floor and one familiar figure, short and stout as a fireplug, sitting at a table by herself.

I buy myself a beer on tap at the bar and carry it over to join Jamie. I feel guilty for telling her I would be singing at the Three Hundred Club, as though I'm a featured attraction, a big star, instead of someone Isaiah coaxed to come and sing one or two numbers. I haven't even rehearsed with the Working Poor, unless I count the afternoon last Saturday in Isaiah's barn.

"You're looking good," says Jamie when I set down my beer. I see she's been nursing a glass of Coke.

"Have they played yet?"

"They were playing when I got here. They just now took their break. They're not too bad. Not too bad for country-western anyway. What do you get out of it? It's all the same. Whiskey's my drink; my life's in the sink."

I have to laugh.

"Your boy Isaiah came over and said hello. Wanted to buy me a drink."

I want to ask whether she's seen Catina, which I really, really don't want to ask Isaiah. But she adds, "How did you ever get to know him?"

"I thought I told you."

But no, it was Catina I told. "We were in foster care together. Back in the nasty times. When there were abuse investigations. And scares about satanic rituals."

"Oh, I remember. A whole lot of people got arrested."

"Yes. Our foster father—Isaiah's and my foster father—was the policeman who headed the investigation. And I had to testify at the trials. And I lied because my foster father told me to. And people went to prison, and then the appeals started, and they all got exonerated."

And we kids who testified were the villains. All but Anne. Anne had risen above the scandal. *Ruby Jarvis told me, and I believed her.*

Jamie looks past me. "Don't turn around, but the Queen just walked in. With a guy."

My neck goes rigid with the effort not to turn. All that saves me is the appearance of Isaiah and his band. They stride up to the bandstand in black jeans and tacky gold satin shirts, grinning at the ripple of applause they get, and strike up a number I don't recognize, maybe one of the summer top hits that's too new for the retro station. Whatever, it has a heavy bass line and a relentless percussion, and several couples get up to dance or at least to flail around the dance floor.

I watch Isaiah's fingers dance across the neck of his guitar, picking out a melody while he listens to his sidemen and winces when the bass player misses a note and has to jump to catch up.

Back in the groove, Isaiah takes time to scan his audience and finds me.

The number comes to an end with another smattering of applause. While the dancers wait to see what happens next, Isaiah and his guys confer briefly, then begin a slow, insistent repeating phrase. Isaiah steps up to the forward mike.

"Folks, we got a treat tonight, we got a real voice here with us tonight, and she's gonna sing a number with the Working Poor." His eyes are on me, daring me. "Give a hand to Ruth!"

Real stage fright isn't something I've felt for a long time. Butterflies, of course, on the first night of a new gig, wondering if everything will pull together and the electrical sound system and the amps will work and all of us hoping for a friendly audience. I didn't expect what I feel now, with Isaiah's eyes willing me to the bandstand while his guys repeat the insistent phrase, slower, harder. My bones have gone soft, but I manage to push my chair back and stand and walk across the dance floor in a wavering spotlight and hesitant applause, with everyone probably wondering what they're in for.

Isaiah gives me a hand up on the bandstand and puts his arm around me to make me face the audience. When he kisses me on the cheek, I hear a murmur from the tables around the dance floor. It's clear that Isaiah is a local favorite. Now the guys slide into the beautiful sad chords of "Hickory Wind," and Isaiah steps back and takes up the melody line, and I close my eyes and sing.

After the first bar I'm all right. I'm at a mike with a band behind me, and maybe it's a band that's only a step up from a garage band, but still it's a band, and I'm performing, and I will by god make these Versailles people fall in love, if not with me, at least with the hickory wind. I sing the aching melody and feel the energy ignited by an audience, and I open my eyes and see Jamie at her table just behind the dance floor with her face working and, beyond Jamie, Anne Albert with her face a mask, and the blond man sitting by Anne with his back turned to the bandstand. At the sound of my voice he whips around in his chair, and if anything could have made me lose my place in the line and the lyrics, it's the sight of his face because it's Brazos.

··· ···

"He called you Ruth."

I nod. My two names are too complicated to explain, too complicated for me at this moment. Brazos is too complicated for me. I lived beside him and played music beside him for ten years, he's as familiar to me as the red suede skirt and vest I lost, and I owe him a lot, and he has a right to be angry.

"Not one goddamn word from you. Not one goddamn word!"

Isaiah's hand comes to rest on my shoulder.

"The last place in the world I ever thought you'd be! Versailles! This hole in the sagebrush that Gall and I dragged you out of! Calling yourself *Ruth*!"

"It's my name."

I'm standing on the bandstand, and Brazos has to tip back to glare at me. I want to ask him about Gall. Brazos and Gall go way back. If anybody knows what became of Gall, it will be Brazos. But I can't find the words, and my pulse throbs in my ears, keeping a beat with the pulse I see in Brazos's face. A circle of silent faces observes us from the ring of tables around the bandstand.

Isaiah slides his arm around my waist. "Hey, man, we got a set to play."

"Who the hell are you?"

"He's my brother," I say, and Isaiah's arm tightens.

Brazos's face changes, as though he's working out a difficult arithmetic problem in his head. "Ruby, you and I have to talk. I've got to take Annie home. Will you be here when I come back?"

Annie.

The moment stretches like an elastic band toward a snap. A bald man in a suit is making his way through the tables toward us.

"Yes. I'll wait."

"Everything okay here, Ike?" asks the man in the suit.

"I think we got it worked out, Jimmy."

132

The suit turns to Brazos. "You finished with your business here?"

Brazos nods. "You promised to wait, Ruby."

He returns, stiff legged, to the table where Anne Albert is crying and puts his arms around her. The man in the suit says something to Isaiah over his shoulder as he starts back toward the bar, and Isaiah answers him, "Yeah, yeah."

"You gonna sing again?" Isaiah whispers, and I shake my head. But I remember how it felt, *in performance*, with an audience, the escape from my old battered self.

"Later. Not now."

Isaiah lets me go, and I step down from the bandstand. By the time I get back to Jamie, he and his guys have charged into an old standard with plenty of rhythm and percussion to break the tension, Proud Mary keeping on rolling, and a few couples get up to dance, although faces still look my way and whisper.

"Are they gone yet?" I ask Jamie, and she nods and touches my hand.

"You've got the strangest friends. Goddamn musicians anyway. They never seem real to me. Like they're onstage all the time. Like they're in a movie. Who in the state of Montana is that guy?"

"His name is Brazos Keane. He's a spoiled rich kid from Boise. Do you want a beer?"

"No. If I drink one, I won't stop."

··· ···

The bar is getting ready to close when Brazos returns. Jamie has crossed her arms on the table and looks as though she is ready to rest her head and go to sleep. When I asked if she had talked to Catina, she had shrugged and shaken her head.

The people who ordered fresh drinks at last call are finishing them, and Isaiah and his guys are unplugging and covering and storing instruments and amps. Isaiah glances over his shoulder when Brazos sits at my table, but he goes on coiling electrical cords.

Brazos wears a threadbare white shirt and jeans and brings with him that sense of disjointed time. Surely I've carried that very shirt to a Laundromat and brought it back to our motel room and ironed it for him. And seeing Brazos and Isaiah at the same time in a bar in Versailles is time traveling me back ten years. It's hard to know what's past and what isn't.

I ask the only question I have for him. "What happened to Gall?"

"His father came and took him back to Boise on a medivac plane."

His words are slurred, and I know he's a little drunk. One of the bar staff is turning chairs upside down on tables and shooing out the last of the clientele. Isaiah's guys are leaving, but Isaiah comes over and sits down with us.

Brazos ignores him. "Anywhere we can go to talk?"

I try to think. Does he have a hotel room, or is he staying with Anne? *Annie.* His blond head—the blond head I saw a few days ago in Anne's driveway.

Isaiah leans across the table and speaks directly to me, ignoring Brazos. "We can go to Mrs. Pence's if you want. I'll make you coffee."

"What about Mrs. Pence?"

"She's a night owl. She's probably playing the piano."

... ...

Ray Pence smiles down at us from his photograph in the foyer. What possible good news can he expect from us? Brazos, Isaiah, Jamie, and I, who have trailed each other from the Three Hundred Club in our various vehicles.

Mrs. Pence is playing the Debussy étude on the Steinway behind the closed door of the piano room. Brazos pauses to listen to the rich notes rising from the Steinway's long soundboard. I see the foyer through his eyes, the contrast between the wealth of the Steinway's sound and the shabby wallpaper, the umbrella stand, the stairs and the bannister rail.

Shabby could be a word for life on the road, but Brazos comes from a different world. Once he drove us past the house in the

Boise Highlands where he grew up, a block from the house where Gall grew up, and the country club just down the street.

I hear Isaiah grinding coffee beans in the kitchen. By the time the rest of us file in with the notes of the Steinway fading behind us, he's filling the pot with water and setting the filter.

"My mother had a kitchen a lot like this," remarks Jamie. She pulls out a chair for herself, sits at the table, smooths out a wrinkle in the oilcloth, and yawns. "Ah-ah. What time is it? Two thirty? It's been a long time since I was out and about at this hour. Does she always play the piano in the middle of the night?"

"Since you *asked*," says Brazos, "Gall agreed to go home, and Bill and I got him as far as the airport, but he took off running again. Finally, the Anchorage police caught him and locked him up and sedated him."

No one speaks.

"By the time his dad could book a flight to Seattle the next morning, they had Gall so drugged up that he didn't know where he was or who he was. And you'd run off, nobody knew where."

Silence, except that the old coffeepot starts to growl.

"His dad had to charter that goddamn medivac plane to get him down to Boise. And on the flight he *lapsed* some more. And now he's in a—what do they call it—*care facility* in Seattle. I went to see him. He didn't know me. Didn't know anybody. He's—"

He clenches his fists on the tabletop in his effort to find words.

"He's *gone*! His brain is blown! Nobody home! Gall! The best fucking country tenor since Gram, and he's not *there* anymore."

Brazos, the perfectionist of the Rivermen, the dreamer who saw that the Rivermen had a real shot and wrote the songs and got Gall sober enough to perform and several times talked Bill out of quitting and going back to Boise. He taught me to how to live on the road. How to live on potato chips and salami and how, when we were camping to save motel money, to take a bath in a bucket. Taught me how to perform. Tonight he's been drinking, and he's rigid with tension, anger—and grief.

But I can't feel anything yet. Gall. Gone. His brain blown. Not *there* anymore.

"What was he using?" asks Jamie.

Brazos looks at Jamie as if he'd forgotten she was there. She just looks back at him.

"We don't know. He'd been doing heroin after coke in Seattle. And there was talk around Anchorage about bad heroin."

"Did you talk to anybody at the facility? What are his chances?"

"Nobody knows a damn thing. They told me about a kid that came out of his coma after three weeks."

"So—"

"For Gall it's been three fucking months! And the kid that came around after three weeks? He lost his fucking hearing!"

Isaiah sets a cup of black coffee in front of him. Brazos stares at it as though he's never seen a cup of coffee before. I'm trying to absorb the idea of a musician losing his hearing.

"Anybody else?" says Isaiah. Jamie and I shake our heads, and Isaiah shrugs and pours himself a cup.

"So, how long have you known Anne Albert?" asks Jamie as pleasantly as though normal conversation is normal tonight. Jamie with her fireplug poise, Isaiah with his coffeepot—no wonder Brazos looks unfocused.

"Since we were kids. My mother and her mother were best friends. Annie's brilliant, but she went through a lot of troubles in her teens—her mother moved over to Montana with her, which is how she ended up in foster care here in Versailles for a year or two—"

He loses his thought and turns on me again. "And you, making more trouble for her, like running off from Gall wasn't enough for you—you *bitch*—"

"That's enough of that," says Isaiah in a voice I've never heard before.

Brazos pushes his chair back from the kitchen table, and Isaiah's on his feet, and I see Jamie gather herself for whatever happens next.

What happens next is Mrs. Pence in the kitchen door. At some point the Debussy étude must have come to an end. She's wearing her embroidered Chinese dressing gown, and her hair hangs over her shoulder in a thin white braid. She looks like an ancient china doll as she gazes, frail and surprised, at the scene in her kitchen.

"How nice to see you're having friends over, Ruth."

"Yes," says Isaiah. He sets the coffeepot back on the stove and comes around the table to put his arm around Mrs. Pence's shoulders. "They're friends all right. But they're getting ready to leave."

Brazos has pulled himself back together. He stands and sets his coffee cup in the sink. "Sorry, ma'am. I appreciate the coffee."

He looks at me. "First I knew you had a brother," he says, and he's gone. We hear the front door open and shut behind him.

24

On Saturday, while Mrs. Pence's piano students come and go, I think about mowing the lawn again or at least pushing the mower over the brown stubble. The air is sultry, but the smoke's not as bad. Maybe the crews have gotten the fires under control, or else I'm getting used to the fumes.

From the shade of the blue spruce in the backyard, I can look along the side of the house and see a narrow slice of the front sidewalk. The blonde "Für Elise" student—Madison Albert—wheels up on her bike with her satchel of music, and a minute or two later a younger girl, probably the stumbling "Song of the Volga Boatmen" student, crosses the sidewalk in the other direction. She calls to somebody, and soon I hear a car pulling away. Her mother, I suppose, picking her up after her lesson.

Late July. Unrelenting sun. I feel beads of sweat trickling through my hair and down my neck, and I retreat to the deeper shade of the porch and retrieve my cup. The coffee is lukewarm.

Piano students coming, piano students going, the eternal circle of motion that never seems to change. I haven't seen or heard from Brazos since last Saturday at the Three Hundred Club. Probably he's still angry. He'd planned to drive back to Boise soon. Maybe he's already gone.

Summer's almost gone . . .

The kitchen door bursts open behind me. I jump and turn, slopping coffee. The "Für Elise" girl, Madison, wild-eyed, seems as suspended as a strip of silent film on pause, her hair falling out of its ponytail, soundless words pouring from her mouth. Behind her the screen door hangs ajar. Then motion resumes, the screen slams shut on automatic hinges, and she's running toward me and screaming.

"It's Mrs. Pence, I don't know what's the matter with her, I couldn't find you, I ran all the way upstairs and looked for you, I didn't know what to do, it's Mrs. Pence—"

She's still babbling, still explaining, as I race through the kitchen where the familiar range and refrigerator and sink have turned into strangers, down the hall where Ray Pence smiles from his photograph, and into the piano room.

Mrs. Pence half-lies against the practice piano bench where she fell. Her mouth ajar, her lips blue. I hook her dentures out of her mouth with my finger and drop them on the rug, then ease her away from the bench until she lies flat on the rug, pinch her nostrils, and bend to breathe into her mouth until her chest rises and falls as I lift my mouth from hers. *Again. Again. Count slowly. Again.*

"I didn't know what to do, she was okay and talking about the arpeggios, and then she just dropped over, and I think she hit her head on the corner of the bench, but I don't know, and I didn't know what to do. Mr. Pence, Mr. Pence, I didn't know what to do!"

Who is she talking to?

Someone looms between me and the window, a dark shadow in the corner of my eye—"You need me to spell you?"

I shake my head, breathe deeply into her mouth again, and manage to gasp between another breath and the next, "Ambulance?"

"I already called."

Isaiah's dark fingers on her wrist, checking her pulse. I can't break my rhythm to ask how he got here. I can see Mrs. Pence's dentures, a pair of yellowish grotesques, where I dropped them, and a wet nose on my arm that is Jonathan, but the voices over my head are babble.

"Mr. Pence, I didn't know what to do, and I was looking everywhere for Ruth, but I couldn't find her, and I was afraid I was all alone—"

"Madison, you did just fine."

"Is she going to be okay?"

"We'll hope so."

Breathe again. Count slowly. Breathe again. My vision darkens. Her dentures seem to rise and fall on the rug as I raise my head to breathe deeply and bend to breathe into her mouth. I've been breathing and counting forever, I'll go on breathing and counting forever.

"You okay?"

I nod between breaths. Then, where there was only the frightened girl's babble and the deepening veil over my eyes and the rhythm of my counting, a burst of shouting and lights and clanking metal.

Somebody's getting between me and Mrs. Pence, pushing me aside.

"It's okay, we got her now."

A pudgy man with a beard and ponytail fits a mask over Mrs. Pence's face, while his companion, taller and slimmer, attaches a hose and turns on a pump. Her chest rises and falls as the pump goes to work. The pudgy man pulls a stethoscope out of his pocket, plugs it into his ears, and listens for a minute or two.

"Got a heartbeat. Okay, one, two, three."

Together they lift Mrs. Pence on a white-sheeted stretcher and set it on its wheeled rack, the pump wheezing the whole time.

Silence where there had been racket. I stand and wish I hadn't when the pianos start to tip over. Isaiah catches me and steers me to a bench.

"Put your head down," he tells me as I get a glimpse of the "Für Elise" girl's face, Madison's face, bathed in tears.

"Oh, Mr. Pence," she weeps.

"Is your mom coming to pick you up?"

"No, I'm on my bike."

"We'll drive you home."

Isaiah leaves to pull the Pontiac out of the garage, and Madison sits beside me on the piano bench. "Ruth, I was so scared!"

"I know. I was scared too."

"How'd you know what to do?"

I wonder myself. Bill the Drummer, I half-remember. Somebody had OD'd, and Bill the Drummer started mouth-to-mouth and coached me between breaths to spell him.

"Is Mrs. Pence going to be all right?"

"I don't know."

Isaiah is back. "I hope that was your bike in the middle of the front sidewalk. I loaded it in the trunk of the car. Ruby, are you okay now?"

"Yes."

At least I'm not dizzy, although it's a shock to walk out the front door and find it isn't dark yet but broad late daylight and the Pontiac its stately self by the curb, the lid of its trunk slightly raised where Isaiah had to batten down Madison's bike with a bungee cord. He's getting into the driver's side when Madison screams, "My backpack!" and goes running back to fetch it.

"God," says Isaiah.

Madison climbs into the back seat, and Isaiah shifts the Pontiac into gear and is pulling away from the curb when there's another frantic squeal: "No seatbelt!"

Isaiah seems to mull deep and serious thoughts before he says: "No. Once upon a time there were no seatbelts in cars."

"Really?"

"Really. It's not that far to your house. I'll drive careful. You'll be all right."

Madison's house turns out to be only a few blocks away, on another cottonwood-shaded Orchards street, a smallish bungalow with flaking gray paint and a scorched lawn. I wait in the Pontiac while Isaiah helps her get her bike out of the trunk and walks her to her door. A couple of boys stop riding their bikes in figure eights to watch, and I recognize them as the kids who hang around the mailboxes.

Madison Albert. What is the connection with Anne?

"Her mother was Francis Albert's first wife," Isaiah explains when he comes back to the Pontiac.

"Why did she call you Mr. Pence?"

"Because it's my name."

He's silent then, keeping his attention on his driving until we reach the grade and turn down toward Main. Then he adds: "She's one of my high school students. She'll be a junior this fall."

Magpie nest, full of shiny things hidden in the dark. Isaiah had had a name, and it wasn't Pence. I'd known his name once, but now it dances, elusive, through the twigs and feathers and droppings of the magpie big mess.

More than my mind can hold.

The familiar town lies below us. There stretches the shopping mall, there lies the campus, there waits the hospital. Perhaps it's the late sun playing a ghost's waltz across roofs and treetops and the slow current of the Milk River that casts it all in a strange new light, while Isaiah and I, locked in our ancient chariot, hurtle toward whatever rises to meet us.

25

"Let's walk," says Isaiah.

The air hangs warm and smoky along the hill overlooking the Milk River. I don't know where we're headed or even which direction until I locate the Big Dipper, like a cup with a long handle, hovering over the dark bluffs beyond the Milk River and hoarding its invisible water like the pitiless drought itself, and I realize that we've driven north, over the Milk River bridge, into a part of town that's strange to me. It's not really late, although the houses on both sides of the street are lighted. When we come to the end of the residential street, we're looking across a small park set in a ring of ornamental lights on the very crest of the hill.

The light poles are too high, or the light globes too frosted, for me to see my feet, although I feel I'm walking on grass toward a small indistinct structure, perhaps a gazebo, on the far edge of the park. Then I stumble on a shallow depression in the grass and nearly fall.

"Careful." Isaiah catches my arm.

My eyes adjust enough to the dark to make out a series of long narrow trenches along the side of the park that overlooks the river, seven or eight trenches beyond the one I nearly fell into. Are they empty graves?

"Rifle pits."

"*Rifle* pits? For *what*?"

"For fighting off Indians," he says, and catches me before I fall into the next trench. "We can sit in the gazebo. There's a bench."

The gazebo smells of cedar. The bench faces out, overlooking the lights of downtown and the reflections on the surface of the water where the Milk River flows on its endless journey. Isaiah digs into his shirt pocket and takes out the makings: papers, lighter, baggie of cured clippings from which the familiar sweet scent rises. He rolls his joint and lights it, and I see the red glow as he takes his drag and breathes out.

"Want some?"

I take a hit and breathe in the smoke and feel its reassurance, like the calm face of an old friend.

"They're talking about legalizing the shit in Washington State this fall," he says, when I hand back the joint.

"Does that mean you're going to quit growing it back of Mrs. Pence's garage?"

Isaiah laughs.

We sit in silence for some time, feeling the calm from the smoke, until I say, "Was there an attack?"

"No, but they thought there was going to be."

I wait, but he's thinking his own thoughts.

"The Nez Perce Indian War of 1877," he says after a moment. "The Nez Perce were on the run from the U.S. Army, all the way from Washington and across Idaho, and they fought the army at the Big Hole in western Montana and fled across Yellowstone Park and up into the Judith Basin, and folks here in Versailles thought they were likely to keep riding north and attack the town, so they dug the pits and posted lookouts, but nothing happened. The Nez Perce veered east, over by the Bear Paws. Instead of crossing the Milk River into Canada, they stopped to rest, and that's where General Howard caught them."

He tells me a little more, about the broken treaties and the refusal of the Nez Perce to give up their homeland, their enforced resettlement, and the revolt of the patriot warriors, while I half-listen and imagine those lookouts on the plateau, watching the prairie for any sign of war ponies, while behind them in their pits crouched the waiting men with rifles. The Milk River and the outline of the bluffs would have been about the same as today. Fewer lights, of course. Far fewer.

Would those lookouts and riflemen have been relieved when dawn broke and no Indians on ponies appeared as faraway specks that materialized out of the bunchgrass and sagebrush? Or maybe they had been spoiling for a fight and were disappointed. What was it about fear?

Isaiah stirs, as though I had asked aloud. "Brad Gilcannon died, you know."

"No. I didn't know."

"A couple of years ago."

Brad gone. For a long time he had seemed, at least to me, as permanent and certain a presence as the prairie that enclosed Versailles. The policeman who kept us safe. The local hero, until his investigations went sour. Now I feel a curious absence, like an empty space next to me.

"What did he die of?"

"Heart attack." After a moment he adds, "I've always wondered if he really believed all that shit."

"What shit?"

"The covens. The satanic rituals."

I think about it. "I always thought he did. *I* believed it, except the part where I said I'd seen it. I guess I believed Brad."

"You were how old? Nine?"

"Eight. Nine by the time I testified."

The evening has darkened, and the lights of downtown below us are pinpricks. A car drives past us, following the beam of its headlights, and turns past the park to take the street down the hill. Isaiah makes a sound somewhere between a chuckle and a choke. "You loved Brad, and you believed him. And he believed Anne."

I wait for his next question, but he doesn't ask it. *What did Anne believe? Where did it all start?*

The car leaves a silence behind its passing. The prairie is a field of darkness. An enemy has gathered on the horizon. I see the glint of moonlight on their rifles, hear the snorts of their ponies and the restless dancing of unshod hoofs. The fear on the plateau above town is like an inflection spreading from man to man. *We have to be ready! The Indians are coming! We still have some time but not much time. We have to act!*

"Seems like a long time ago in some ways. In some ways not so long."

"No," Isaiah says, and I'm not sure which he means.

"What I keep coming back to," he says. "Brad must have believed it. If he didn't believe it, why did he do what he did?"

"You mean, file all those charges and so on?"

He nods. Whatever he's thinking is distant.

"There must have been a prosecutor. And a judge." I'm trying to remember. Were there juries? I hadn't appeared before a jury. They had taken me into chambers to tell my story to the judge.

"They must have all believed Brad. And his witnesses. Seems pretty damned improbable when you think about it now."

"Did *you* believe any of it?"

He's silent for a long time. "It was scary as hell," he says finally. "All those grown-ups in suits looking like the end of the world was coming. It was scary that they were scared."

He pauses. "What I didn't believe," he says, "was that I'd seen any dead babies. Or fires on the altar or people running around in black robes. Or having sex in church. I was what, eleven? Even when I was eleven, something like that would have tended to stick in my mind."

I have to laugh, and Isaiah puts his arm around my shoulders.

"That's better," he says.

"What do we do now?"

"I'm going back to the hospital. You're going home and get some rest."

"I want to come with you."

"I'll need you to spell me in the morning. And you need to take care of Jonathan. And water the garden."

What we talk about instead of what we need to talk about.

"Your name wasn't Pence."

"No." Long pause. "The name on my birth certificate was Isaiah Pride. I changed it to Pence when I turned eighteen."

"Why?"

"I wanted a name that was at least part of what I knew I was."

··· ···

"She has a good pulse," the doctor on duty had said. "We've got her on oxygen, got her on a drip, made her comfortable. She may never regain consciousness, but then again she may. And then we'll see."

Dr. Brenner was waiting in the lobby, the robot with a heart. "Can I do anything for you, Ruth?"

"I don't know," I said, and I dropped down in the chair beside him.

"How's Isaiah holding up?"

"Not great."

"He's a good boy."

Then Dr. Brenner surprised me by taking my hand, until his grip told me it was his hand as well as mine needing to be held, and so I held it until an aide came to tell me that Mrs. Pence was settled in a hospital bed with her oxygen and her iv pole and I could see her.

"Talk to her," advised the night nurse. "You never know what they hear, but sometimes it seems to soothe them to hear a familiar voice."

Isaiah and I fall into a routine, one of us sitting at Mrs. Pence's bedside and the other going back to her house to take in the mail and the papers and feed Jonathan and catch a few hours' sleep. Although Isaiah insisted on that first shift, by the next shift we've traded, so I, the natural nightwalker, sit with her through the small hours.

"What kind of a musician are you," I tease him, "that you can't stay up all night?"

He grins and shakes his head. "I don't know what I'll do when school starts and I'm teaching all day. I may have to trade back with you."

"At the college?" I'm surprised. I know the fall term won't start for another two weeks.

"When my school starts. Mike Mansfield High School. Faculty meetings. Lesson plans. That shit."

Taking a cue from the night nurse, I buy a portable CD player and hunt out some classical piano discs, mostly Beethoven and Liszt piano concertos. By my second night of sitting beside Mrs. Pence, I learn how to place a pillow at the back of one of the plastic vinyl chairs, sit back, and use the other vinyl chair as a footrest. I sip water and listen to Liszt over and over while I watch twenty-four-hour cable news with the volume off and think my thoughts.

Such as how could I have been so blind?

The night Isaiah and I followed the stretcher into the emergency room, for example. Against a background of running feet and urgent intercoms, a nurse cornered Isaiah with a form on a clipboard, and he pulled himself together to answer her questions.

"Next of kin?"

Without hesitation. "Rosalie Bohn."

"That's her married name? You wouldn't know her birth name?"

"Pence."

Rosalie. The one-name girl with the voice like a bell. Rosalie Pence.

The name was a clap of thunder in my head that reverberated for a long time. My old fantasy returned, the one where the girl with the voice like a bell gets off the Greyhound bus in the Versailles dust with her hair streaming down her back and her baby in her arms. I made the leap: could that baby have been Isaiah? That would mean—I'd never checked it out—that Isaiah had been the California baby, and I was born here in Versailles.

I have no proof. His name on his birth certificate had been Isaiah Pride. And yet so much fits together. Mrs. Pence's fondness for Isaiah and his for her. The lengths to which Mrs. Pence had gone for me, rescuing me from under her blue spruce and taking me into her own home. Paying for my crow's clothes, helping me to find work.

My white bedroom on the second floor of Mrs. Pence's house—could it have been Rosalie's?

A stir from the bed, faint as an air current, interrupts my surmises. The face that lay on the pillow for three days, almost as white as the pillow, with oxygen hooked to the hawk's nose and the hawk's eyes closed, now turns toward me.

"Mrs. Pence!"

"Rosalie?"

"It's Ruth."

A sigh.

The hawk's eyes open to wander the room. "I've been listening to Liszt for days," she whispers, "and I'm sick of him. All that rubato. Why can't he get hold of himself?"

I'm on the verge of laughing as I get up to stop the CD player and rummage for the disc of Beethoven piano concertos and change the Liszt for it. "Is this better?"

She listens through the first several phrases and recognizes the piece. "At least he's got backbone," she whispers and closes her eyes.

Morning is breaking through the east-facing windows, red streaks against pale blue. Isaiah is due any moment. For once I have something to tell him besides the stark *No change*. I'm giddy, hilarious. *She's going to recover! Even if, as the doctor kept repeating, she's nearly ninety, after all.*

Rosalie. She had hoped I was Rosalie.

When Isaiah doesn't appear in the doorway, I glance at the bed and see that Mrs. Pence seems to be sleeping naturally, her chest rising and falling beneath the white hospital coverlet, so I slip on my backpack, steal out to the elevator, and ride it down to the lobby.

I leave the elevator just as Isaiah pushes through the glass doors into the lobby. The day is lightening behind him. To my surprise, Jamie is with him, his arm around her shoulders, her arm around his waist. They must have run into each other in the lobby. Jamie's face is blank, Isaiah's anguished.

"She's dead," says Jamie.

"No! That's just it! She's alive! She opened her eyes ten minutes ago, and she talked to me! She said she was sick of Liszt!"

"Not Mrs. Pence," says Isaiah. "Catina. Catina is dead."

26

A sad-eyed Jonathan meets me in Mrs. Pence's foyer with his stub of a tail wagging in slow motion. I set down my backpack and stroke his head, and he licks my hand. All looks undisturbed since last night, when I let Jonathan out the back door and filled his food and water bowls and called him back indoors before I fled with my pillow and blanket to Isaiah's apartment to sleep on his couch. Isaiah hadn't spoken to me, but he let me stay.

This morning the umbrella stand and the coat rack are waiting for me in Mrs. Pence's foyer, and the stairs with the walnut bannister rail offer the dim second floor to me, but the objects have lost their substance. Even Ray Pence's faded smile seems forced.

Jonathan patters down the hall behind me and up the stairs, where I drop my soiled shirt and underwear into the hamper and sort out fresh clothes to change into. Instead of getting dressed, though, I sit for a moment on the bed.

White walls, white curtains, white furniture. Above the dresser hangs the print of the cathedral in the trees with the storm clouds gathering above the blue. Storm clouds gathering.

Nothing to do but get dressed. Clean blue jeans, a T-shirt. When I go to the mirror to brush out my hair and braid it, I see the little Polaroid of the sullen young man I found between the glass and the backing—when?—last May, for god's sake, and now we're starting September. His baleful eyes have been watching me from the time I stuck him to the mirror and mostly forgot about him.

I study the snapshot for more clues. What I can see of the backyard looks much better tended than its current dried-out and paint-flaking condition. The blue spruce is so much smaller; the picket fence behind the young man is freshly painted. And what of him? The pack of cigarettes rolled in the sleeve of his T-shirt suggests an outdated toughness, a belligerence I associate with retro movies. He's looking for trouble all right, and his muscled arms and shoulders, his thumbs hooked in his belt, tell me he thinks he can handle trouble. Imagine his surprise to find himself taped to a mirror in this white room.

Stay on the mirror, Baleful Face. Don't come down and look for trouble with me.

··· ···

Yesterday Isaiah and I had followed the ambulance that carried Mrs. Pence—I couldn't think of her by a more familiar name—from Versailles Memorial Hospital to the Orchards Villa nursing home. Moving her to the Villa was the right thing to do, her doctors assured us. At the Villa she would get the skilled nursing care and the therapy she needed, which Isaiah and I couldn't provide for her. Besides, we both had to go back to work. There would be bills. Medicare would cover her for a while, but neither Isaiah nor I knew for how long. So much I never knew I'd need to know that I couldn't take it in.

Would she recover, we asked again and again, and got the same answer: Well—she's nearly ninety.

Mrs. Pence herself had been weak but cheerful, observing all the mysterious fittings and appurtenances of the ambulance and thanking the young driver when he adjusted her stretcher so she could raise her head and see better. In the room where we settled her at the Villa, her hawk's eyes noted the aggressive cheer of rose-colored walls and flowered curtains and framed prints of children playing in summer meadows, and she whispered that it was all very suitable. I plugged in her little radio that I'd brought along and set it where she could reach the knob, and Isaiah showed her how to push a button and raise her bed to sit up, and we both promised we'd be back to see her in the evening, and she held Isaiah's hand as he kissed her on the forehead while the Villa nurse waited in the doorway.

He had not spoken a word to me on the way home, and I wondered if he blamed me and for what.

Jonathan follows me downstairs and past the door to the piano room toward the kitchen. I hesitate, and so does Jonathan. The lonely pianos, all by themselves.

The upright Kimball, the spinet, the beautiful Steinway. No, I won't touch her Steinway, but I strike middle C on the Kimball and hold it for a long time, and it reverberates while Beethoven glares out from his niche, angry at what is happening, I think.

The note fades. Just as my birthday has come and gone. Isaiah had brought over a small bakery cake and lit candles for me to blow out, and he and Mrs. Pence had sung "Happy Birthday" to me. I think of striking middle C again and don't.

In the kitchen, where morning sunlight falls on the ancient sink and stove and shelves and highlights the chips and scars of years of use, I open the back door for Jonathan and add a scoop of dry food to his bowl and pour water for him.

Then I fill a bucket with water at the sink and carry it out the kitchen door to the back yard. Jonathan follows me as I water the rows of lettuce and carrots and onions and Isaiah's burgeoning marijuana plants. It takes me three trips from the kitchen sink to the little garden with buckets of water. Given the watering restrictions, I don't dare to use a hose, and the sun is hot and I'm sweating by the time I finish.

I drop the buckets and sit on the back steps in the narrow strip of shade. Jonathan flops down at my feet while I look across the brown lawn that stretches past the garage and the blue spruce to the picket fence that is worn and scabby now but once was freshly painted. People say the grass will revive and grow when the rains come in the fall, but I fear we're coming to an end of some things.

"Ruby?"

I shade my eyes, but the sun reflects off the pale siding of the house, and all I can make out through the glare is a dark figure rounding the corner and through the side gate.

"Ruby? I rang the bell and didn't get an answer, so I took a chance you'd be back here."

Something familiar about that voice, that walk.

A tall big-boned man climbs the steps and sits beside me. He's wearing Levi's and a blue chambray shirt with the sleeves rolled above heavily muscled forearms. Dark-hazel eyes, deep vertical creases below his cheekbones. Hank of dark hair that falls over his forehead.

Bill the Drummer.

I levitate back to that last night in Anchorage, Bill the Drummer and Brazos cursing each other outside my door, and I have to lay my hand down on the wooden step and feel its grain to remind myself I'm sitting on Mrs. Pence's back porch in Versailles, Montana, isolated in the middle of the sagebrush on the northern prairie, and Bill the Drummer of the Idaho Rivermen is sitting beside me.

"How'd you get here?" is all I can say.

"I drove. Well—yeah, that must sound stupid. Brazos asked me to drive up here and help him pack up Annie's house and move her back to Boise."

I haven't seen or heard from Brazos since his outburst when I sang with the Working Poor, and I don't know what to say to Bill. In the silence a robin flies down and pecks at the damp soil around the carrots, and a squirrel ripple-humps his way along the back fence and pauses with his tail up.

What are you looking at, squirrel? What's it like in your world? Mine is upside down.

A song from some old songbook . . . *I wish I was . . . a squirrel . . .*

"You and Brazos must have made up after your fight."

"You heard us in Anchorage that night? Well—kinda, I guess. But what he also told me when he asked me to help pack up Annie was that he'd found Ruby."

I raise my head, find Bill's eyes on me.

"He said he'd found Ruby in Versailles, Montana, and she was singing with some half-assed band with a guy she said was her brother."

"Not that half-assed!"

"You're looking good, Ruby. You doing okay?"

. . . away I'd sail . . .

How to answer Bill's question. No. I'm not doing okay. And it's not making it more okay to be in the here and now in Mrs. Pence's backyard, where the grass is dying and Jonathan grieves and squirrels and robins go about their squirrel and robin business, and at the same time be thrown in the *then*, where Bill was a fixture as familiar and dependable as the electrical cords he wound up and the amps he stowed and the drum set he dismantled and packed whenever we moved from gig to gig.

And now Brazos, taking Bill's help for granted in moving Anne all those miles to Boise.

"What is it?" Bill says. "Brazos and Gall?"

"Partly."

I don't know how to tell him about Mrs. Pence or Isaiah or Catina, none of whom he knows, and so our silence stretches while the morning sun rises overhead and our strip of shade narrows. The temperature will hit 100 degrees, 110, by noon. The smoke in the air is heavier than yesterday's. Forest fires and grass fires all summer, just like every summer. The aides at the Villa talked last night about fires near Yellowstone burning out of control. Things are out of control here on the back steps too. Oblivious, the robin moves on to the onions, thinks of something else he has to do, and wings off.

If I look up, I'll find Bill's eyes on me, so I look at his hands instead. A drummer's hands but also the hands of someone who works with his hands, as good with a hammer or a screwdriver or even a pair of barber scissors as he is with his drumsticks. He must have been working with his hands recently because one thumbnail is blackened.

… I wish it would rain …

Catina. How I wish I could cry for her, but I can't, not a drop.

"Why are you here, Bill?"

"I wanted to see you."

I look up, and I do find his eyes on me, and I can't break his gaze, and I realize he is probably the person left in this world who knows me best.

"What you need to remember," says Bill, "is that Brazos is always having to help people. You, for example."

I remember. Brazos urging me through the high school equivalency exam. Brazos pushing books on me to read. Teaching me to sing harmony. Teaching me how to sing in a band.

"And now he's helping Anne? And he believes everything she tells him?"

"Something like that. He's known her since they were kids."

"Brazos said Anne is brilliant."

"She was. Is. Ruby—look, you scared us half to death when we were already half-scared to death over Gall. His father had flown up to help, and he cried when he saw Gall. It took all of us to get him from the jail to the medivac plane, and he was crazier than a screaming coot, fighting the straps and cussing us and trying to kick us, but we wrestled him on board, and we watched the plane fly off. And when Brazos and I got back to the motel—he'd told me what he'd done to you, which was what sparked Gall's explosion. And I was burned as hell at him and said so—well, *yelled* it at him—and maybe it finally sank into him because in the morning he came with me to look for you, to see if you were okay. And you weren't there. We searched your room. Brazos was—I never saw Brazos look like that. Never want to again. Your clothes were still there. Your goddamn *toothbrush* was still there."

"I'm sorry," I whisper.

"Yeah."

It's a moment before he can continue, and his voice wobbles. "Then Sharyn followed us in and looked back of a panel under the bathroom sink and said Gall's wad was gone. And I knew

156

the Rivermen were over and done. And I was so damned scared I'd never see you again."

"I bought my airline ticket with Gall's money."

We both just sit there. The sun keeps rising inexorably, and the strip of shade along the back of the house narrows until the line between shade and sun falls across my bare feet and Bill's feet in the same old Justin cowboy boots that I remember from Rivermen days—*one of those boots hitting the TV screen*—and the memory feels like an electrical surge.

The squirrel makes a leap for a branch of the neighbor's maple tree and chitters and scolds down at whatever angers him on the other side of the picket fence, a cat perhaps, and Jonathan wakes up and charges the fence, yapping.

"I packed your clothes and brought them back with me. I brought your red suede outfit, in case you want it. In case you decide to keep singing with your friend and his band."

What else had Brazos told him?

"He's my brother!"

"Your brother."

"He *is* my brother!"

27

On Monday I creep back to campus with the retro station on the Pontiac's radio playing Loretta Lynn and Jack White's "High on a Mountaintop." I can hardly bear to listen. I lock the Pontiac and drag myself up the three flights of stairs to the Office of Student Accounting in the black clothes that feel strange after wearing the same pair of jeans for almost a week.

The office feels strange, too, although the coffeepot is perking and Jamie is making the rounds of her plants with her watering can. We're both early. When the coffee is brewed, she pours us each a cup and sits beside me in Catina's chair, at Catina's workstation. The closed door to Anne's office is a surly presence, but Jamie says nothing, and I say nothing, and the cups of coffee sit in front of us and cool.

We both look up when Dr. Brenner lets himself in. Jamie starts to get up, but he waves her back and pours his own coffee and pulls up a chair to sit with us.

"How's your grandmother, Ruth?"

"Oh—better," I say, surprised. Then I wonder why I'm surprised. All the longtime residents of Versailles have elephants' memories. My story hadn't been a secret to anyone but me. "She tires easily, but the physical therapist visits her, and she eats real food."

And tells me what to do about her piano students.

Dr. Brenner nods, and Jamie looks up—"That's good to hear."

"And Isaiah?"

"I don't know. He doesn't talk to me."

"Hard on him."

The three of us breathe in the tranquility of spider plants and travel posters and the silence of the third floor. A silence to be shattered next week by the beginning of the fall semester and the rush of students.

"I'm afraid there's plenty of work ahead for you, Ruth," says Dr. Brenner.

Plenty ahead that I haven't allowed myself to think about. Medical bills, nursing home bills. Will the house in the Orchards have to be sold? What about the pianos?

Unexpectedly, he reaches over and pats my shoulder. "In the meantime we've got to get the situation in this office straightened out."

"Mrs. Albert—?" asks Jamie.

"She won't be coming back," says Dr. Brenner.

His words sink in.

"Her friend is helping her pack up her house and put it on the market. He's taking her back to Boise with him. So, Jamie—"

Details of the office: dust on the file cabinets, one of the framed posters hanging slightly askew, brown edges on the fronds of the spider plants. So much for tranquility.

"—I believe her friend plans to clear out her office this morning. Once he's finished, you may as well move in. It'll be a temporary appointment; you'll have to apply for the position, but that can wait. Ruth—"

I drag my attention back from the fronds of plants.

"—you'll have to apply for your position too. If you want it, that is."

If I want it. He's waiting for my answer. I nod.

Dr. Brenner picks up his coffee cup and stands. "Right. Good. We'll borrow Zella from the registrar's office to help you girls through the fall rush."

His office door closes behind him.

I look at Jamie, and she looks at me.

"So. Zella," she says. "Do you know her?"

"No."

"Eech."

That was at eight o'clock. Jamie and I have pounded steadily at our keyboards to make a dent in the backlog of student data that piled up during the past black weeks until ten o'clock, when we are jolted by a thud and crash at the outer door. It opens on Brazos, who has just dropped a stack of unassembled cardboard packing boxes, and Bill the Drummer, who pushes a dolly on creaking wheels.

Suddenly the Office of Student Accounting feels overwhelmed by large young men. Surly Brazos won't look at me, and Bill's face is carefully neutral, although he gives me a surreptitious two-finger wave.

Anne follows, looking unlike herself in a limp T-shirt and shorts and flip-flops. Her face is pale, and her lips tremble.

"Where?" Brazos asks her.

Anne points at her office door, and Brazos shoulders his way past my computer station, with every muscle of his face and body taut with anger. Anne unlocks her office, and they all go inside and shut the door, and Jamie and I are alone again with our computers and our backlog. But the air feels too dense to breathe, and not just from the lingering smoke from the fires. I'm hearing a high vibration that seems to have started between my ears, a whine in a minor key that swells and sinks and swells again. My head can't contain it; I want to rid it from my head; I can't bear this tension that hums like a wire in the wind. Thin smoke-tinged air separates me from Jamie, who peers into her computer screen and shows no sign that she's affected by any whine or hum.

Something smashes behind Anne's closed door, a waterfall of broken glass. The door is hurled open, and Anne runs out, nearly falling in her flip-flops. Brazos is right behind her and tries to take her arm, but she flings him away.

"Everything! Everything I have is broken!"

"Annie, I didn't mean to break it! You know I didn't mean to!"

She stands sobbing by my computer station. Brazos tries again, and this time she lets him gather her to him. Against his chest she's small and blonde and fragile, with white pipe straws for arms and legs.

Brazos glares at me over Anne's head. "Are you satisfied yet?" The whine is back, the wire in the wind.

Dr. Brenner looks out of his office to see what's going on, and Brazos tucks Anne under one arm and confronts him with cocked shoulders and braced legs.

"That liar. *Ruby!* Calling herself Ruth. You know she's a liar, don't you? So what did you do? You used her to make Annie miserable and have to quit her job, just when she most needed her job!"

He's so angry I think he must be the wire in the wind, but Dr. Brenner, taller than Brazos by a couple of inches, just looks down at him with the detached interest a robot might take in a human's unaccountable rage. How can Dr. Brenner stay so calm when a red film rises over my vision?

"Egging her house! Scaring her half out of her mind!"

I see Brazos through the red film. I'm on my feet. Jamie's computer manual, three hundred pages of fine print on gray paper she left on a filing cabinet, finds its way into my hands, and with both hands I heave the manual at Brazos, and it hits him on his shoulder, where it bounces off and lands on the floor in a ruffle of exhausted pages, as though it has carried out an arduous task.

The manual couldn't have hurt Brazos, but it obviously startled the hell out of him because he turns in bafflement, his face reflecting his sight of a girl whose strings he used to pull to make her move but now, for some puzzling reason, has cut the strings and started throwing computer manuals at him.

"Brazos Keane, you spoiled bastard! Don't you dare call me a liar! I might be a thief, but I'm not a liar, and you damned well know it!"

His mouth opens and shuts. Opens and shuts.

"And it wasn't your money I stole!"

"Young man, you'd better leave," says Dr. Brenner, like a reprise. First he had to chase Dustin away from the office and now Brazos.

Brazos pulls himself together—"Oh, we're leaving all right!"

He catches Anne by the hand and heads for the door, but Dr. Brenner says, "Mrs. Albert," and she stops.

"Have you turned in your keys?"

She stares at him as though she doesn't understand what the word *keys* means. Then she digs in the front pocket of her shorts and draws out a set of keys and looks at them for a moment. Closes her fingers over them. Then, slowly, she opens her fingers and hands over the keys.

"Thank you," says Dr. Brenner.

She doesn't answer but stares at him as though she wants to remember his face. Then Brazos draws her away, and they're gone.

Bill the Drummer has watched the whole scene from the doorway of Anne's office. Now he speaks in a voice that's carefully matter-of-fact.

"I can pack up the rest of her stuff and finish getting the paintings down, but I can't carry the rugs and chairs downstairs by myself. I'll have to wait till Brazos can come back and give me a hand."

He's holding an electric drill.

"I'll give you a hand," says Dr. Brenner. He takes off his suit coat and hangs it on the back of Catina's empty chair, and he turns back the cuffs of his shirt, and then he looks from me to the fallen computer manual, shakes his head, and follows Bill back into Anne's office.

A choking sound from Jamie. She's laughing and rocking back and forth in her chair, trying to contain herself.

"I have now seen everything," she gurgles. "I have seen everything that can possibly happen in this goddamned office."

··· ···

"Just when you think nothing will change, you look around and notice that everything's changed."

Jamie holds the key Dr. Brenner gave her in the palm of her hand, looking at it as though she expects it to levitate and fly away. When it doesn't, she says: "What the hell. We might as well take a look and see what she left behind."

I follow reluctantly as she unlocks the door and opens it into a dusty emptiness and sneezes.

"Bless you," I whisper.

"Holy shit," she says.

Her voice echoes across the bare room. Anne's desk remains and her desk chair and her computer, which probably are the property of the college, but the rugs are gone, and so are the armchairs and the paintings and even the curtains. All that is Anne's is the blue color of the walls, but I feel like a trespasser in a forbidden space.

"I wonder how long it took them to pack all her precious shit. After they broke her lamp. Did you ever see this room, the way she had it fixed up?"

"No. Well—I got a glimpse through the door once."

"I hope they'll at least repaint the walls for me."

I see darker-blue blotches on the walls, unfaded squares and rectangles where Anne's paintings had hung, and the holes where Bill the Drummer removed the screws that held them up, and I'm thankful it is Jamie, not me, who will move into this haunted room.

"So you'll be an administrative assistant now?"

"Looks like it. What about you?"

"I don't know."

Jamie gives me a strange look. "What don't you know? You don't want the permanent appointment?"

It's what I meant. But I don't know what I meant. A tangled something has webbed itself around my thoughts. A stick turned into a snakeskin. Mrs. Pence turning into my bedridden grandmother. Catina burned to ashes. James McMurtry singing "Bear Tracks" on the Pontiac's radio ... *bear tracks, coming after me.* Red suede coming to Versailles, Montana, coming after me. And now

I've started throwing things at people. Maybe Dr. Brenner will fire me when he gets back.

What Anne knows. What she feared I knew and would tell when I came back to Versailles.

"Are you okay?"

I don't think so, I want to say. Instead, I say, "I don't know how you can stand to move into her office."

"She never got to me the way she got to you. It's just an office. I'll hang up some plants and posters and spread my files around, and it'll—" She pauses. "That was a stupid thing to ask. How could you be okay? I'm not okay. I just pretend to be."

Her eyes are brilliant, and I have to turn away. I don't want to see her grief. *You should be sorry, Ruby Jarvis. You have a lot to be sorry for.* I hadn't stood by Gall. I hadn't taken the Pontiac that afternoon and gone looking for Catina instead of telling myself I'd see her at the office, where I could warn her about Dustin. I hadn't cruised past the Goodwill with an eye out for her, and I hadn't checked out the shopping mall in its zero-tolerance air-conditioning. Or—I saw myself looking up Jim Belasco's address in the phone book and driving to where he lives in the East Orchards, looking for Catina, or walking the few blocks and climbing the rickety stairs to Isaiah's apartment and knocking on his door—would she have been there?

"Maybe I'll be fired and I won't have to think about the office."

"I don't think you'll be fired. I very much doubt it."

Jamie wanders over to the window and looks out at street and sidewalk and the tops of fir trees. Her voice, when she continues, is matter-of-fact.

"So pull it together. Pretend you're okay. At least both of us will be getting bigger paychecks. There's that."

She turns from the window and shrugs.

28

The courthouse is smaller than I remember it. Once upon a time Brad Gilcannon led me by the hand past the bronze Chippewa Indian on horseback who guarded the front of the courthouse facade and observed the traffic on Main Street with his inalterable gaze. Brad led me across a marble foyer and up a grand marble staircase to the judge's chambers on the second floor. I thought those stairs, with their ornate brass rails that soared aloft on either hand, were grand enough for a palace. Brad was in uniform because he was going to testify later. He winked at me and squeezed my hand for reassurance, and I felt frightened, but also important, because Brad was escorting me and I was going to be a big girl and tell my story to the judge.

The bronze Indian and his horse still oversee Main Street, but stains disfigure the marble foyer, and the staircase seems shrunken, its treads hollowed and stained by generations of footsteps. Now Isaiah's feet and mine are contributing their miniscule wear toward deepening the hollows in the treads as we climb toward the early-morning shadows.

A balcony with a brass rail runs all the way around the stairwell, forming a U-shaped hallway with doors to chambers on either side and the main courtroom at the end of the U. Its double doors stand open to a metal detector, where a uniformed security guard waves us through, first me and then Isaiah, and into the courtroom.

Fluorescent lighting overhead, walls paneled in dark wood. Rows of public seating form a semicircle facing the judge's bench and a raised section for a jury. I scan the backs of the heads of a handful of spectators and recognize Dr. Brenner's bony shoulders and cropped gray head. Beside him, much shorter, Jamie's head and shoulders. When I slide into the row of seating behind them, Jamie glances back and nods.

Isaiah sits by me, but his face is closed. He hardly spoke a word when I came to take his place yesterday with Mrs. Pence at the Orchards Villa, although he nodded when I told him the time the arraignment was scheduled, and he was ready and out the door of his apartment when I stopped to pick him up this morning.

This is the first time I've seen Isaiah in a suit and tie. I wouldn't have thought he owned a suit, although maybe he wears a suit when he teaches. This suit is dark and perfectly pressed, and it makes him look unfamiliar and remote.

Dr. Brenner, now, the strange thing would be to see him not wearing a suit. He always looks as though he'd been unfolded from his closet that morning, suit and all. And here I am, thinking about men wearing suits. So I won't have to think. Won't have to wonder. Wonder how much Isaiah blames me. Blames me for not looking for Catina that afternoon. For not trying harder.

Jamie turns and whispers, "See the man in the plaid shirt? Opposite us? That's Jim Belasco. Her father."

Words. Plaid shirt. Father. Not someone I remember seeing at the laying of the ashes. A thick shock of curly gray hair and glasses and a little paunch. He wears a necktie with the plaid shirt. But my attention is wandering. I'm watching from the ceiling. Seeing suits. Men in suits spreading their papers on their respective tables. They seem friendly with each other, speaking back and forth in low voices across the space between their tables. A middle-aged woman climbs the steps to a platform to the right of the judge's bench, where she seats herself behind a keyboard. Something is about to happen.

What happens is that Dustin is led in, handcuffed and shackled, which brings me down from the ceiling with a thud. Dustin's face lacks color, in contrast with his bright-orange jumpsuit, and his eyes are fixed on someone seated behind us. Then he's guided to a chair next to one of the men in suits and made to sit down with his back to us, and I breathe out.

I feel Isaiah's tension beside me like a knotted fist, and I don't dare look his way. More is happening. We're all getting to our feet because the judge has come in. He seats himself behind his bench, and we all sit down again. I have not seen a judge since the one who questioned me in his chambers when I was nine. I remember him as elderly and kind. This judge is youngish, with rimless glasses and dark blond hair like Dustin's.

Words. Words. I try not to float away. Behind the judge an American flag hangs, unfurled, and also the Montana state flag, with its plow and its shovel and its pick posed against a green pasture in front of the Great Falls of the Missouri. *Oro y plata*, reads a banner across the bottom of the flag. Gold and silver. What we value. Fame and fortune. Dustin and his attorney have risen to their feet. The judge asks a question, and Dustin must have answered because the judge nods. Now the other attorney rises from his table, and I pick out a few phrases. *Your honor, a serious crime here ... potentially first-degree murder ... may ask for the death penalty ... bail not recommended ...*

And now Dustin's attorney. *He's lived here all his life ... never lived anywhere else ... not a flight risk, nowhere to go ... nature of the crime ... he's not a threat to anyone else ... parents will put up what they've got ... take responsibility for him ...*

Dustin and the attorneys sit again.

"Bastard," says Jamie, and Dr. Brenner glances down at her.

"Bail set at two million dollars," says the judge. He raps the bench with his gavel, and that's that.

"The bastards!" says Jamie, too loudly.

But the judge is gone. Dustin's attorney claps him on the shoulder and says something that makes him smile at the faces he'd spotted in the back of the courtroom before he's led away with his rear end just as high and tight in the orange jumpsuit as it had been in blue jeans.

The morning is still young, but the courthouse steps sizzle with the heat of Versailles and lingering smoke from the forest fires. Even the bronze Indian seems to quiver with the heat and smoke. He's said to be Chief Stone Child of the Chippewa, from the Rocky Boy Reservation, and I imagine him swinging down from his horse and hunting himself up some shade and maybe a wet towel to breathe through.

Summer's almost done for, though. The leaves of the young oak trees on the courthouse lawn have turned a burnished red. *Winter's comin' on* ... The old lyrics are stuck in my head.

"They won't have no trouble posting a couple million?" Jim Belasco asks Dr. Brenner, who shakes his head.

"Old Man Murray's owned that junkyard east of town for years. That land is prime commercial development if anybody can pry him loose from it. Any bail bondsman will advance him the two hundred thousand cash he'll need to get his grandson out of jail."

"Old Man Murray wasn't in court today," Jim Belasco observes.

"No. He doesn't get out much these days."

"Kid's folks was there, though. I saw them setting in back. Helluva thing."

A slight breeze ruffles Jim Belasco's gray curls—Catina's curls—as he stands at the top of the courthouse steps, pondering. "And not that she wasn't asking for trouble," he says suddenly. "I told her, I dunno how many times I told her, but she couldn't listen, oh hell no, no more than her mother could."

Isaiah makes a strangled sound in his throat.

"I have to get out of here," he mutters and takes off running down the courthouse steps. I can't run in my heeled office shoes, and I have to hope he's headed for the parking lot where we left the Pontiac and not—where he might—my thoughts won't go any farther. But he's in the parking lot, waiting by the Pontiac, when I get there.

He holds out a hand—"Let me drive."

I give him the keys and walk around to the passenger side and get in. Isaiah sits behind the wheel and sticks the key in the ignition, but he doesn't turn it.

"Fuckfuckfuckfuckfuckfuck—"

He beats his forehead against the chrome Indian head on the horn button while I wonder why the horn doesn't sound. Maybe it's so old it doesn't work. I can't remember whether I've ever tried to use it. The chrome Indian is taking quite a beating. Isaiah's going to raise a powerful welt on his forehead, and here I am thinking about chrome Indians and whether or not the Pontiac's horn still works. Chrome Indians, bronze Indians, Indians everywhere, turned into statues and hood ornaments. Also elk, turned into wallpaper.

Finally, Isaiah slumps against the wheel. "Maybe you'd better drive after all," he says, so I get out again and walk around the car while he slides over on the bench seat.

"Where do you want to go?"

"You decide."

I pull out of the courthouse parking lot and leave the bronze Indian supervising the traffic on Main Street. The radio wakes up, mid-song, with a Reckless Kelly hit, which Isaiah slams off. I drive north and cross the Milk River bridge and then a few more blocks along a residential street until I draw up to the curb by the little park with the gazebo that overlooks the river.

"Do you want to walk?"

He shrugs, but he gets out and waits for me.

I have to pick my way in my office heels across the desiccated grass and stubble of weeds, but by full light of day I easily make out the depressions of the rifle pits, where long ago the men of Versailles crouched with their rifles and waited for the Indians to ride north across the prairie and attack the town and where I had nearly stumbled in the dark. Daylight exposes the gazebo as a ramshackle shelter in need of repair. Birds have been nesting in its rafters, and a stray twig floats down and catches on a splinter. The little bench is streaked white with dried droppings, and I worry about Isaiah sitting there in his good suit, but he doesn't seem to notice.

We sit. Sunlight falls through cracks in the roof of the gazebo and speckles the board floor. I take shallow breaths in the dusty air and wonder what a passerby might think, seeing a man and a woman in dark formal clothing sitting on a bench in a decrepit gazebo and gazing straight ahead without speaking. What are they doing there, in the heat of the day? Why do they look so glum?

"Isaiah, have you known about us always?"

Just when I'm sure he won't answer, he says, "Pretty much."

I wait.

"It helped that I learned in college how to do research. I tracked down my birth certificate in Monterey. It didn't give a father's name, but my name was given as Isaiah Pride, and my mother was Rosalie Pence."

A pause. The air feels dense. My imaginary passerby waits to hear what happened next.

"I guess she didn't know what else to do, so she brought me back here," he says. "For a while we lived at"—he hesitates— "Grandmother's house. I can sort of remember. Mostly I remember hearing the music, the piano. And then we—anyway. I was three when CPS took me. I got bounced around for a while and ended up with Brad."

Below us the Milk River flows on its unhurried way. Isaiah watches something, a flight of birds that swoops above the river and sinks and seems to dissolve like the reflection of a dark cloud into the current.

"I can't remember you before I met you at Brad's. I don't know why."

"I can remember you. I'd walk up the hill to visit Grandmother or Brad would drop me off, and you'd be having a piano lesson. Do you remember that?"

"I remember the piano lessons."

Playing hands alone on the practice Kimball from John Thompson's *Teaching Little Fingers to Play*. The solemn tone of the piano. C, D, E, C, D, E. Sing with the notes. *Here we go, up a row.* Good. Play it again.

"Brad was always good that way. Other ways, not so much. Remember our fights? But he made sure I got to see Grandmother. Or more like it, made sure she got to see me."

"He dropped me off for piano lessons, but that was all."

"By the time you moved in with him, he was up to his neck in charges and trials and testimonies, and you were part of the testimonies. He probably wanted to shelter you from anybody who might twist your thinking one way or the other."

Isaiah studies the surface of the river. From here it looks like cast metal. Where did the birds go?

"What a bastard Brad could be. But I don't know if he deserved what he got or not."

"Isaiah, did you know my father?"

I've always thought that maybe my father's name was Gervais. Because why the odd spelling, which Brazos had told me was French? If my mother picked it at random, wouldn't she have spelled it *Jarvis*?

"No. But I've always thought he had to be somebody in Versailles because we'd been gone from Monterey almost three years before you were born."

A screaming confrontation.

Like you gave away the other one?

I hate you!

"She gave you away when she got pregnant with me?"

"Probably."

"What about your father?"

"All I know is, obviously he was black. I was three years old, remember. What would she have told me?"

"Maybe your father's name was Pride?"

"Maybe."

A golden oldie. A voice singing about kissing an angel good morning.

"Not that dude," Isaiah says, as if he reads my mind. "Charlie Pride had left Great Falls and was living in Texas by then. More likely it was Rosalie's bad joke."

I wonder about Rosalie Pence. How had she felt about Isaiah's father? About leaving him behind in California? *Had* she left him behind in California? Maybe he died in a car wreck. Maybe he was killed in whatever war was going on thirty years ago. Maybe he killed his brain with bad heroin. If I'd had a baby with Gall, would I know how she felt?

"The best thing that happened to her was going to prison. You need to know that. Even if it was a crock that put her there. She sobered up and got her head straight—straighter anyway—and then Jerry Bohn got her sprung, and he married her, and I think that's worked out okay for her."

"You've been in touch with her?"

"No." He hesitates. "Dr. Brenner keeps me up. He was a professor of mine when I was in college, before he went into administration."

The imaginary passerby waits to hear the rest of the story. He's going to be disappointed. The sun has worked its way westward and dazzles the river through the remains of the smoke. Monterey was a long time ago. Rosalie Pence and her troubles were a long time ago. Our troubles are now. Sweat trickles under my dark clothes, and I think about driving home, taking a shower, and driving up to the Villa to take my turn with Mrs. Pence. My grandmother.

"Why do you think she—Grandmother—didn't take us when Rosalie went to prison?"

"Rosalie gave me away," he says. "Put me up for adoption, which didn't happen. You? I don't know. CPS came and took you away. Maybe Rosalie had, what, some kind of veto power?"

"Maybe."

He shakes his head and studies the river. "I guess it's getting to be that time of year," he says.

. . . summer's almost gone . . .

"Anyway," he said.

Anyway. Anyway.

Anyway.

What we talk about when we can't talk about—

"Catina," I said.

"Yup."

. . . winter's comin' on . . .

"She was so goddamn alive," he bursts. "And she by god didn't deserve what she got. Life for her was one experiment after another, and I was one of her experiments."

He's looking at his hands, clenching his fingers. "I should never have let her leave and go home that night."

"I should have looked for her."

He reaches over and takes my hand and holds it. Our hands so much alike, dark and pale, big piano-playing hands. We sit together while the imaginary passerby wonders who we are and why we're lingering so long and where we might be going, until the air in the gazebo grows so hot and suffocating that we get up and walk across the dying grass to the Pontiac, where the chrome Indian on the hood has been keeping watch over us all afternoon.

29

Madison's rendition of "Für Elise" has improved after working on it all summer, but she still misses the accidental F sharps that Mrs. Pence had circled in red for her. She misses the first F sharp, and her fingers stumble on the beginning of the long chromatic scale, and when the doorbell rings, she stops. It rings again, and I get up to chase off whoever is interrupting her lesson.

Bill the Drummer, carrying a suitcase, has left the porch and is circling around the house toward the backyard where he found me last time. When he hears the door open, he turns, grins at me, and climbs the porch steps with the suitcase.

"I brought your clothes."

"Oh. I thought you'd gone back to Boise."

"Brazos and Annie did. Um—are you going to let me come in?"

"I'm giving a piano lesson." I hesitate. "But it's almost finished."

Madison hits another F natural instead of F sharp as we enter the piano room, and Bill winces. He sets down the suitcase and makes himself comfortable in the rose wingback armchair where mothers observing their daughters' lessons usually sit. Where Mrs. Pence sat in the evenings, listening to her radio.

Bill the Drummer, once so unobtrusive a part of the Rivermen, is taking up more space in this room than I would have thought possible. His hazel eyes, fixed on me. His dark brows, his heavy fringe of dark eyelashes—I remember Sharyn the Screamer calling him Mr. Eyelashes, although it never got her anywhere with him—his Levi's and his familiar old Justin boots and the gray linen shirt he was wearing when he and Dr. Brenner moved Anne's armchairs and paintings and rugs out of her office. What

I thought would be my last sight of him was that gray shirt tightening across the muscles of his back when he bent to pick up his end of the rolled-up rug and loosening when he stood to follow Dr. Brenner, who carried the other end of the rug, out the door.

The sound of the drill I had mistaken for the sound of the tension in the room that day. Tension in this room today. How can Bill look so at ease?

To silence the sound of tension, I turn my back to Bill and sit on the piano bench beside Madison as she starts over, and I point out the accidentals with the tip of my pencil as she comes to them, and she actually plays to the end without a more serious mistake than slowing down on the sixteenth notes.

"You've made the same mistakes so many times that your fingers have learned to play them. You need to practice a few measures, over and over, until your fingers relearn the right way."

Madison looks at her fingers and makes a face, but she rises and gathers her music books.

Bill grins. "I never thought I'd see you giving piano lessons. What got you started as a piano teacher?"

"My grandmother had a stroke, and I've taken over her students until they can get on a real piano teacher's list."

"Hey, I'm sorry!" He sounds as though he really is sorry. "Is she going to be okay?"

Madison has her back to us, stuffing her music books into her backpack, but I know she's listening. "We don't know yet. We hope so."

"I'm really sorry, Ruby. And I was hoping I could talk you into coming back to Boise with me."

I'm so surprised that I can find no words. "But Brazos—"

"He'll get over it. We won't be the Rivermen again, but we'll play music."

"What makes you think I'll get over it? He called me a liar! He said I egged her house!"

Madison lets out a mouse's squeak. She whirls around with a last music book in one hand and her backpack in the other, fuming with the righteous indignation of a fifteen-year-old, and shakes the backpack at Bill while he stares at her from the rose armchair.

"Did you say Ruth egged Ugly Anne's house? You listen, Mister. That's a lie! Ruth never egged Anne's house!"

"Wait a minute! It wasn't me—it was Brazos said it when he was angry, which is a bad time to say anything."

"Who's Brazos? Some guy? Then he's a liar because Ruth never egged Anne's house, and I know she never egged Anne's house!"

"Because you know who really did it?" Bill suggests.

That stops her. I watch her face as she adds up her thoughts to an uncomfortable total. Finally, she jams the last music book into her backpack and heads for the door but turns to fire her last shot—"All I'm saying! Ruth never egged Anne's house."

The front door slams.

Bill shakes his head, half-smiling in a way that deepens the vertical lines under his cheekbones. "What set her off?"

"I have no idea."

"Ruth. Ruby. Why do you have two names?"

"You asked me once before. I don't know. It just happened. I think my mother named me Ruth and started calling me Ruby for some reason, but Mrs.—my grandmother—went on calling me Ruth. Sometimes it feels like I'm two different people."

"Hmm." He ponders for a minute with a hand propped under his chin. "Do we know for sure that Annie's house got egged?"

"It must have been. Dr. Brenner went over and helped her clean it up."

"Ruby"—Bill leans forward in the rose chair—"what you need to understand about Anne is that she's broken. Really broken inside. I didn't grow up in the Boise Highlands, I never knew her or Brazos and Gall until we started high school, but they knew her from way back, and I think Brazos always had a crush on her. Remember him talking about the girl he loved who moved away to Montana and married somebody else?"

I do remember.

"And he told me that something was broken in her from when she was really little. Her mother put her in counseling because she thought men were following her. She'd hide and spy, trying to spot the men. When she was a little older, she thought her mother was trying to kill her. That's when she went into foster care. And they got her on medication, and apparently she did really well there."

Yes. She had done really, really well. Brad's star success story. "And Brazos wants to fix her?"

"Yeah. He's kept track of her all this time. But he can't fix her. No more than he could fix Gall. But it's deeper than that. It's like he wants to join her somehow. He wants to believe in her fears."

I can't make sense of what Bill is trying to tell me. How would you *join* somebody who thought men were following her? Or *join* somebody who thought her mother was trying to kill her? If you could, why would you want to?

Join in hiding, now, would be something else. In a big cardboard box in the blackberry brambles behind Brad Gilcannon's house, where the air is thick and dim and smells of ripening fruit, and someone might call and call your name because no one knows where you are. Or at night, hiding under your covers where the air has a moldy smell, and you listen for the stealthy footsteps, wait for the intruder's knife blade to your heart.

Shards from a glass lamp. *Everything I have is broken.*

Anne knows something that has nothing to do with dead babies and satanic rituals and people having sex in church, and so do I, even if neither of us knows what it is we know. Will I ever know? Will she?

Meanwhile, here is Bill, the quiet workhorse of the Rivermen, who checked the electronic gear and counted the electrical cords. Bill, who serviced the van and wouldn't let Brazos and Gall squander the money he needed to gas it up, even though Brazos always drove it. Kept track of our gig dates and got us there. Kept track of us. Kept his own counsel. Trimmed my hair. I wonder if he ever thinks of the girl in Albuquerque.

Bill has sprawled back in the wingback chair where the mothers usually sit, incongruous but clearly comfortable. He smiles at me so the vertical lines in his cheeks deepen again.

"You're not going to throw anything at me, are you?"

His drummer's hands. His hands in my hair. Hank of dark hair hanging over his forehead. Watchful dark-hazel eyes. It occurs to me that for ten years Bill never missed a thing while I missed so much.

"So it looks like I can't talk you into coming back to Boise with me," he says, "but maybe I can talk you into letting me buy you dinner?"

30

"How old were you when your mother went to prison?" asks Jamie.

"Nine. She was there for three years, so I would have been about twelve when she got out."

"You were living with Brad Gilcannon all that time? So you were old enough to remember all the trials and appeals and then what, the overturned convictions?"

"Yes."

We're sitting over our salads in the food court, in the relief of getting away from Zella. Now that the fall session has begun and we're back on the hour-long lunch period, Zella likes to eat downtown or out at the mall with her friends from the registrar's office. She no longer bothers to invite Jamie and me along.

"It must have been awful," Jamie says.

Brad was gone a lot during the early years. Later I understood he was testifying at trial after trial, going over his legwork again and again, going over his research. He came home late, and his wife kept their little boys out of his way while he ate his dinner. But the prosecutor had been winning conviction after conviction in those days, and Brad was buoyant. It was later that his world turned sour.

"Did you ever get to see your mother? During her trial? Or after?"

"No."

She hadn't wanted to see me, although I wasn't told that at the time.

Losing a child. What could be worse, Mrs. Pence said. She asked about Jamie again last night, wondering how her custody case was going.

"Jamie, what would make a mother give away her children?"

"Well—could be different reasons, I suppose. Seems to me it would have to be something pretty bad. Maybe if she couldn't afford to keep them fed?"

"Maybe."

"Or—maybe somebody raped her and got her pregnant, and she couldn't stand to look at the baby because she saw its father in its face? God, I can't imagine."

"I can't either. Maybe if I ever had a baby I'd understand more."

"I keep wondering—what Prairie Rose will remember."

"It's strange for me. Whole patches are just gone. I'll be told what was happening at a certain period, and it's like hearing about a movie I never saw. Other times everything is so vivid that I feel like I'm time traveling."

"Hmm."

I see that Jamie is trying to imagine time traveling.

"The spookiest times are when I don't remember anything and then all of a sudden I do remember."

The nest of dry needles under the blue spruce.

Bill the Drummer's hands in my hair.

"So a lot of what's going on now could be a blank to her later."

"Or not."

I can't tell if there's something Jamie hopes Prairie Rose will remember or fears she will.

··· ···

The Working Poor are booked to play for a wedding reception in Broadview, twenty miles east of Versailles. The guys talked of canceling, what with Isaiah's having to cut their practices short because of his grandmother, but the wedding date had long been scheduled, and in the end they decided they could go ahead and wing it if they had to. It wasn't like it would be a critical audience, probably a lot of drunks. Would I play keyboard and sing? I said okay, hoping that playing music would lift me out of my doldrums, and so late Saturday afternoon, after the last piano lesson, I drive out to the barn to practice with the guys before the gig.

I hadn't bothered to do much more with myself than change out of my piano lesson clothes into jeans and a shirt and braid back my hair. After our practice I planned to drive up to the Villa and sit with Mrs. Pence until she fell asleep, then drive back to her house and wake up the pianos and play for myself for a few hours. My days are piano lessons and Mrs. Pence on weekends, the Student Accounting office and Mrs. Pence on weekdays, regular as a squirrel on a wheel. Welcome to my world, squirrel.

I park in the weeds and take my time walking across to the barn. The sun is bright, but the days are getting shorter, and the air has a nip. I look for the llamas, but maybe they've gone to their barn for the night. On the other side of their pasture a bird rises from a flock that looks like thick black fruit clustered in a box elder tree. The bird soars, circles, and returns to the flock. Things in the bird world are in flux, and the flock is getting ready to leave. *Let's get the flock outta here.* How long will I have to remember that?

Inside the barn I find Isaiah and Stu and Brian doing nothing and looking morose. Brian, the steel player, gives me a halfhearted two-finger wave, but Isaiah and Stu just sit on their hay bales and study their feet while the last of the sun slants through the cracks in the barn's siding and stipples them with patches of light.

I see they'd started to unpack their instruments and amps and then stopped. "What's going on?"

"It's what's not going on," says Brian.

Isaiah abruptly stands up from his hay bale, flicks a stray wisp of hay off his shirtsleeve, and reaches for his guitar to stow it back in its case. Stu follows suit, shrouding his bass and zipping up the shroud.

"We may as well spool up the cords," says Isaiah. "Get it over with."

I hook my thumbs in the belt loops of my jeans and wait for one of them to tell me what has happened. Something dire, from the way they're acting. Something awful. Although from the point of view of somebody like me who has lived through the past spring and summer, *dire* and *awful* are relative terms.

Isaiah finally latches up his guitar case and slings the strap over his shoulder. "Terry's quit us," he says.

"They've got a baby due any day. His wife put her foot down," says Brian.

"I tried to call you, tell you not bother driving out from town, but you'd already left."

It sinks in. Terry is the drummer. He quit. No drummer. "So now what?"

"So now what is nothing! No Working Poor! You ever hear of a band with no drummer?"

Of course not.

Brian, folding up his steel, says over his shoulder, "Unless you just happen to know a drummer who ain't currently playing somewhere, Ruby? Preferably one who's out of high school and doesn't have a curfew?"

I don't answer. My thoughts unfold like paper flowers in water, one depth after another. When I finally look up, cold autumn sunlight still stipples the instruments and amps and hay bales and dusty floor, and all three of the remaining Working Poor stare at me in dawning surmise.

··· ···

I shut off my phone and ask myself what I've done. Even when I tapped in the number he'd given me, I'd been sure that if he did answer, it would be from somewhere on the highway between Versailles and Boise with his truckload of Anne's belongings. No, he'd say, although being Bill, he'd manage to sound regretful. No, he wouldn't be coming back to Versailles. It was too bad about my brother's band, he knew these things sometimes happened, but he wouldn't be available to fill in.

Instead, a surprised pause and "Uh—sure, why not? Where'd you say you were practicing? Have you got a set of drums out there?"

So I'm dragging Bill the Drummer from the Rivermen into the Working Poor, impelling the two halves of my life into an uneasy conjunction, and Isaiah and Brian and Stu are unpacking their instruments again and talking in low nervous tones among themselves.

"Holy shit, the drummer from the Rivermen," Stu had said, and began telling me what I already knew. "You guys were getting to be the real deal! You'd cut that CD, and you were getting reviews, and there were alternative stations, not just in Alaska but down here, that were playing your tunes."

We wait.

Then the barn door opens on a sunset and Bill the Drummer in silhouette. Something lurches in me as he hesitates there, a dark shape of a man against the glow, to let his eyes adjust from the glare of the road. Then he closes the door behind him, and the glow is gone, and he's taking his time through the dust and chaff toward our makeshift bandstand, a tall guy in a gray shirt and boots and Levi's with a lock of dark hair hanging over his forehead.

He shakes hands with Isaiah and Stu and Brian, who rise from where they've been sitting on the bandstand, and he puts an arm around my shoulders and gives me a hug.

"So what've you been playing?"

The guys tell him: they've been doing covers of popular country, also the wedding standards that everybody is sick of, like "We've Only Just Begun" and "Bridge over Troubled Water," but also some old Nanci Griffith tunes they like. "Lone Star State of Mind." "Once in a Very Blue Moon." Once in a while they go way back. Gram Parsons and the hickory wind. The Carter Family even.

"Play a little for me," says Bill. "I'll see what I can pick up on. These the drums?"

The drums are Terry's, which he left behind at the last practice and hasn't yet come back for. There's some discussion. "Terry's going to throw a fit if we—" "Well, why the hell should he? He's the one who ditched us"—while Bill waits for them to hash it out and I feel the absence of warm weight where Bill's arm had been. It hadn't been a *hug* hug, more like the friendly handshakes he'd given the guys, and I'm trying hard to stay in the barn and not go time traveling. Bill's arm around me. The fine long shape of Gall's hands—*Gall*—the shape of Gall's shoulders, the shape of his skull, the brush of his hair across my face. Then that night, the heavier alien shape of Brazos, his weight on me—and from there the situation with the Rivermen went from bad to terrible.

What Bill asked me, the night he took me to dinner. *Did you tell Brazos not to?*

"Ruby! Are you going to sing?"

We run through "Lone Star State of Mind" while Bill finds the drumsticks where Terry dropped them, listens for several measures, finds a rhythm, and joins us. We're ready to play it again, together, at a faster tempo than Griffith recorded it, to make people want to dance to it. My voice sounds harsher, in my own ears, than Griffith's joyous lyricism. Maybe not what a wedding party would want to hear, if they listened to the verses. But I stand and sing to the hay bales and the drifting dust motes, and I hear the drums and cymbals behind me, tentative and then more assertive, underlying the strings and the steel and the vocal with their certainty and stitching us together.

We come to the end. Brian adds a little riff on the steel and grins ear to ear. "Great friends you've got, Ruby!"

Bill looks as unassuming behind the borrowed drums as he always did with the Rivermen. "Not too bad," he says, and it's heady praise.

··· ···

When I walk into Mrs. Pence's room at the Villa that evening, she seems to be dozing, while a Brahms piano sonata plays softly on her little radio. I see that she's been brought her dinner on a tray, but she doesn't seem to have touched it, and I don't want to wake her, so I sit in the pink vinyl armchair by her bed and lean back and try to let my mind take a rest.

Playing music helped. Even in the barn, without an audience, playing music took me somewhere else. Somewhere aloft that the birds know about and where nobody has to think. But I realize I'm tired. How many piano lessons today—eight? None of Mrs. Pence's students have found another teacher, nor do they seem to be looking hard for one. And practice in the barn had gone on later and later, all of us wrapped up in our woven patterns of sound, and I reached the Villa too late to chat with Mrs. Pence over her dinner tray.

And I haven't eaten. I take a stick of celery from Mrs. Pence's tray and crunch.

"Rosalie?"

Her eyes are open, searching the ceiling. I take her hand.

"It's Ruth."

She turns toward my voice. She doesn't pull away from my hand, but she looks bewildered. "Ruth," she repeats, and for the first time I doubt she recognizes me.

··· ···

On my way to campus on Monday morning, I catch the last few bars of Reckless Kelly playing "Idaho Cowboy" on my retro station. Reckless Kelly, now there are a couple of Idaho boys who came out of a homeschooling life in the Sawtooths and made it big in Austin, Texas—what if Gall had been dead set on moving to Austin instead of Anchorage? And then comes the news of the forest fires south of us and to the west of us, still burning out of control, thousands of acres, hundreds of evacuations, property destroyed, livestock lost. The smoke doesn't seem as bad to me as yesterday, but maybe I really am getting used to it.

I'm not getting used to the new climate in the Office of Student Accounting. Zella from the registrar's office is a stocky woman in her forties, freckled and sandy haired and incapable of silence. She tries to convince Jamie and me of the conspiracies she's certain threaten us all—her favorite at the moment is that the contrails left by jet planes across the skies are in fact poisonous chemicals being filtered down by the government to destroy our minds.

Jamie retreats to Anne's old office and shuts the door, but Zella talks to me, or at me, when she isn't talking out loud to herself. If it isn't conspiracy theory, she's narrating her progress on her data entries. "Okay, now I'm on page 7, at last I'm about to turn to a new page. Oh, just look at all those numbers! We must be getting more students enrolled in this dump. Wonder how long it'll take me—oh, not too bad, not too bad, maybe I'll be done by lunchtime—" And she has a talent for inopportune observations at the wrong moments. When Dr. Brenner arrived at the office on her second morning at work and greeted us with his usual "Good morning, girls," as he poured his coffee, Zella brayed at his departing back: "Don't you just hate it when he calls us 'girls'? Or when he says, 'You girls'?"

I know he heard her. But what could he do, when his request to hire a permanent clerk still hasn't been approved? At least he hasn't fired me, although he looked at me and shook his head again when he came back to the office the day I threw the computer manual at Brazos.

The Working Poor had practiced most of Sunday but shut down early enough for me to leave for the Villa in time for Mrs. Pence's dinner. We all felt we were more than ready for the wedding gig next weekend, our sound more than better, and I knew it was the certainty of Bill's rhythm and his sensitivity to the tenor of the drums and the whisper of the cymbals that made the difference. When I first sang with the Rivermen, I hadn't realized that drumming wasn't just keeping time with sticks, and at the memory I wince over my keyboard. Zella sees me and interrupts her monologue—"Whaja do? Make a mistake?"

So much I learned with the Rivermen. In a sense Gall and Brazos and Bill had raised me. They took in the sixteen-year-old and taught her what they could. And what had the sixteen-year-old done in return? To Gall and all that lost talent? To Brazos, so driven and determined and now so enraged?

She'd grown up was what she'd done.

31

The morning slips by. Clatter in the corridor signals the lunch hour, and Zella throws the cover over her computer and tears off to find her friends from the registrar's office. Jamie's door stays shut. She's been increasingly withdrawn. I can't remember when her next custody hearing is scheduled, but I'm sure it's much on her mind.

Dr. Brenner emerges from his office, sees me sitting alone, and stops.

"How are you, Ruth? How's your grandmother?"

Grandmother. Just when I thought I had been staying so calm, I feel my tears spring with the word.

He pulls out Zella's chair and sits down beside me. "What's the matter, Ruth?"

It's a moment before I can speak. When I do, it's with an unraveling of words that can't be coherent. Everything. Piano students, one after another. Gall with a dead brain and Brazos with a burning anger, Isaiah with a broken heart and Catina's bright colors taken from her with her life. And now Mrs. Pence, my grandmother, who seemed a bit brighter last night, although I'm still not sure she knew me, and who asked again for Rosalie. Laced through it all, in a way I don't understand, with the persistence of time past and the whisper of the cymbals, is Bill the Drummer.

Dr. Brenner listens until I fall silent. Then he pulls one word out of the heap of shards.

"Rosalie. Your mother. Are you in touch with her?"

"No."

"Hmm." He studies me with his strangely magnified eyes behind his glasses, pondering, and then he says: "When did you eat last? Let me take you to lunch, Ruth."

He leads me out of Admin to the parking lot and holds the door of a gray Prius for me, and then he folds his long bones into the driver's seat and drives away from campus to downtown Versailles and a restaurant called Bloom, where sunlight falls through plenty of windows and smoke doesn't seem to have filtered in. We're seated at a table by one of the windows, and Dr. Brenner orders soup and sandwiches for us both.

The soup is creamy and hot and thick, with chunks of potatoes and onions. Dr. Brenner waits until I drink most of it before he says, "I think it's time that Rosalie steps up."

What in the world could cause that to happen? "Why—I don't—I mean, why do you care?"

The robot face allows its ghost of a smile. "Your grandmother—Mrs. Pence—was very good to me when I was a boy." He drinks soup, lays down his spoon, and holds up a knotted hand. "You wouldn't know it now, but my mother thought I might be able to play the piano in church, so I took piano lessons from Mrs. Pence for a couple of years. The lessons didn't take, but Mrs. Pence did."

"I see," I say, although I don't.

He takes another spoonful of soup. "She smoothed off some of my rough edges. She talked to my folks. Convinced them that I should get a college education, which was unheard of in my family. She even lent me the money for my first semester's tuition. By the way, in those days she had a little money from Pence's life insurance, and you should check whether any is left."

"Is that how you got to know Isaiah?"

Again the almost-smile. "That was later. Isaiah came up here to college on a football scholarship—he was a standout high school running back, did you know that? And he took classes from me. Mrs. Pence, now, advised me to go back to college and get my doctorate. And she was very good to my wife when she first came to Montana. My wife is from England, you know, which is why I always wait until I get to the office for my coffee."

I didn't know. So much I don't know about Dr. Brenner. That robots have wives. English wives at that.

"I knew how much she worried about you and Isaiah." He sets down his cup. "Eat your sandwich, Ruth. You've lost weight this summer. I haven't seen much of Rosalie for several years, but I know Jerry Bohn pretty well. I'll drop by his office and talk to him this afternoon." He glances at his watch and adds: "None of this is your fault, Ruth. Don't take all of it to heart."

Then, to my astonishment, he smiles a real smile. "And don't throw anything at anybody else."

··· ···

Piano lessons, three or four weeknight students. Then the drive up to the Villa to sit with Mrs. Pence over her dinner tray and coax her to nibble a little of the macaroni and cheese, to take a bite or two of limp green beans. She does seem to enjoy her hot sugared tea and lets me pour her a second cup. I don't think she knows me—"Rosalie?" "No, it's Ruth"—although she treats me with the grave courtesy she shows toward the nursing assistants and the aides.

Then the drive back to her house with another out-of-date tune playing on the Pontiac's retro country station—Patterson Hood singing about incest and lost love with the Drive-By Truckers and their soaring steel behind him—and then the routines, filling Jonathan's food bowl and water bowl and letting him out for his backyard run and giving him a little attention when he comes back into the kitchen, scratching his ears and rubbing his stomach. Then a glance through the refrigerator for whatever food I remembered to buy, maybe bread and cheese, then the minimal tidying the kitchen needed, and then, finally, finally, an hour or two to myself in the piano room.

I have begun to relearn Haydn's "Hungarian Rondo," and I am concentrating on advice Mrs. Pence gave me before her stroke, to keep my fingers curved and close and to lean into the keyboard for power. Even on the practice Kimball, the rush of sixteenth notes through the rising crescendos fills the room with wild sound that seems to escape the constraints of the keys, fighting to break through walls and windows and ceiling and into its natural element of night wind and endlessness, where all sounds live on, where Haydn himself plays the rondo amid a cacophony of street noise and bombs and screams and barking dogs. I had looked with longing at the Steinway concert grand, knowing the increased volume its big soundboard and the length of its strings would give to the rondo, but I would never touch Mrs. Pence's piano behind her back, and so I lean into the Kimball and tear through the crescendos and the restraint of the diminuendos and free myself in music. I come to the end and lift my hands from the keys and lose myself in a room full of tones sinking back down to rest.

Jonathan leaps up from under the piano bench, barks once sharply, and growls. I turn and freeze.

Dustin Murray stands by the spinet, watching me. Whether he knocked or rang the bell, I don't know. I hadn't heard a thing above the crashing ripples and chords of the rondo. But here he is, in the room with Beethoven's bust and Mrs. Pence's framed BMus diploma and the pianos and me. A part of my still-functioning mind notes that he's as pale as a ghost of himself. He must have lost color during his incarceration and whatever it was, house arrest and monitoring, that he's still supposed to be under. Otherwise, in ordinary Levi's and a T-shirt, he looks just like himself, Dustin Murray, the cute guy with the tight ass.

Well, no. His stillness says he knows he's where he should not be. Maybe he also knows he's what he should not be: the angry boy who waited under Catina's apartment stairs with his hunting rifle.

"I didn't know you could play the piano."

I can think of no response.

His mouth works. "I needed to—hey, I gotta sit down."

He's about to cry. He drops into the rose wingback chair and struggles to control his face.

"I need to talk to you," he finally manages. "Because you"—his voice wobbles and breaks—"you knew how much I loved her. And now they want me to—"

That's where he loses it and gives himself up to ugly racking sobs. I wait. I don't know what else to do. It may be a minute or two, it may be longer, before he sobs himself out and raises a wild and tear-streaked face.

"They want me to—"

"They? Who are you talking about?"

"My attorneys! They want me to, how do they say it, enter a plea bargain. They think they can get the county attorney to go for a lesser charge if I"—his voice trembles again—"plead guilty to it and they don't have to have a trial."

"I see."

"But I'd get thirty years! Maybe twenty with parole! Even then, I'd be forty-four when I got out! Forty-four! And those sons of bitches—excuse me, but that's what they are—trying to tell me I should be glad not to get a life sentence. Forty-four! How am I supposed to be glad about that?"

How to get him out of the rose wingback chair and out of the house is my only thought. "No, of course you're not glad."

He looks up, as grateful as Jonathan for a sympathetic word. "I thought you might understand. I thought maybe you'd be willing to tell them, *explain* to them, how much I loved her. Because you know how much I loved her."

"Yes. Yes, I know that."

"I knew you'd understand, and if you can talk to them—tell them that all I want is to have her back—" He's losing it again, struggling to swallow his sobs. "If I can't have her back, they may as well give me the death penalty and get it over with!"

"I'll tell them. I'll tell them you loved her. I promise. But—" What to say. "Dustin, you've got to get some rest, and I have to get some rest, because I have to go to work tomorrow morning.

If I promise to tell them how much you loved her, will you go home now and let me get some rest?"

"Uh—sure." He sounds surprised. "I know you gotta go to work. I'll leave now. Since you promised me."

To my relief he's on his feet and turning to the door.

"You're a real nice lady," he says, "even if you do hang out with that blackie."

I follow him to the foyer, wait until he closes the door behind himself, and then watch through a crack in the living room curtains to see him climb into his lonely Mustang, turn on his headlights, and drive away. Then I lock the front door, scolding myself for not keeping it locked always—I should know better, except that it's such a nuisance with piano students coming and going—and then I go to the kitchen with Jonathan bristling and growling at my heels every step of the way, and I lock the back door. Then I find my phone and call Isaiah.

32

The uniformed cop arrives about three minutes after Isaiah, which was at a dead run from his apartment to Mrs. Pence's house with his phone clapped to his ear. He's still breathing hard when I open the door to let in the cop and lead him back through the house to the kitchen table.

The cop has a youngish face beneath the blue and silver bill of his uniform cap. He opens his notebook on the kitchen table and jots a few notes as I describe Dustin Murray's visit, and he shakes his head when I get to the part about his wanting to be executed and get it over with.

"Sounds like he's more of a threat to himself than anybody else," the cop says. "Apparently he thinks he can trust you. You could probably take out a restraining order against him, but it might give him the idea that you've turned on him."

Isaiah growls something about the little son of a bitch, and the cop, who obviously knows him, says: "Take it easy, Ike. I'll look up the terms of his bail, and we'll keep an eye on your sister's place. How's your grandmother doing, by the way?"

Isaiah paces around the house after the cop leaves, turning off lights and checking windows and looking out at the darkened street. I look out once and see the outline of a prowl car parked a block away with its dome light off, and I feel suddenly and profoundly drained. I grope my way back to the kitchen, turn on a single lamp, and sit at the table with my head in my hands. Maybe I won't go to work in the morning after all. Maybe I'll cancel the piano lessons and stay in bed all day.

Isaiah joins me at the kitchen table. "Is there anything to drink in the house?"

"I don't think so."

"Grandmother used to keep Henry Weinhard's for me." He rummages in the back of the refrigerator and finds a bottle. "You want one?"

"Is there another?"

He brings out a second bottle, pops the caps off both, and hands me one. He takes a deep draft, and I sip, and we both look at the empty air around us.

"The cop knows you?"

"We played high school football together."

A silence.

"Dustin Murray. I hope they fry him, the worthless little prick. Coming over here to cry on your shoulder. *Please! Tell 'em I loved her!* What did he think that was going to accomplish?"

Time drags on. Isaiah finishes half his bottle of ale. "Ruby. Bill. What's going on between you and him?"

"What do you mean? Nothing's going on."

"Come on! We've all seen the way he looks at you. Why do you think he's drumming for the Working Poor? It ain't for my pretty face. Or Stu's or Brian's."

I have to laugh. Maybe it's the ale.

"Ruby," he says. "Go for it. You deserve some good."

I get up and hunt out linens, blankets, and a pillow for Isaiah's night on the sofa. *You deserve some good, Ruby.* What Dr. Brenner said. *None of this is your fault, Ruth. Don't take all of it to heart.*

Even Dustin. Now there was a testimonial to live up to: *You're a real nice lady.*

No. A lot of the shit of my life might be my fault but not all of it. I might be tired out of my mind, too tired to sort it out tonight, but I'm not going to call in sick and cancel piano lessons and stay in bed all day. A time will come to sort out blame.

··· ···

Isaiah had folded his sheets and blanket and left early to shower and shave at his place and dress for a day of teaching, but he had posted a note to the refrigerator with a musical note magnet.

My football buddy cop called me. They spotted Dustin Murray's car parked on the Milk River Bridge and found him leaning over the rail and looking at the current. They decided it was reason enough to haul him in. Maybe the judge will revoke bail. Not that I think the little prick would have the guts to jump.

"Poor Dustin," I sigh, when I tell Jamie over lunch what had happened. I should have known better.

"Poor Dustin, my ass. He feels sorry enough for himself without you feeling sorry for him."

We're in no hurry; we've come to the lull in the data entries at the end of late registration. Jamie's custody hearing is next week, and her attorney is hopeful, and she feels better, and we both think we've earned a little slack.

Jamie takes another bite of the hamburger she splurged on and stirs a little more sugar into her iced tea. It looks like she's suspended her diet for the day.

"Ruth, do you ever wonder whether feeling sorry for people is what's got you in trouble over the years?"

No, I haven't. But now I think about it. Who else have I felt sorry for in years past? Brad Gilcannon's wife? Maybe a little sorry for her but mostly in looking back and being glad I didn't have to live her life. More likely feeling sorry for myself.

Maybe feeling guilty is a way of feeling sorry for myself?

The din of the food court ebbs. Jamie and I are running late all right. Like getting used to the smoke, I've gotten used to the sounds of campus that were so maddening during my first weeks at work. The noise of women's shoes and women's voices punctuating their day as they arrive for work in the morning, take their coffee breaks, hurry out to lunch and back, and clatter out again at five. In between the clatter voices are lowered in the offices, where women sit at their silent computer screens in the faint hum of window air conditioners and the tap-tap of keyboards. Voices drop but never quite cease when the occasional student wanders in or a male executive in a suit passes through. Codes ripple between offices; words float here and there; threads of conversation connect from coffee breaks or carpooling. Like a miniature reflection of Versailles itself, the campus secretaries and clerks know what there is to know about each other and about the men and the one or two women they work for, factual or otherwise.

And here I am, letting my mind drift off into campus noise instead of answering Jamie's question.

Maybe feeling guilty is a way of feeling sorry for myself, but feeling guilty as a reason for accepting punishment is more accurate.

I hadn't answered Bill's question either.

... ...

Gall has gone with Sharyn to her room, and I'm alone in ours, counting the elk on the wallpaper to keep my mind off the pain in my abdomen. Thirty-two elk, I think. All thirty-two have spreading antlers, so they must all be bulls. Each has his own little grove of low-growing firs that he seems to be walking through, leaving a little patch of blue sky behind him. Nothing but blue skies for these elk.

Maybe I've miscounted. I start over.

A tap at the door, and it's Brazos, followed by a draft of Anchorage chill. He doesn't wait to be asked in, but at least he pulls the door shut behind him while I pull my knees up under my chin and shiver.

How'd he seem to you tonight?

I shrug. It's hard to say how Gall seems from one night to another. He'll be in a stupor during a set, forgetting his chords and his words, while Brazos and I improvise a harmony to cover for him and Bill tries to hold us together with the drumbeat. Or else he can't contain himself—he's jumping up and down and playing and chattering, and we can't keep up with him.

Did he go with the Screamer tonight?

Yeah.

I'm sorry, Ruby, Brazos says. He sits heavily beside me on the bed and pats my bare leg. What the hell are we going to do about him?

Brazos emanates worry. I can feel it seeping out of his pores, and it would seep into mine if I didn't hurt so badly. It occurs to me that there are probably another two or three elk behind the mirror over the dresser. I'll have to count again. It's not that I don't feel sorry for Brazos. I guess I do feel sorry for him. He and Gall have been friends a long time, since preschool in Boise maybe. Thirty-four, thirty-five elk? Something is trying to gnaw its way out of my abdomen.

He's telling me about the girl he loved in Boise who moved away and married somebody else, and some dull part of my mind that isn't counting elk tells me that explains a lot about Brazos. He never gets involved. Everybody else does. Even Bill the Drummer fell for that girl in Albuquerque.

He acts like a bastard to you, Ruby. How do you stand it? I can't stand it, and I love him too.

Brazos kisses me. He tastes of the rum he's been drinking, and I try to say no. Yes, Bill, I'm trying to say no. I do say no. You're hurting me, Brazos—I can't bear your weight. But I try not to whimper when he turns me on my belly and pulls down my cutoff jeans and tears the elastic of my underpants, and his hands on my breasts are not Gall's hands; he is bigger boned than Gall, bigger and heavier; we're half-on, half-off the bed; he's probing, cunt hole, butt hole; I'm begging no, no, I hate it there, and the pain is no longer just in my abdomen but screaming from the place where he is bucking into me and calling not my name but Gall's name, while the indifferent elk roam the walls around us. And then the door opens, and Brazos pulls out of me and turns, and there, watching, is Gall.

··· ···

198

"Where the hell do you *go* sometimes?" says Jamie. "We'll be in the middle of a perfectly normal conversation, and I realize that you're ... somewhere else. I never saw anything like it."

A promise is a promise, and it's not pity for Dustin or any belief of mine that telling his attorney how much he loved Catina will help him avoid prison, but my promise to him, along with Isaiah's cop buddy's warning, *Don't give him the idea that you've turned against him*, that makes me leave work early and takes me up a flight of stairs between two brick buildings on lower Main that leads to a balcony overlooking a parking lot and a sign on a door that opens off the balcony: JERRY BOHN, LLD, ATTORNEY AT LAW.

Bad, bad idea, I knew after I combed the newspapers for the name of Dustin's lead attorney. But Jerry Bohn is a lawyer, right? Who is he to pick and choose whose story he'll listen to for, what, ten minutes? Just a few minutes, I told his secretary over the phone. Ten minutes. It has to do with Dustin Murray.

I take a minute to catch my breath and look down at the parking lot and the alley that leads past the back doors of retail stores toward Main Street. Garbage dumpsters and leftover packing cases and windblown leaves. One of the doors opens, and a woman, foreshortened in black stretch pants and a gold sweater, comes out with a sack of trash and a burst of late-afternoon canned country music. A real oldie. Tanya Tucker singing about the man who keeps asking a little girl, *What's your mama's name?* I realize it's the back door of the Alibi when the woman drops her trash into a dumpster and returns, shutting the door and cutting off the sad swooping instrumentals behind the lyrics and leaving me with another song stuck in my head.

Jerry Bohn's office is brighter than the shabby balcony would have suggested, more what I would expect for a man who lives in a house on Lila Drive, maybe too much for a public defender. Maybe he also takes other, more lucrative cases. Dustin Murray, with his rich grandfather, probably is a lucrative case.

The secretary I spoke with on the phone sits behind a well-polished desk of dark wood, and her computer and the printer on the credenza behind her look expensive. Fluorescent lighting, of course. A gilt-framed mirror on the wall behind the secretary's desk reflects her talking to a young woman in a red shirt. It's not until I notice the woman's dark braid hanging over her shoulder that I realize I'm seeing myself. In the heat of late September I've given up my crow's clothes for cotton shirts and khakis, and now I don't recognize myself.

"Jerry will be right with you," the secretary says. She smiles and gestures toward a sofa and a coffee table with a few magazines, but already the inner door is opening, and I see a tall man in his shirtsleeves, with a chiseled face and graying hair that touches his collar. I suppose I've seen him before, at Dustin's arraignment, but I wouldn't have known who he was, and in any case all the attorneys mostly had their backs turned to the spectators.

"Ruth?" he says. "Or Ruby, which?"

"It doesn't matter," I reply, although I'm beginning to think it does, and he holds the door for me and gestures me toward one of a pair of cream leather chairs arranged in front of the wide desk. After I sit down, he takes the other chair.

"So. Ruth Gervais." *Szcher-vay*. "You had a visit from young Murray."

After telling Isaiah and then Isaiah's cop buddy about Dustin's visit, I can relate it without elaboration and well under my ten minutes, while Jerry Bohn listens without interrupting. I come to the end, my locking of the front door, and raise my eyes from where I had been keeping them, on my hands folded in my lap, to Jerry Bohn's face.

Bluish-gray eyes, a blade nose, a wide mobile mouth. A face that my mother, angry and afraid, saw for the first time in a prison conference room.

"Were you afraid, Ruth?" Jerry Bohn asks.

I consider his question. "All I could really think about was how to get him to leave. Afterward, maybe, a little afraid."

"What did he think"—he interrupts himself—"I don't suppose *think* is the right word."

"I don't know what he thought. But I promised him I'd tell you he loved her."

I've had my ten minutes, and I start to rise from the luxurious buttery leather of the chair. But Jerry Bohn raises a hand.

"It's just as well you did, Ruth. If Dustin had blindsided me by asking whether you'd talked to me when you hadn't, there's no telling what he'd decide to do. I can tell you, and I tried to tell him, he's damned lucky the prosecutor didn't put the death penalty on the table. And now this stunt of his on the Milk River Bridge. Not that he was much danger to himself. The river there isn't more than waist deep. But with luck we can keep him locked up for his own sake until we can get him evaluated. How did he strike you? Did you think he was in control of himself?"

"I—no, I guess I didn't. Although I never really knew him before he—" And now I'm taking more than my ten minutes, telling Jerry Bohn about Dustin with his putter and his golf ball across the street from campus. About the day he sat on the floor outside the Student Accounting office until Jamie kicked the door open and pinched his rear end. About the afternoon when Catina crouched in terror on the floor of the Pontiac as I drove away from the Goodwill store.

"That was when I started to worry. Up until then I just thought he was good-looking and dim."

Jerry Bohn had scrawled a note or two on a pad, and now he glances back over it. "We'll try to get his bail revoked for a while at least. "So, Ruth—"

He's weighing something he's about to say. An old hippie, somebody had described Jerry Bohn to me, this graying man with the top three buttons of his shirt undone and his suit coat and necktie hanging over the back of his desk chair. I had gone online and combed through some of the old newspaper coverage of the trials and appeals after I made the appointment with him. A young crusader, he'd been called back then, who had fought to overturn the satanic ritual and child abuse convictions. He had won my mother's release from prison and fallen in love with her and married her. Now his dark eyebrows show a few white hairs, and he's got lines of weariness around his eyes, and he could use a shave, and saving people is still his line of work. Saving Dustin from himself, I guess.

And he's, more or less—no. No more or less to it. He's my stepfather.

A stepfather whose stepdaughter is a stranger to him. A stranger who, long ago as he well knows, was driven past her mother's house and said, *Yes, it happened in that house.* What must he be thinking?

He glances at his watch, and I know I've overstayed, but all he says is: "I've been looking forward to meeting you, Ruth. George Brenner speaks highly of you. We'll talk soon."

··· ···

Jamie surprises me by lingering in the office on Friday afternoon until she's sure Zella has covered her computer and left for the day. Now she turns from the window, where she had been watching the street and making sure that Zella hadn't changed her mind and come back.

"This came in the mail," she says. "I wanted to show it to you."

She hands me a rectangular blue envelope, and I see that it's addressed to Ms. Jamie Warren at 620 West Montana Street, Versailles, Montana, in a clear handwriting with black ink.

"Go ahead and open it."

I hesitate, then draw out an all-occasion card decorated with birds that I think are penguins until I notice their curious black and red beaks. Puffins? What a strange card. I turn it over and see it's from a set of free cards sent by a charitable organization hoping for a donation. Then I open it to a different handwriting, a child's uneven cursive in pencil.

Dear Mommy—

I look up at Jamie. Her eyes are brilliant with unshed tears. I turn back to the card.

My teacher is helping me to write this letter to you. I miss you. I hope I can come to see you soon. I love you.

Your daughter,
Prairie Rose

33

The wedding reception gig at Broadview is set for Saturday evening, and the Working Poor have agreed to meet at Isaiah's barn that afternoon for a final run-through before we pack up the instruments and head out. I rescheduled my piano students and visited Mrs. Pence while she was being served her lunch, since both Isaiah and I will be playing music later, and now I'm driving out to the barn with my retro station fading in and out of reception, with Dylan singing about the jingle-jangle morning through bursts of static.

Except it's not morning; it's a midafternoon jingle-jangle of sharp sunlight cutting through bronze cottonwood leaves to dance on the windshield of the Pontiac, and my thoughts are as sharp edged and sporadic as the static. The smoke in the air has cleared, and the good news on the radio reported that the wildfires to the south are under control. Until next fire season, until next fire season.

No llamas in their pasture behind the barn, no birds forming flocks in the trees, only a few dry leaves floating down as testament to what's coming. We haven't had a hard freeze yet, but the weather's changing, with something ominous in the darker-blue band taking shape over the western horizon. *It's a hard freeze—a hard freeze.* Are those the words from a real song, or did I dream them?

Bill, I told Brazos not to, and I begged him to stop, and if he'd been thinking about anybody but himself and Gall, he might have heard me. True, I wasn't a sixteen-year-old anymore, being raised by three twenty-something fathers. I was twenty-six and old enough to say no, and maybe I should have fought harder to stop him. But I didn't want him to do what he did.

I wasn't feeling sorry for him, Jamie. I was miserable with pain and grief, and within thirty-six hours I would be undergoing emergency surgery in Versailles Memorial Hospital in Montana. I understood Brazos's grief. I knew he loved Gall, had loved him longer than I had. But I didn't want him to do what he did.

I haven't seen or heard from Bill since he took me to dinner after our practice session in the barn. Not that I expected to see him, but my wandering mind loops out and circles back, searching for reasons. When he took me to dinner, he still had a truckload of Anne's belongings to take down to Boise. Probably that was where he went. Once in Boise, with its vibrant live music scene, why would he come back to Versailles?

"When he took you to dinner that night—did you have a good time?" Jamie asked.

··· ···

Dinner with Bill the Drummer. I can't relax. Being near him in the cab of a pickup truck. Trying to think of him as Bill and not as Bill the Drummer of the Rivermen, while Gall and Brazos, two gaping dark absences, ride with us. Bill is too present. His hand on the steering wheel, his hand dropping to the knob of the shift when he changes gears. Although he's scrupulous about giving me my space. No touching of my hand, no brushing against my shoulder. After he parks at the restaurant, he gets out and holds my door for me but doesn't try to help me with the long step down from his pickup, a big Toyota Tundra with a canopy, to the pavement.

The restaurant is on the Milk River, with a deck that extends over the current. A girl in black jeans and a black T-shirt leads us to a table on the deck, by the railing, where the warmth of the day yields to the faintest of air currents and where she leaves us with menus. Only a few other diners. Tables with cloths and overhead globes of light that reflect on the river with an illusion of stillness spread across its surface.

Bill might be keeping his hands to himself but not his eyes, and when I look up, he smiles at me.

"Ruby."

I tell myself to say something. "What have you been doing in Boise?"

A pause. Water lapping at the edge of the deck.

"I was working construction," he says, "and hanging out with my mom."

Inside the restaurant music is playing, something saccharine with strings that swells when a waiter comes out with a tray of drinks and fades when the door closes behind him. Bill has picked up a menu, and he glances at it, and I see the darkened patch on his thumbnail is growing out.

He returns to me. "Ruby, when we couldn't find you that morning, it was—all that kept me from either killing Brazos or leaving on my own was knowing how bad he felt. So we said goodbye to Sharyn and packed up the gear and shipped it home and sold the van and bought tickets to Boise."

"But you quit a job to help Brazos?"

"Oh, hell, I got over wanting to kill Brazos." Bill smiles at me again, and the warmth unsettles me. "Mostly got over it. And I can always find a day job. And there's always a band somewhere that can use a drummer."

A waiter comes with water glasses to take our orders, and Bill looks a question at me, and I shrug. I'm not sure I can eat.

"Give us another minute. Bring me a bourbon—Mark, if you've got it. Ruby, you used to like white wine?"

"Whatever."

But *whatever* isn't going to do it. Act like a normal person. Straighten your back. "Tell me about your mom."

By chance I've raised the right topic. Bill smiles a little to himself, thinking of his mother. "Oh, she's—my mom is cool. My dad died when I was twelve. He was career military and gone so much I hardly remember him, and so my mom basically raised me. She was, well, still is, a nurse practitioner, and she taught me to cook and do my own laundry, which has come in real handy in my life since."

A mini jet boat rips past us, spraying a slosh of white water against the deck and misting the air over us, and everyone at the other tables looks up.

"Damn them," someone says distinctly.

"Anyway. My mom's an old Boise girl, and after my dad died, she brought me back from wherever we'd been living, Fort Bragg I guess it was, and she bought"—he grins, remembering—"she bought us this house. It wasn't exactly on the wrong side of the tracks, but it sure as hell wasn't the Boise Highlands. It had been, can you believe? somebody's crack house, and it"—he shakes his head and laughs—"it was beyond bad. My mom and I gutted it and remodeled it. My mom and a twelve-year-old boy, pretty much by ourselves. She lives there to this day."

"I never knew any of this."

"No, I don't suppose so."

He's watching the curving wake of the jet boat getting fainter and farther away and finally disappearing under the Milk River bridge.

"I started drumming in junior high band. Went on drumming in high school and got to know Gall and Brazos and Annie. Had a couple years at Boise State and probably should have stayed longer, but Gall and Brazos were starting the Rivermen by then, and the music, well, called."

"Did you have a girlfriend in Boise?" I ask, again to keep him from what I fear he wants to talk about.

A longer pause this time.

"There was a woman. Named Teresa. God, I was young in those days."

"Is she still there?"

"No. She died. Some kind of fast cancer. And that was when I left Boise with the Rivermen. I was twenty-one."

I'm stricken to have asked. "I'm sorry. I didn't know."

"No."

His smile is gone. But he's looking at me as though he expects me to evaporate as easily as I disappeared from that motel in Anchorage. Without a word.

But then he says: "Ruby. That night in Anchorage. Did you tell Brazos not to do what he did to you?"

... ...

I pull myself out of my head and get out of the Pontiac and walk across the lot to the barn, shivering when an unexpected nip of wind scours my face and bare arms and rattles the weeds. I should have brought a jacket. Isaiah's white pickup and the minivan Brian and Stu use to get back and forth are parked by the barn. So they're here but no Toyota Tundra.

Isaiah stands on the makeshift bandstand in a shaft of thin sunlight that haloes his silky black curls. He tilts his head to listen as he tunes his guitar, notices me, and gives the G string a final twang.

"Is that what you're going to wear tonight?"

I'd shaken jeans and a T-shirt out of the laundry hamper that morning. "No. I'll change."

Brian is adjusting the height of his steel, doing something that requires a screwdriver, while Stu sits on the edge of the bandstand and thumbs through a SHAR catalog. No hurries here and no worries apparently.

But Isaiah has a sardonic eye on me. "Look behind me," he says.

Behind him? A scattering of chaff across the floor, chill sunlight falling through the high window that once had been the door to the hayloft. The instrument cases. The set of drums.

"Look closer."

The drums. I recognize them. Tama Imperialstars with deep-red poplar shells and the specially sealed chrome fittings. I remember the day they were purchased for a quarter of their worth at a pawnshop in Billings, Montana.

"Those aren't Terry's drums. They're Bill's!"

"Right," says Isaiah. "He drove all the way to Boise, two god-damn days, with his truckload of Anne Albert's shit, and he unloaded it for her, and then he drove back up here, another two days it took him, with his own drums. Now he's trying get some sleep before we practice."

Somewhere in the ether Bob Dylan sings about a jingle-jangle morning, and Gram and Emmy Lou sing about love that hurts.

34

We drive east to Broadview in two vehicles, Brian and Stu with most of the instruments in Brian's white van and Isaiah and me with Bill in his pickup, with Bill's drums under the canopy in back. I'm crammed into the narrow rear seat with my knees against the front passenger seat and my garment bag spread across my lap. My plan is to wait and change clothes after we get the instruments set up. There will be plenty of time. The wedding party reserved the bar and restaurant at Rowdy's, starting at nine, and we can expect the celebration to continue until two in the morning, when the bar has to close.

The sky has lost light, although occasional clumps of box elders or hawthorn brush are silhouettes against a pale gray. Closer to the asphalt are dim shapes, shapes that sometimes have eyes and move. Bill's headlights cut across sagebrush on the curves and return as the highway straightens. I can make out partial outlines of Bill's head and Isaiah's, and I know they're discussing something but not what it is, and I wonder, as I've often wondered, whether either remembers the other from that long-ago night at the Alibi.

Then a nest of lights ahead, with scattered outliers, and the BROADVIEW POP. 597 sign and speed limit signs and then the amenities of the town strung out along the highway: a motel, a tractor dealership, a food market, an incongruous Starbuck's. Isaiah points, and Bill makes the left turn at the traffic light and pulls into the parking lot at Rowdy's. The white van pulls in right behind us.

I have never been in the bar at Rowdy's, and yet I feel as though I've walked into it a hundred times. It's almost a parody of itself. Recessed lighting and dark paneling hung with mounted elk heads that stare out, glass-eyed, at the clientele hunched over their beers at the bar or at a few scattered tables. Caps and flannel shirts and suspicious eyes on these strangers, one of them black, who are carrying instrument cases and mysterious equipment into their space. I think of lines from old western movies: *Hey! Sodbuster! Whadda ya think you're doin' here?*

But the bartender comes around the end of the bar, a big guy with a dark beard who obviously knows Isaiah—"Hey, Ike, howza goin"—and they shake hands, and the bartender points us to the back room, where tables with white paper tablecloths are grouped around a bandstand with an open space for dancing.

"The ladies room, where you can change—"

Why do restrooms in country bars all smell the same? The odor of disinfectant soap overlying something fetid. Scarred linoleum tiles, never quite clean, that evoke the fumes of a filling station pump. I let down the changing table—changing table, up-to-date!—so I can drape my garment bag over it. Then I unbutton my shirt and pull off my jeans and hang them on the hook on the back of the door while a young woman with long dark hair watches me from a clouded mirror. She's a taller woman than her mother. She has a straight nose, without the arch of her mother's and grandmother's noses. Does she look like her father?

New black jeans from the garment bag, new red cowboy boots, and a dark-red silk shirt. My hair loose to my waist and waving slightly from being in a braid.

I had lifted the fringed red suede skirt and vest from the suitcase Bill brought down from Anchorage, and I unfolded the leather and smoothed out the creases and spread the skirt and vest out on the bed. The suede had stiffened over time, and the afternoon light picked out a few worn patches in the nap but none so bald that bar lighting wouldn't conceal, and I thought about stepping into the skirt and zipping it and slipping on the vest like a familiar second skin—somebody else's skin—but I knew I would never wear these clothes again. I hung them in the bedroom closet opposite the painting of the cathedral in the trees where storm clouds gathered and the sullen young man glowered from his Polaroid, and I made a hasty trip to the shopping mall for new jeans and boots and then to the Goodwill, where Catina's ghost followed me through the sale racks until I found a silk shirt that actually fit me.

Out in the dimly lit banquet room a couple of women are decorating the tables with plastic flowers and white disposable cameras and laying out trays of crackers and dips and toothpicks and salami slices. The guys have finished setting up the instruments and amps on the bandstand. We'll have time for a little supper before the show.

Bill is seated behind his drums, frowning over something underneath the smallest snare, but he looks up and sees me and rises to his feet.

Slow motion, time doing its thing. Bill steps down from the bandstand and walks toward me between tables set for the bridal party. In the background Isaiah and Brian and Stu seem not to move.

"You didn't think I'd come back from Boise?" When I can't answer, he touches my cheek. "I'm not going anywhere, Ruby."

When he turns back to the bandstand to fiddle with his drums, one of the women carrying a tray of nibbles winks at me. "He looks like a keeper to me, honey."

··· ···

How to perform for a crowd of happy drunks: first, hope they stay happy.

The wedding party rushes into the banquet room ahead of the throng, the bride with her veil askew and lots of white lace over a hoopskirt and the groom in a black tuxedo jacket and Levi's and cowboy boots. Groomsmen in tuxedo jackets and Levi's and boots, bridesmaids in billowing lilac lace. Several little girls, also in lilac lace, are hastily sidelined near the food. Then the onslaught of family and friends, going through a semblance of a receiving line and ordering drinks from the cash bar.

Isaiah introduces the band—"Stu on bass, Bill on drums, Ruby on the keyboard, and Cryin' Brian on the steel."

We look pretty good, I think. At least I'd coaxed the guys out of their awful gold satin shirts and into plain black linen.

We start with "Moon River" for the bride's dance with the groom, heavy on keyboard and steel and augmented by whoops and whistles from the crowd, and switch to "Daddy's Little Girl" for her dance with her father. We sound fine, but it hardly matters. These are happy folks.

And so the evening progresses. The temperature in the banquet room soars, even though somebody opens a door that looks out at the parking lot. We take a fifteen-minute break every hour and use the restrooms and wipe the sweat off our faces and sample the salami, which one of the barmaids says has been made from antelope meat. It's nearly midnight when we get the whole crowd line dancing to "Louisiana Saturday Night," while Brian makes faces over his steel that mime retching at the music and the sight of bridesmaids trying to kick-dance in hoopskirts.

Then it's past midnight, and we're playing "Indian Outlaw" to a thunder of cowboy boots on the board floor, and everybody's hopping and stomping, when a man with a beard and a fatigue jacket with American flag patches on the sleeves throws a bottle across the room and hits a long-haired fellow in a sleeveless leather vest with snake tattoos up and down his arms—*Draw, sodbuster!*—and Isaiah and Bill and Brian and Stu get up and stand in front of me and their instruments, and the bartender and a couple of his burly friends turn up the lights and storm over to break up the battle. "Hey! Bunce! Jackson! None o' that in here!"

After that the room thins out, some to see the bride and groom off to wherever they're going on their honeymoon and others to watch Bunce and Jackson duke it out in the parking lot. Isaiah glances back at me and nods, and I get up from the keyboard and join him and his guitar at the front of the bandstand, and we sing the songs we want to sing. In harmony, alto and baritone over the throb of snares and whisper of cymbals and richness of bass and steel. "High on a Mountaintop." "Lone Star State of Mind." "Love Hurts."

Then Bill and Isaiah are giving each other high fives over the drums as a smattering of applause rises from the survivors in the audience, and that's when I see, in the back of the room, Jerry Bohn in a chambray shirt and Levi's, looking more like an old hippie than an attorney at a wedding reception. He strolls up to the bandstand and nods at Isaiah and me.

"I wanted to hear you play," he says, "so when I heard you were booked out here, I cadged an invitation." He touches my hand. "I'll call you next week," he says.

35

Time with its own motion. Sunday afternoon, and Bill and I sit on Mrs. Pence's porch steps, eating peanuts and watching the weather move over the porch roof and on eastward. The forecast had spoken cautiously of rain.

"Did you see Gall or Brazos while you were in Boise?"

"Gall, no. He's still in that facility in Seattle. Brazos, yes. He helped me unload Annie's furniture at her new place."

So much I want to know, so much I don't know how to ask.

"Did Brazos say anything about Gall? How he is?"

"He says the doctors are starting to see some muscle flickers. His eyes move back and forth. But he can't speak, and they don't think he can hear anything."

Bill cracks another peanut and tosses the shell into a pile of fallen leaves. The sky has deepened to purple. Down by the mailboxes the bicycle kids are practicing their wheelies.

"I don't know a hell of a lot about these things, but a coma that's lasted this long can't be good."

"No."

"We had a real shot, you know. The Rivermen had a real shot, that is. But then Gall's meltdown."

"Do you think the Working Poor has a shot?"

"Probably not. We'd need a songwriter, for one thing. We'd need to get away from playing covers."

We.

Bill looks at me, straight on. Warm hazel eyes, dark lashes. "I didn't love Gall, not the way you did and Brazos did. And not that I'd wish what happened to him on anybody, but he was a mean arrogant bastard, and there were too many times I was ready to walk off and find somewhere else to play music."

I think about the words. A spoiled bastard and a mean arrogant bastard. "Brazos always talked you into staying."

"Well, yeah, he did! Where was he going to find a better drummer?"

Bill grins and tosses away another peanut shell, but it's no more than the truth.

"Also—" He doesn't finish the thought. Cracks another peanut.

"Gall might have been a mean arrogant bastard, but god, the talent. The voice he had. Ruby, who the hell are those kids by the mailboxes, and do they always hang around there?"

Just as he speaks, the older boy tries another wheelie, hits loose gravel, and takes a spill. He untangles himself from his bicycle and gets to his feet, rubbing himself and checking his elbows, while the younger kid points at him and lets out a cackle that we can hear from our seat on the porch steps.

"I see them there a lot. I think they're Madison Albert's little brothers. They live a few blocks away."

"The 'Für Elise' girl?"

"You remember her?"

"The one who couldn't hit F sharp? The one who had a meltdown over the house egging?"

A sudden gust of wind torments the bare maple branches across the street and drives a cascade of dead leaves off the roof of the porch with a rattle that might have been rain. Sure enough, a few wet spots darken the gravel walk.

"When I asked you the question I did," Bill says, "I didn't mean—"

A pause.

"—I didn't mean, did you *fail* to say no. I meant, was Brazos listening?"

"No. He wasn't listening."

"Damn him."

216

We sit for a time, listening to the thrashing of branches overhead and sporadic raindrops slapping at the porch roof. Down by the mailboxes, the bicycle kids pull their jackets over their heads, but they aren't giving up. I wonder if their mother will be able to move into a better house now that Francis Albert has divorced Anne and Anne has gone back to Boise with Brazos.

He's already got a new girlfriend, Madison had sneered. I hate him!

Bill lays his hand on my knee, and I shiver.

"What do you see yourself doing now, Ruby?"

I surprise myself with my answer. "Living here, in this house. At least for a while. Taking care of the pianos. And hoping my grandmother can come home, at least for a while. I won't have her forever." After a moment I add, "And playing music."

Thunder explodes like a bombshell out of the west, powerful enough to splinter the air over Versailles. Its reverberations roll over our heads, turning the sky the color of a bruise and pouring down torrents of rain and hopping hailstones. The bicycle kids abandon the mailboxes and pedal off as fast as their legs can churn.

Bill laughs, long and exuberant, and I feel his enjoyment of the storm and the sight of the fleeing kids through his hand on my knee.

"What do you see yourself doing?" I ask, when I can make myself heard over the rain and hail.

"Staying in Versailles for a while. Finding a day job. Playing music."

"Even in bars like Rowdy's?"

"Hell, it was kind of fun. Your guys are pretty good, you know. Or would be, if they could practice more. Ruby, have you ever thought of singing Gall's tenor parts? Dropping your range down even half an octave?"

"No. Really? Do you think I'd have the voice for it?"

"Yeah, I do. And with that big baritone of Isaiah's, we'd have a helluva vocal sound."

We watch our jingle-jangle storm until the rain starts to slacken, and Jonathan, standing on his hind legs to watch us through the screen door, whines anxiously.

"I have a theory," Bill says, "about the house egging."

··· ···

Time with its own motion. Monday afternoon, and Isaiah and I sit in the matching cream leather chairs in Jerry Bohn's office. Isaiah had finished his classes at Mike Mansfield High, and Dr. Brenner let me leave the Student Accounting office early. The rain tapered off during the night, but the window that looks out over Main Street shows the dripping facades of old brick commercial buildings and a slice of sodden sky.

Jerry Bohn, in his shirtsleeves, sits behind his desk with his back to the window. "The thing is," he says, "she's been hurt pretty deeply too."

He glances at the framed photograph on his desk. I only see its black velvet backing and stand from where I sit, but I can guess whose picture it is.

"There will be expenses," says Isaiah. "It's hard to know what the total might come to. Our grandmother has her little social security check and Ray Pence's pension check, and she did have some income from her piano students, although that's fallen off as she's gotten older, and now, of course—well, that's how it is. I'm a high school teacher. Ruby is a data entry clerk. The nursing home will take Grandmother's social security checks and the pension checks, but they'll need more. And there's the expense of keeping up the house. Do we have to sell it? *Can* we sell it?"

"Did your grandmother give either of you a power of attorney?"

I don't know what a power of attorney is, but Isaiah says, "No," and adds to me, "You'd know if she gave you one."

"And of course we still hope she'll be able to come home," he goes on. But she'll need more care than Ruby and I can give her unless one of us quits a job, and even then—"

"I'll have some of this researched for you," says Jerry Bohn. He makes a couple of notes.

When he first ushered us into his office, he had caught us up on Dustin Murray's status, his bail revoked pending psychiatric evaluation, which, Jerry Bohn said, might even play in his favor if it came to a trial. I felt Isaiah go tense beside me and prayed he wasn't going to explode over anything's playing in Dustin Murray's favor.

"So don't worry about any more visits from him, at least for a while," Jerry Bohn said, "and we'll give you a heads-up if there's a change."

Now he says, "We can work out the financial situation. Yes, the house might have to be sold, down the road. Do you have any idea of its value?"

"I don't," Isaiah says. "It's old, and it needs renovation. The kitchen looks like it was installed in the 1930s, and the plumbing is almost as old as the house. The pianos, of course, are valuable, especially the Steinway."

Selling the pianos. The Steinway.

Jerry Bohn leans back in his chair and glances again at the photograph on his desk. Steeples his fingers. "The finances are one thing. George and I talked about the other aspect of the situation, and it's murkier. What, exactly, are you hoping to bring about between the two of you and your grandmother and my wife?"

I speak before Isaiah can. "It's not about Isaiah or me—it's about our grandmother."

It's almost the truth. Almost? Well, no.

Jerry Bohn waits gravely while I find words to explain to this decent man what I hope for. "Mr. Bohn, I haven't lived with, or talked to, my mother since I was eight years old. I turned twenty-seven in July. That's almost twenty years, and it's been longer for Isaiah. Twenty years is a lot of time, and a lot that's just—over and done with. I don't know her now, and she doesn't know me. But my grandmother isn't over it. I don't think she recognizes me now. But every night when I visit her"—I have to pause and take a deep breath—"she says, 'Rosalie?'"

Jerry Bohn closes his eyes for a moment and opens them again. "I see," he says. He massages the bridge of his nose. "I'll see what I can do."

I hesitate. But when will I have another chance to ask? And who better to ask than a man who has been an attorney at law in Versailles for at least twenty years?

"Mr. Bohn, did you know my father?"

In the startled silence I have time to regret my question and wish I could ask more questions and watch emotions I cannot not follow as they play across Jerry Bohn's face.

"No. I didn't." He meets my eyes. "There's a lot—as you say, over and done with—Rosalie and I have never spoken about. I do know"—another long hesitation—"she was badly damaged by Isaiah's father. She has never spoken his name, but he was the reason she left Monterey and came home to Versailles."

"I see. Thank you."

A rap of rain against the window, the dregs of the storm passing over Versailles. We're all on our feet now, and Jerry Bohn reaches across his desk to shake my hand and to shake Isaiah's hand.

We drive in Isaiah's pickup from Jerry Bohn's office to the Orchards Villa, where we spend an hour with Mrs. Pence. She's sitting up in bed with her dinner tray on the adjustable arm, and she seems a little brighter than she had the night before. She always knows Isaiah, of course, and smiles up at him and clasps his hand. With me it's "Rosalie?"

And this time I say, "Yes," and see a tremulous smile light her face.

"I was so afraid," she says, "that you had gone away with Mark Gervais."

A startled exchange of glances between me and Isaiah. "Have we got a real name?" he mouths.

··· ···

Daylight has faded, and streetlights are winking on when Isaiah parks at the curb by the familiar picket fence. When I get out, he kills the headlights and turns off his engine and follows me. A lot on his mind, I suppose. I find my key—yes! key! I remembered to lock up! Thank you for that, Dustin! I unlock the front door, and Jonathan is greeting us in the foyer when Isaiah says, "Play some for me, Ruby."

He relaxes in the rose wingback chair while I play Haydn's rondo. I've been working on it off and on, and it's getting better, although I still can't afford even a glance away from the music to Isaiah. He had looked dead tired. Of course he'd had a full day at the high school and then the meeting with Jerry Bohn and the visit at the Villa. I play the last notes and let the sound linger as long as I can hear it before I turn on the piano bench.

Isaiah opens his eyes. "Damn, you're getting good."

"You want a beer? I picked up a six-pack of Henry's this morning."

"Sure."

I fetch us each a Henry's from the kitchen, and we sit in silence for some time, Isaiah in the wingback chair and I on the piano bench.

"We have a name," he says after a while. "Maybe we have a name."

I nod.

"You ever wonder what kind of life Rosalie might have had if she hadn't left Monterey and come back here?"

"Yes. Often." And I tell him about the box of clippings I discovered, long ago, in the closet of the rental house north of the river in Versailles.

"They must have mattered to her if she saved them. What do you think became of them?"

"Trashed. Along with her records. She was living in that house when she was arrested, and she never went back."

"All that talent."

Like Gall. All that talent.

Isaiah straightens in the armchair and belches a little from the Henry's. "You think she ever plays music now? Sings?"

"No idea."

"I've been thinking," he says, "about songwriting."

"Songwriting? Who have you been talking to? Bill?"

He laughs. "Hey, I took a poetry writing class in college. I wrote a couple poems." Then he asks, as Bill had, "What do you have in mind for yourself, Ruby?"

I take a slow sip of ale. "It depends, doesn't it. Whether Grandmother can come home."

"And Bill?"

I could brush him off with *Bill? What about Bill?* Instead, I try to explain, maybe to Isaiah, maybe to myself, what I've been feeling.

"The Rivermen were like fathers to me, at least in the beginning."

Again I'm hearing Patterson Hood with the Drive-By Truckers singing "The Deeper In," about incest and love and loss, which isn't exactly what's troubling me but has something to do with the way I had loved Gall and what happened with Brazos and how I can be drawn to Bill. I hadn't told Bill the details with Brazos, only that it happened, and maybe Brazos told him more, but Jamie, yes, I'd told Jamie more. Sounds to me, Jamie said, like there was more going on between the two of those guys than either one of them with you.

Isaiah listens to my stumbling attempts at words and says, "Bill's a great drummer, and he's a good man. Take your time."

Time. It was mid-May when I came back to Versailles. Now it's mid-October. I drink more ale and think about yesterday's rain and whether it came in time to save the lawns and trees of the Orchards. Poor shattered trees. Scattered thoughts in the magpie's nest. Shiny fragments. I catch at one.

"Something I've always wondered and never asked Grandmother—why does she have all that mismatched sterling silverware? There must be a dozen different patterns. A couple of forks in one pattern, five or six in another, a few teaspoons in still another, assorted knives, all jumbled together in the top kitchen drawer."

"I know the answer to that."

"You do?"

"I wondered too, and so I asked her, and she told me. Turns out she had a whole flock of great-aunts in England, and none of them ever married, and they all had sets of sterling silver tableware. One by one they died and passed what silver they hadn't lost or forgotten to their niece, who was Grandmother's mother. Then *she* died, and when Grandmother came to Montana, she brought all the odd knives and forks and spoons with her."

"So that's one mystery solved."

"Yup. How many do we got to go?"

36

Rosalie, Rosalie, Rosalie. What were you seeking in Monterey? Fame and fortune? Was that what you yearned for? And what did you find?

Now you live on a sagebrush prairie, in Versailles, Montana, in a house overlooking the Milk River. What do you do all day while your husband and rescuer, Jerry Bohn, goes about his work of rescuing others? You've cast off your children. You've told your mother that you hate her. Do you have friends? Do you listen to music? What music? Do you still sing, even to yourself?

What is worse than a singer who has lost his hearing? Maybe a singer who still has her hearing but has silenced her voice?

I hear thunder, not the explosive clap that set off yesterday's storm but more of a quarrel among night clouds. I get out of bed and go to the window and see lightning flash and vanish over the filigree of bare branches and darkened roofs of the Orchards. Maybe it will rain again.

Jamie said that paranoia is a way of making the world make sense. A way of believing that events are connected. We'd been talking about Zella and the contrails left by jet planes. When I asked Jamie what she meant, she explained that if you believe people are conspiring against you, you can also believe that the conspiracy is the reason for everything that happens to you. Better, she added, to think the government is trying to kill you with contrails than to think something random that you can't control is happening all around you.

Better than what, I had wondered, to think that hostile Nez Perce were riding across the prairie toward you? Or that the

Satanists were after you? Or that your mother was trying to kill you?

Booze makes it worse, Jamie said. Believe me. Was your mother a drunk?

Probably.

I go back to bed, hoping I can sleep.

Fame and fortune. *Oro y plata.* The Rivermen came close to catching the gold but not close enough. What was left but to self-destruct?

Bill's eyes are a warm dark hazel. He is smiling, and I feel his smile when he kisses me on the lips and then draws back to search my face.

No? he says.

Yes.

But I feel ashamed to be saying yes.

What are you trying to do, Ruby? Fuck your way through the whole goddamned band? One minute Gall is so angry that he is jumping up and down and screaming; the next minute he's sobbing in Brazos's arms. *I thought she was a kitten, a dolly, a sweet sweet dolly, but she's a bitch!* He tears himself away from Brazos and drives his fist through one of the wallpaper elk and runs out into the long late northern daylight. And Bill and Brazos will chase him all over Anchorage, get him to the airport and lose him again, and finally, with the help of the cops, lock him up and call his father.

I'm sitting up in bed with my hands full of wadded sheets, realizing I've been dreaming, so I must have been asleep.

··· ···

I'm bent over my keyboard the next morning, staring into my computer screen, when I feel my phone vibrate in my pocket. Zella, ever alert for other people's business, leans out of her chair with her mouth open when I answer and scowls when I carry the phone out into the corridor.

Jerry Bohn sounds weary. "Ruth, she's not ready to talk to her mother yet. But I think she's willing to talk to you and Isaiah, and we can see how that goes. Maybe later she'll feel she can take that next step."

I thank him, and we make tentative arrangements for such a meeting, provided she doesn't decide at the last minute that she can't go through with it.

"She's had a hard time," Jerry Bohn says, "more than she's been able to bear."

Jerry Bohn hangs up, and I call Isaiah, knowing he'll be in class but leaving him a message. Zella watches me suspiciously when I return to the office and put away my phone, but at least she doesn't ask outright, and I sit at my computer station and pretend to absorb myself in the screen. Maybe, like Jamie's connect-the-dots view of conspiracy theory, there's a hidden message in the rows of names and numbers that explains Rosalie's anger at Mrs. Pence and Isaiah and me.

I told the judge my mother was part of the coven that abused children. And he believed me. I was eight years old—well, nine years old by the time the trials got under way—and I believed Anne and Brad, and I loved Brad. Now I see a shadow on the computer screen, a reflection of my own face, my eyes, and I try to imagine the face of a young woman almost twenty years ago who had been trapped and publicly condemned and knew she was going to prison for years because her own child, the one of her children she had kept and tried to raise, had testified against her. She wouldn't have been drawing many fine distinctions.

But why would she hate Isaiah, who had refused to testify? *I ain't going to say I saw no dead babies when I didn't!*

My old fantasy, the girl in the rain with her baby in her arms, leaving behind any thought of a career as a singer in Monterey and getting off a bus in Versailles, Montana. Isaiah is thirty now. Thirty years ago, would a biracial baby born out of wedlock have been a greater shame than such a baby would be today? Why had she named him Isaiah Pride? Why had she given him up when she knew she was pregnant with me? A thought floats up. What if Brazos had gotten me pregnant that night? What would I have done?

And what of Mrs. Pence? All I knew were the hateful words I had overheard, flung like nails being driven into a board and meant to hurt.

Isaiah and I will keep the appointment, and Rosalie will show up and talk to us or she won't.

"I don't know about this office," says Zella. "Apparently I'm the only one who ever does any work."

......

Bill is bunking with Isaiah until he finds a place of his own, and he has learned what time I'm likely to come home from the Villa and put in my hour or two at the piano. On his first visit he accepted a bottle of the Henry's I had started keeping for Isaiah, and after that he brought a bottle of Maker's Mark with him. Now he pours himself a little Mark and sits in the rose wingback chair and listens. At first the whole room seemed disturbed by his presence, Beethoven scowling down from his niche in disapproval and the Steinway in silent reproach under its cover, although Bill never speaks, never reacts when I play the same two or three measures over and over to get the fingering right, and gradually Beethoven and the Steinway and I have gotten used to his presence. When I finish practicing and the last tone fades, he will look up and smile and carry his glass out to the kitchen and say good night.

Tonight he lingers. Sips the last of his whiskey.

"Ruby, what if Gall came out of the coma—got his voice back, got his hearing back, got back to being Gall again. What would you do?"

"Have you heard that? That he's coming out of it?"

"No. I'm just saying what if."

"Well—I'd be glad."

"What if he came to Versailles and wanted to talk to you?"

"I'd talk to him. Sure."

"And—"

Gall. The tawny hair that brushed his collar, the line of his jaw I had followed with my fingertips, the breadth of his shoulders. The nights when he held me and kissed my hairline and called me his kitten, called me his dolly. His breakdown was only months ago, but those nights were long past.

"There was a time I believed in song lyrics. I still think in song lyrics, but the music is what I believe."

Bill looks into his empty glass. After a moment he nods and rises to his feet. "Ruby, this house has a gutter problem," he said. "We'd better take a look tomorrow."

··· ···

During the drought of the spring and summer I hadn't given a thought to the state of Mrs. Pence's rain gutters. Now that rain is falling nearly every night, following the thunder-crashing deluge that had overflowed creeks and runoffs and caused landslides down the eroded hillsides north of the river—in one case a whole mobile home sliding down a hill—I'm ducking through a cascade of water overflowing the gutters every time I leave the house, and my piano students arrive in the foyer shivering, with wet hair and wet backpacks and jackets.

Bill studies the gutters. "Like the Arkansas traveler," he says, "we gotta patch the old roof till it's good and tight," and he climbs into his pickup and drives off.

"Arkansas? What is he talking about?" asks Jamie. She and I have been driven by Zella into a conspiracy of silence in the office, and so Jamie often drops by Mrs. Pence's house after work to catch me up on her latest information about her upcoming custody hearing. Her chances are looking good. Dr. Brenner is coming in person to the hearing to speak about her excellent work and reliability and sobriety.

"It's just an old song." I hum a bit of it for her.

"You musicians. I swear you speak a whole different language from the rest of us."

Now that I'm looking at the gutters, I see they're brimful of leaves and broken branches, through which rainwater pours and where a few green weeds have taken root and stick up their heads in defiance of coming frosts. At one corner of the kitchen porch, a gutter has pulled free from the roof and drains its water onto the lawn.

"Does he come here often?"

"Who, Bill? He visits sometimes. You're as bad as Isaiah."

"Ha."

··· ···

Bill returns with an extension ladder strapped to the top of his pickup. He climbs out, carrying his toolbox, and ducks through the drips from the gutter to open the toolbox on the porch.

"Do you still carry barber scissors in the tray?" I ask, and see him stop with his gloved hand on a hammer. Then he picks up the hammer and just touches the tip of my braid with it on his way back to his pickup for the ladder.

Jamie and I watch from the lawn as Bill extends the ladder, sets it against the side of the house, and climbs, step by step, with his hammer hanging from a rear pocket by its claws, until he reaches the gutter and scoops out a handful of rotten leaves and mud with a primal odor. Freed, a stream of black reeking water gushes from the spout.

"Bring a trash bag," he calls down, and Jamie goes to fetch the roll of trash bags from the kitchen.

More rain is expected. I smell the leaves and water from the gutter and see gray sky through bare black cottonwood branches and, at the top of the ladder, Bill's back and shoulders in his dark windbreaker and his long legs in Levi's. I take a step closer to the ladder and see the bottom edges of his rear pockets, heavily worn, and the frayed place where the inseams of his Levi's cross at the crotch, and I wonder if I want to know more about the woman named Teresa who died in Boise and know I'll never ask him.

"Do you still have the barber scissors?" I call and see the ladder lurch before he steadies it by grabbing the roof.

"When I'm at the top of this ladder is maybe not the best time to be asking me that."

And then Jamie comes back with a trash bag, and she and I hold it open while Bill drops down murky handfuls from as far along the gutters as he can reach. He moves the ladder again and again and fills that trash bag and another, and he nails back the gutter that had pulled away from the side of the roof, and by that time it's almost dark and rain has started to fall again.

Jamie says good night and goes back to her car and drives away. I watch Bill climb down the ladder for the final time, watch the stretch of denim over his legs and the sway of the claw hammer from his rear pocket with each step, and I watch as he folds the ladder and props it against the side of the porch to return to the equipment rental place in the morning.

He strips off his filthy work gloves and drops them on the porch and turns to me and weaves his fingers through my hair at the base of my braid.

"Ruby. Ruth. I kinda like that name. You think we ought to go inside and get out of the rain?"

"Yes," I say, as I had in my dream.

... ...

Isaiah and I climb the stairs to the balcony overlooking the alley behind Main Street. As before, we're coming from work, Isaiah from Mike Mansfield High and I from the Office of Student Accounting, which I left early, to Zella's overt disapproval. Isaiah's acoustic guitar is slung over his shoulder, and our hands find each other and clasp as we open the door with the gold letters. JERRY BOHN, LLD, ATTORNEY AT LAW.

His secretary recognizes us and smiles, and Jerry Bohn himself opens the inner door and gestures us inside. He takes in the two of us, our clasped hands, and the guitar.

"She's in the conference room next door. Please remember she's fragile. I'm sorry, but I don't think she'll talk to you. She had agreed, but then, just now—well. You can try. I'll sit in, and I'll try not to interrupt you."

Pale cream walls in the conference room, framed photographs of dignitaries on the walls, many of the dignitaries with beards, a long walnut table, and, seated at the far end of the table, a woman with a cloud of dark gray hair and downcast eyes who wears a white lace sweater.

"Please, sit down," says Jerry Bohn behind us, and Isaiah unslings his guitar, and we sit at our end of the table.

No one speaks for a long minute. I can't see Jerry Bohn, but I sense his tension, and just when I think he'll intervene, Isaiah pushes back his chair, picks up his guitar, and starts tuning it.

Ping, ping, ping, rings through the conference room. Then Isaiah strikes a badly flattened note from the E string—deliberately, I think—and I see the woman flinch, and I'm pretty sure Isaiah sees it too as he retightens the peg. So she still has an ear.

I'm remembering my struggles with the CPS woman. Throwing myself on the floor, catching at the legs of chairs to keep from being taken away. *Mommy!* Remembering the invisible cord that drew me across the bridge over the Clearwater that night, trying to reach her before Brad caught up with me in his squad car. It wasn't quite the truth and not quite a lie that I had told Jerry Bohn. All that has passed isn't past. The cord that draws me to the woman at the opposite end of the table might be frayed, but it's there.

I note her face, which once was beautiful. Then I see the shape of her hands and her slightly arched nose. She is our grandmother's daughter, Rosalie, who once was the girl in Monterey with a voice like a bell.

Isaiah finishes tuning his guitar, and I get up and stand beside him. "Ruby and I thought we'd sing a little to you," Isaiah says. His fingers move over the strings, playing a line of melody and then finding the chords as we lean toward each other and sing about the hickory wind that blows through the pines and the oaks, Isaiah's big baritone in harmony with the tenor I've adapted from Gall. Bill was right about our vocal sound. We're bringing a helluva sound to that conference room, enough to ring the dead ears of the bearded dignitaries in the photographs on the walls. Remember, remember, the pines and the oaks, and remember that we play music and sing not because we expect fame and fortune but because that's the air we breathe.

The song comes to an end. The bearded dignitaries recede into their frames. Rosalie's mouth opens, but she does not look up or speak. Jerry Bohn suddenly is at her side.

I step back. Isaiah is picking at his strings, pretending to search for notes, which I know is an act because we practiced it half the night. He finds the melody he's looking for, plays it and reprises it. His eyes are fixed on Rosalie. He takes a step toward her and teases her by beginning the reprisal, breaking it off, and beginning again.

"Will you sing for us?"

She looks up with widening eyes, and Jerry Bohn draws a sharp breath.

Silver threads and golden needles . . .

Isaiah and I searched online through old newspaper accounts, and we're pretty sure this was at least one of the songs she sang at the Monterey festival. Now Isaiah begins the melody one more time, and a thin voice joins him. He coaxes her with the guitar, and she gains strength and pushes back from the conference table and opens her mouth like the singer she is. After the first verse I sing a quiet harmony on alternating lines, and Isaiah joins in, and we see her face soften and cast off years, and we hear her true mezzo voice soar on the solo lines . . . *I dare not drown my sorrows* . . . and we come to the end.

She hides her face in her hands.

Jerry Bohn holds her, kissing her and murmuring to her. He nods us toward the door, and after a few minutes he joins us in his office.

"I've never heard her sing," he says. "We've been married for nearly fifteen years, and I've never heard her sing."

"She has a beautiful voice. Still."

Jerry Bohn shakes his head. I see that he's on the verge of crying himself. "Well. As I said, she's fragile. When she heard you were back in Versailles, Ruth, she was beside herself. Frightened. Furious. Cursing. Hospitalized for several days. Well. We'll see what happens next."

Isaiah and I walk down the stairs to the alley in silence. He had left his pickup in the parking lot, and now he cases his guitar and stows it behind the front seat, and we get in and sit for a moment.

"Bill's right," Isaiah says. "We've got quite a sound."

I'm thinking about men who love damaged women. Jerry Bohn and Rosalie. Brazos and Anne. How far the men who love damaged women will go to keep them safe and what the safekeeping might do to the damaged women.

"Isaiah. Do you think I'm damaged?"

"No more than the rest of us." He hesitates. "Are you worried about yourself with Bill?"

I nod.

He takes my hand. "Don't be. You're all right, Ruby."

A spatter of rain hits the windshield like weather that can't make up its mind. My mind is on the Polaroid of the sullen young man, still stuck to the mirror in the white bedroom. Bill, naked, stopping to study it.

Who is he? He looks like you, Ruth. Or you look like him.

Isaiah leans his head on the steering wheel, and it takes me a minute to realize he's laughing.

"What?"

"Bill! He came back to the pad at three in the morning, and that dude was walking on a *cloud*!" He starts laughing all over again. "And you're blushing!"

"I am not!"

"You are too!"

He takes my hand. "We'll make it through this, Ruby."

"Yes."

We sit for a time, watching the rain on the windshield try to decide what it wants to do, and I think about Isaiah's broken heart and Gall's burned-out brain and Grandmother's pleasure at my deception. Rosalie.

Bill.

"It was three in the morning? Really?"

"It was!"

He's laughing as I have not heard him laugh since Catina's death. "You want me to ask him his intentions?"

"Stop it!"

But what can I do but laugh with him as he turns the key in the ignition and drives down the alley from all we might never know and turns on the grade toward the Orchards and whatever is going to happen next.

Source Acknowledgments

Paul Clayton, Larry Ehrlich, David Lazar, and Tom Six, "Gotta Travel On." © Carlin America, Inc., The Bicycle Music Company.

Charlie Daniels, "Ole Slew Foot." © Universal Music Publishing Group, Spirit Music Group.

Colonel Sanford Faulkner, "Arkansas Traveler." 1850.

Dallas Frazier and Earl Montgomery, "What's Your Mama's Name." © Sony/ATV Music Publishing LLC, Universal Music Publishing Group.

Burl Ives, "Wooly Boogie Bee." © Pickwick Group Ltd.

Loretta Lynn and Patsy Lynn Russell, "High on a Mountaintop." © BMG Rights Management (US) LLC.

Guy Massey, "The Prisoner's Song." 1925. © Shapiro Bernstein & Co., Inc.

Dick Reynolds and Jack Rhodes, "Silver Threads and Golden Needles." © Sony/ATV Music Publishing LLC, Carlin America, Inc., BMG Rights Management (US) LLC.

Nanci Griffith, "I Wish It Would Rain." © Sony/ATV Music Publishing LLC, Universal Music Publishing Group.

IN THE FLYOVER FICTION SERIES

To order or obtain more information on these or other
University of Nebraska Press titles, visit nebraskapress.unl.edu.

CPSIA information can be obtained
at www.ICGtesting.com
Printed in the USA
LVHW03s0915120718
583455LV00002B/2/P